THE BLEEDING WOODS

THE BLEEDING WOODS

BRITTANY AMARA

47NORTH

This is a work of fiction. Names, characters, organizations, places, events, and incidents are either products of the author's imagination or are used fictitiously. Otherwise, any resemblance to actual persons, living or dead, is purely coincidental.

Text copyright © 2025 by Brittany A. Marasciulo
All rights reserved.

No part of this book may be reproduced, or stored in a retrieval system, or transmitted in any form or by any means, electronic, mechanical, photocopying, recording, or otherwise, without express written permission of the publisher.

Published by 47North, Seattle
www.apub.com

Amazon, the Amazon logo, and 47North are trademarks of Amazon.com, Inc., or its affiliates.

EU product safety contact:
Amazon Media EU S. à r.l.
38, avenue John F. Kennedy, L-1855 Luxembourg
amazonpublishing-gpsr@amazon.com

ISBN-13: 9781662534102 (paperback)
ISBN-13: 9781662534119 (digital)

Cover design by Caroline Teagle Johnson
Cover image: © Polina Bottalova / Getty

Printed in the United States of America

For my grandma, Elia,
who believed in me before I knew how
to believe in myself

1 | CLARA

The night I killed my parents, I felt no guilt. I was fourteen years old, and the tears I cried were a by-product of human hardware. Humans cry for a lot of reasons. That night, I was stranded on the edge of a snow-slickened highway illuminated only by two upturned headlights and the reddish glow of a friction-fractured guardrail. Shards of glass were embedded under my skin, sending rivers of red from every incision.

I was cold. I was hurt. I was alive.

They were liars.

I descended the icy slope their car had tumbled down, the pastel ballet shoes on my feet filled with clumps of powdery snow. We'd been headed to a dance recital, and I was about to pirouette my way out of the junior company. The show, in my case, had always extended far beyond the stage.

The car produced a plume of black smoke and orange embers. In the front seats, two mutilated bodies dangled, arms limp, eyes agape, and mouths overflowing with blood and saliva.

My parents.

Liars.

I straightened my spine and brought my eyes skyward. The frigid air froze my tears. The blizzard speckled my hair with glittery white evanescence. The quiet abyss of the cliffside void swallowed me whole, a reminder that darkness was home to all demons born to dwell in it.

The quiet did not last very long.

Sirens raged through the winter winds, and ribbons of red light came right along with them. Some kind, foolish soul had called the authorities, and it became abundantly clear that I'd have to put on a show tonight after all. I took my dominant dancing leg and slammed it onto a spire of windshield glass with all my might. Once it was thoroughly, convincingly impaled, I lay face down near my mother and father. Despite every emotion their eternally vacant stares made me feel, I willed myself in the direction of grief.

Tears began to trickle, and soon, the trickle became a roar. I had to play the part, and I had to play it well. There could be no reason to accuse me of malice, no inkling of how or why I could cause an event like this. Thankfully, no one dared—no one except my sister, but she could barely form words, what with her sob-ravaged throat making her voice scratchy and incoherent. Even if I had been swarmed by questions at the time, I wouldn't have known the answers.

All I'd known then, and all I know now, was that I'd missed a pill.

I lived out the remainder of my adolescence as quietly as possible. Placed in the custody of my grandparents, I kept my head down and my lips sealed. I was good. I was hidden.

Kill them all. Kill them all. Kill them all.

A diabolical thing, my deviant self, grew louder whenever I waited too long to repeat my daily dosage. It raged violently against the soft pink gel orbs stockpiled beneath my childhood home. But I was good. I was hidden. Since the night I killed my parents, I've kept it under control, and I will continue to keep it under control until—

Oh no.

A sight I knew I'd someday face mocks me like a carnival clown before a crying child. My inconspicuously unlabeled metallic canister of concentrated control produces not two, not three, but *one* pill upon being diagonally tipped. The terrified child hiding behind my heart convinced herself the supply was infinite, but the adult guiding her knew. She always knew.

I give the canister a few desperate shakes, and the puff of air it produces is as good of a laugh as any. My apartment is a micro-studio one zero above affordable, but right now, it feels infinitely tinier. The walls are closing in, and talons are tightening around my throat. The world is burning, and I am burning with it.

Chemicals.

It's just chemicals. Obnoxiously named, multisyllabic chemicals that no overworked pharmacist in their right mind would bother to investigate. I've investigated plenty and arrived at nothing but dead ends. If I can take them without question, they can make them without question. I'll bring the final dosage to the sleepiest drugstore in the city and act like a customer in need of an immediate refill. I'll play the irresponsible twentysomething-year-old who partied too hard the night prior to remember her medicinal needs. I'll play innocent. No one pays much attention these days anyway. We're all existing in our own pocket dimensions, impatiently waiting for intruders to leave us to our daydreams. I'll become an intruder, and then I'll be ushered out.

It could work. It has to work.

I gather my everyday belongings in a flurry of motion. A cell phone, a wallet, and my final pill, sealed in a sandwich bag. I change into a dainty white top, blue jeans, and a pair of kitten heels hoping to look as harmless as I had in my tutu.

My home city is entropy incarnate. As I step into the exhausting frenzy of fast-paced humanity, I am blinded by buttery midmorning sunlight and overwhelmed by every honk, hiss, and conversation within a ten-mile radius. My presence is mousy, so I am bumped into no matter how hard I try to avoid it.

"'S'cuse me, 's'cuse me—sorry," I mutter. "Excuse me. Sorry . . ."

No one accepts or returns my apologies. They're too busy making it big or making it by, and I'm too busy trying not to be bulldozed by someone tall enough to have their own zip code. It doesn't work out well. My heel catches on a lifted sliver of cement, and I plummet toward a sea of dried gum and discarded cigarettes.

Ire burns in my veins, but I let none of it seep out. I cannot let it, not with my dosage flushing away like this. Silently, with as much control as possible, I rise back to my feet and choose a family-owned drugstore nestled on a street just busy enough to be found. It borders a far more commercial area, one with bigger, flashier pharmacies. The mere fact that I've chosen this one should come across as an act of rebellion against the capitalist tyranny of the neighboring consumerist hub.

A jingling bell welcomes me inside, and suddenly I am ten steps from salvation.

The woman behind the counter has the squat, plump build of a fairy godmother. Her hair is lined with highlights to lessen the appearance of the places its melanin has given out, and it sits in the shape of a neatly styled bowl-cut dome. If not for the white lab coat with her name, *Denise*, stitched below the breast pocket, I'd have taken her for a librarian whose consciousness has yet to escape the 1980s.

I approach her and shove both hands into my pockets, swaying back and forth on my heels. The casual fidgeting is designed to appear as bubbly nervousness with a side of social anxiety. This is the role I've chosen, for now.

"How can I help you?" says Denise, her words riding the tail end of a sharp sigh.

She seems tired. I can work with that. I slip a palm-sized pill canister out from my pocket as quickly as possible. Then, with a sheepish smile, I slide it across the desk.

"Hi. I'm here to grab a refill on my anxiety prescription."

Her eyes move up and down my body like searchlights over a crime scene. "I've never seen you come in before."

She's more investigative than I planned on. I pivot.

"I'm new to the area. I know you probably need a doctor's note, or a fax, or something, but I couldn't get in touch with my home office this morning, and I really need these," I ramble, lining up each point with a shivery hand gesture. "I saved my last pill hoping you might be able to copy and paste it back there. Pharmacies here do that sort of thing, right?"

At her own languid pace, she pulls out a pair of thick eyeglasses and fastens them atop the bridge of her nose. With a purse of the lips, she examines the orb and gives the canister a shake for good measure.

"Do you know the name of the medication? I can't tell what it is by just looking at it, hon."

"Um . . ." I sway once more, throwing my gaze to the ceiling. "I'm really not sure. I'm not good with names. It's not a name brand one, though. I needed it personalized because I've got all kinds of allergies."

"You had it compounded?"

I tilt my head until my ear grazes a shoulder and say, "Compounded?" I know what it means, but few things look as innocent as ignorance.

"Right." She snorts, smiling with sudden amusement. "Okay. I'll run it through the system and see what I can do. I will need your general practitioner's information, though. I really can't move forward without a prescription."

"My psychiatrist prescribed them. I've been calling her all morning, but she's, like, seventy, and the original prescription note was handwritten. I'm still living out of boxes and haven't been able to find it. If I could just get a few pills—even just a week's worth—I would be so grateful."

I could get a week's worth of pills from every pharmacy in the city until I figure out how to properly forge a doctor's authorization. For now, I'm hoping that Denise, with her eighties haircut and retro-chic glasses, will be too caught up in nostalgia to criticize my imaginary psychiatrist's old way of handling patients. She clicks her tongue, then her pen, to scribble something on the lid of my pill container.

"Get me that note as soon as you can."

I perk up, but not enough to insinuate excitement. Only relief. Respectful, health-conscious relief. "Of course. Thank you so much," I say.

She nods, then slides a form layered in triplicate across the counter. "Write down your name and contact information."

It's almost too easy. A friendly wave and a farewell jingle from the doorway bell send me back onto the street. The promise of more pills lingers beyond the threshold between today and tomorrow. I'd only have to make it through the next twenty-four hours, and in solitude, I could effectively avoid a repeat of what happened on that highway.

The day moves at a snail's pace, and my senses heighten as the hours pass by. Lights become brighter. Sounds become sharper. Smells become individually divided and precise. Each tick of the clock that hangs above my stovetop is a tock toward complete destabilization. Destabilization and the dangerous curiosity it comes packaged alongside.

When I was under the age of seven, my parents would crush up my pills and pour the dust into the sugariest cereal possible. They demonstrated for me once, hiding their lies in plain sight. After that, they called them vitamins and assured me every growing girl needed her vitamins. Only on the day of my recital did I find out they weren't for growing girls at all. Before the massacre of my parents, I took those pills with a mind made absent by comfort. Afterward, I took them because I didn't want to know exactly what kind of growing *thing* they were for.

Now I feel dangerously close to finding out.

My veins sting as though a string of fiery parasites is rolling within them. The muscles beneath my skin writhe like the tectonic plates of the earth before a quake. Everything is an inferno, and despite the horrific discomfort of it all, sinful questions sit cross-legged at the back of my brain: *Do I want to know what I am? Do I want to know how I killed them so easily? Was it me or the missed dosage that wanted to see my parents splattered across a shelf of ice and snow?*

A siren wails in the distance, but my eardrums quickly tune it out. It is deafeningly loud—loud enough to pull a cry from my throat. I abandon the window and the overcast sky beyond, slink under my comforter, and pile pillows atop my aching head. I close my eyes, listening to the gentle rumble of thunder, and beg sleep to steal me. In any way and every way, I beg for darkness, silence, and freedom from the sensations of my body. I beg for someone to alleviate the pain, heal my horrors, and make me human.

I hope for someone who doesn't exist—someone capable of keeping me *me*.

2 | GRAYSON

No one in this world is good, not really. People pretend to be more than they are, but human nature cannot be changed. We're selfish survivalists caught in a system built to kill us on an orb of misery spinning through a void. Every second of every hour comes with the same assignment: Do what's necessary to make this droplet in the ocean of existence bearable. For that reason, I spend as much time as I can with Clara Lovecroft.

Clara is a sunset in the dead of winter. She is beautiful in every eerie, frigid sense of the word, and she is completely off-limits. The whole Lovecroft family is to be kept at arm's length if I'm to avoid the tongue-lashing of a lifetime. Usually, I'm good at following orders. For them, unfortunately, I falter.

A knock rattles my apartment. Its volume suggests irritation, and its speed suggests urgency. On opening the front door, I find my forbidden best friend of too many years, Jade Lovecroft. She wears a frown like fangs and speaks with a voice like venom. Only those equipped with the antidote come away from interactions with her unscathed.

"What happened?" I sigh.

"I need food," she says.

A glance down at her knuckles clues me into her situation. They are wrapped in ivory gauze, but bruises trickle out from beneath it. They crawl down her fingers like a case of gangrene.

"You need a doctor," I correct her.

She scoffs, shoving her way past me. What she lacks in height, she makes up for with brute strength. Though she's Clara's sister, the two are nothing alike. If Clara is icicles and overcast skies, Jade is blazing sunlight at the height of July, a scorching red-sand desert with inescapable fury. She tramples over the welcome mat and leaves a trail of brown gravel on the white tiles of my kitchen floor. Her hands tear open the cabinets with an unspoken vendetta, and she rips a bag of potato chips from my alphabetized pantry as though the pantry might have wrestled her for it.

"I'm entering another tournament," she announces.

"I thought you were done street fighting." I start on the preparations for a pitcher of lemonade, tossing her the lemons to pulverize.

"I need the money. It's as good a job as any."

"It's a coping mechanism, and a stupid one at that."

She reduces the lemon in her hand to citrusy entrails entangled in the thick spirals of a crushed rind. I curse under my breath and follow it with an apology. I shouldn't have mentioned it; I'm never to bring this topic up first. Jade is sensitive about it year-round, but this weekend marks the ten-year anniversary of her parents' death. It hangs in the air like smoke carried for miles, leaving a noxious stench on all it touches.

Death has a way of tainting life.

Jade was happy once. Her gaze was sharp, and she existed at the center of a singularity. She saw only possibility, only hope. She wanted to be a physicist, a video game designer, and a firefighter. She wanted to rescue animals from kill shelters, become a lawyer for underrepresented communities, and learn how to farm vegetables in inhospitable environments. If no one stopped Jade Lovecroft, she very well may have become president.

Then we received the phone call.

We were seventeen and much too cool to attend a junior ballet recital. It was meant to begin at eight o'clock. At seven, we were buried in a console battling for crudely pixelated coins. At seven fifteen, we were raiding the liquor cabinet for swigs of vodka neither of us could keep down. At seven thirty, red and blue lights were pouring through the windows.

"Jade Lovecroft?" an officer said, his navy uniform pressed to perfection. "Your sister is in the hospital."

Jade snickered, unmistakably tipsy. Then her face blanched at the thought of tiny Clara in a cast. "Did she actually break a leg?"

Someone better equipped to handle the shattering of a teenager's heart should have been sent. Officer Thornefield and his overgrown mustache were not ready. He furrowed his brows, sucked in a breath of preparation, then explained the reason for his arrival like an android attempting empathy for the first time.

Jade cried for weeks. She might have mourned longer if not for the vitriol that developed after she visited the site of the incident. Her grandparents brought her there for closure before moving the last of her things into their lavender-scented, doily-infested apartment. It only opened the wound wider, and Jade's been swimming in blood ever since. Her parents were her Polaris. Without them, she sees no light, no direction, and no hope. There is only agony, anger, and an aimless trek forward with no destination.

"What do you need the money for?" I offer her a glass and an unspoken apology.

She huffs, her breath rattling on the way out. "I got into that criminology program, and pity scholarships will only get you so far."

"Come again?" I drop my lemonade mid-sip, incredulous. "I thought you withdrew your application."

"Yeah, well . . ." She exhales, stalling. "I didn't. It's not a big deal, so don't make it one."

"Can I give you a hug, or will I get a black eye for trying?"

Her knuckles flex, setting off a succession of crackles and pops.

"Noted. Have you told anyone else?" I'm referring to Clara. I raise my brows. She raises hers right back. "She's your sister, Jade. She'd want to celebrate with you."

"Don't give me that. You and I both know the *real* reason you want us on speaking terms, and it has nothing to do with the sanctity of sibling bonds." She launches a potato chip, sharpened into a shard, in my direction.

"I don't like seeing you two like this."

She scoffs. "It's bad enough I had to spend two miserable years living with her after the accident. Must you insist on subjecting me to more of her?"

"Don't you miss her?" I do insist, ironic as it is. "You used to be so close."

"The circumstances changed, and we changed with them. Drop it, Warner."

"All I'm saying is, you might be happier together than apart. There are times when I never want to speak to Joey again, but I'd never be able to just leave him. I get why you moved out of your grandma's place the second you could. The whole place smelled like old-lady soap, and the porcelain dolls were creepy. I get why you want to hold Clara at arm's length, but she needs you more than you realize. She needs you now more than ever, and maybe . . . maybe you need her too."

At the apex of my next inhale, she shoves me into the nearest wall of plaster and holds me to it by my shoulders. Her eyes are bottled lightning, and her teeth are clenched and bared like a wolf's. If I push much further, she won't hesitate to deliver on the promise made by her knuckles moments ago. So I concede, but only partially.

"Clara, Joey, and I are going upstate this weekend," I say. "It's just a quick trip—three nights, tops—in Mom's cabin past Blackstone."

"And?" she growls.

"Consider this an invitation. We could celebrate your acceptance, all the tournaments you've been winning, and . . ." I smile, though the weight gathering in my chest drags it down. It's half-hearted, in the sense that only half my heart escapes the increasing gravity. "We'll be together. This weekend isn't going to be easy for either of you. Even if you're not ready to let her back in, it could be a good way to test the waters."

The way she narrows her eyes is a feral flare of warning. My eyelid aches in preparation.

"Just think about it. I'm picking Clara up in about an hour, though. So if you don't mind, I have to head out."

Slowly, she backs away from the wall, allowing me to peel my bruising back off it. I sweep my jacket up in one arm and hook an indigo backpack onto my shoulder with the other. The flares in her eyes are doused in sunlight. We stare at one another, caught in a standstill but not a standoff. I'm not her enemy. She isn't mine. The only adversary we face is the one all human beings fight against.

She avoids Clara because, by avoiding Clara, she sidesteps the hungry maw of death and memory. She left Clara because, in leaving Clara, she was able to keep the pain of their loss in her periphery.

"Fine." She speaks at last. "I'll come, but only because making Joey third wheel is cruel. I'll keep the kid company. Pick me up at the corner of Aspen and Deadhead after you grab him from school."

Tightening the gauze around her purpling fingers, she starts for the door on footsteps hastened by frustration. I can't help but smile, watching as her platform boots pick up some of the gravel they'd spread on arrival. "See you then, Jade."

"Whatever." She slams the door. That's her way of saying *I love you anyway*.

As Heat Wave Jade dissipates, I pull out my phone to text Clara, wandering into the storm tides of an entirely different natural disaster.

3 | CLARA

I am awoken by the sound of my cell phone. It barks, a beast of digital flesh and pixelated bone. To my utmost horror, the text message that lights up its screen is not from the pharmacy. It is from none other than Grayson Warner.

I'll be there in an hour!

I had forgotten. Amid the chaos of yesterday, I had forgotten our arrangement, the plans we'd made weeks in advance. With shivering fingers, I type out a response, no matter how many pangs it sends through my heart.

Hey, Gray. I'm so sorry, but I'm not sure I'm feeling up to it. I ran out of pills, and I'm waiting on a new prescription.

Bubbles of contemplation manifest as he conjures a response. Disappointed as he might be, it is essential that he be kept safe, and that means he must stay as far from me as possible until I'm properly medicated for . . . whatever condition I carry.

No worries! You left a few at my place the last time you stayed over, though. Want me to bring them by?

My throat seizes up, cutting off my windpipe fast enough to coax a cough from my lungs. *Had* I left a few at his apartment? When would I have done something so careless? I suppose Grayson has a way of making me feel normal enough to overlook such things. I respond with record-challenging speed, thanking him profusely. He sends back a smiley face.

I take a few meditative breaths while changing into a presentable outfit. Movement is a difficult but necessary evil right now. I keep it breathable and loose to avoid any excess touching of the skin beneath. It burns bare, and layers are making it much, much worse.

My eyes catch the corner of a densely packed duffel bag kicked to the left of my bed. I'd packed it when Grayson first invited me on a trip beyond the city's borders. I had been excited. The noise here is suffocating—a boa constrictor of sound. I was looking forward to the quiet.

Blinding streams of sunlight pour in through the windows, and each one hurts more than the last. There is no time to mourn the weekend I could have had. I kick the duffel farther into the gloom, tug a few fingers through my tangled hair, and race for the lobby of my apartment complex to meet Grayson at the door. On the edge of the doorman's desk, I spy the twenty-dollar tip he must have slipped them to gain entry without a key card.

"M'lady." Grayson enters the space wearing a grin and a metaphorical suit of shining armor. Though he is no more than three years older than me, his soul is a skyscraper, and he extends it beyond his flesh proudly.

"Gray." I breathe his name. "Thank you so much. You have no idea how much of a lifesaver you are."

"Don't mention it." He pulls a sealed plastic bag from his pocket. It contains five translucent pink orbs. Before I can reach out for it, he's centimeters from my face, inspecting my eyes like an ophthalmologist. "You got no sleep last night."

"I got some sleep."

"I could put groceries in those bags."

He's right. He probably could fit his weekly supermarket haul in my lower lids. Unlike the workaholic Grayson Warner, I require sleep to appear presentable. He looks perfect no matter how long he spends carrying briefcases through the city's finer districts. "Really?" I murmur.

"No, no. I'm kidding. You look fine. Just a little tired." Like a mother hen, he pulls a pill out himself, places it on my palm, then produces a bottle of spring water from the satchel hanging at his hip. "Beautiful, but tired. Bottom's up."

I slip the glossy pink orb between my teeth and swallow it without the water. Grayson stares between a series of surprised blinks. I must have looked far too eager.

"What are those for, anyway?" he asks, airy and clueless to the magnitude of his question.

"Anxiety." The Universe, in all its infinite humor, chuckles at me. "Hence the grocery-bag eyelids. Plus, this weekend is the anniversary of . . ."

My parents, hanging slack-jawed from their seat belts. My parents, screaming with infantile instinct despite decades in flesh. My parents, and the lie they'd been telling me since I was born. "We did it to protect you," they had said.

They knew good and well what they were protecting me from, meaning . . . the answer to my problem might be one they can provide. How hadn't I thought of it before? If the pharmacies fail me, my final lifeline is attached to them. They stockpiled the supply that's kept me sated all this time. Conversation of their past was constantly waved away, hidden behind a nebulous, nonspecific veil, but I remember talk of pensions, contracts, and redacted files from behind the bars of our creaking wooden staircase. I remember the way they'd nose-dive into whispers at the chance of being overheard.

"I'm sorry," says Grayson. Sadness and concern dance woefully behind his eyes. They flit across the street, where a coffee shop promises discounted cappuccinos. "Can I buy you a coffee?"

I bury my feelings of realization. I need access to someone Grayson is bound to have better luck with, and coffee will lead nicely into that conversation. "I'd appreciate that," I reply. A silence settles over us as we exit the building and cross the street. Just as his hand hovers over the café's gilded doorknob, I utter a timid, "How's Jade?"

Grayson stalls.

"She's . . ." He blows a sigh through his nose, his eyes glazed over with too many emotions for me to read without subtitles. "She's trying. I asked her to come along this weekend, and she actually agreed to it. If you're feeling better, you should too. It'll give you two a chance to talk."

His intentions are innocent enough. He has no idea that every time I look at my sister, I see myself bathing in the blood that birthed us. Her eyes have always been wrought with suspicion, logically unfounded but atrociously valid. On the surface, I'm the reason they drove out into a blizzard. Below it, darker demons dwell. If I hadn't so often screamed their names in my sleep, she might have gone unaware of them. When I called out, I wasn't mourning them; I was cursing them. In my waking life, I couldn't conceal every sigh of relief at the mention of their deaths. Jade knew vengeance from grief all too well. She knew I didn't miss them as she did, and she hated me for it. When I look at her now, I see someone who sees right through me. Her gaze reaches into the depths of my bloodstained soul.

If all were right with the world, I'd never see Jade again, but desperate times call for desperate measures. "Does she still have Mom and Dad's stuff?"

Grayson purses his lips into a line that glistens with bubble-mint balm. "Where did that come from?"

"I'm just curious. It's been ten years. It's like a morbid milestone. I thought I might take a look at it, if she'll let me." I let a few seconds hang in the air. A groan rumbles strategically through my throat. I'm a drained, nervous Clara in mourning. I'm anything but overeager, anything but desperate. My shoulders squirm into a shrug. The groan becomes a sigh. "Plus, it'll . . . give us a chance to talk."

Grayson's grin tells me everything I need to know. Not only is he prepared to oblige my request, but he is also planning to do so in a way that will give Jade no room for rebuttal. We abandon the coffee shop for an impromptu trip to her den of solitude. To call the drive overwhelming would be an understatement. I squint against each glimmering sign. Sirens and screeches dissolve into complete disarray. My ears ring. My eyes sting. Even with a proper dose of pink making its rounds through my system, I cannot belong here.

"I'll keep her in check. I promise," says Grayson. As sincere as those words are, they are the words of a man with a clouded sense of judgment. "I'm proud of you for this. It's a big step."

"She still hates me."

"She doesn't hate you. I don't think she's capable of it."

"What makes you say that?"

"It's Jade we're talking about. This is still the girl who beat up three boys in your fifth-grade class for making fun of your favorite hair bow. She's still the girl who chased after that ice cream truck for giving you the wrong sprinkles. God, remember that time she yelled at your piano instructor?"

"Please stop, Gray." It hurts. It hurts, and focusing on all her *rights* conveniently excludes all her *wrongs*. She's also the girl who was unwaveringly human in all the ways I couldn't be. She was a constant reminder of my fundamental failings. Then she left. She left me. I wasn't someone worth staying for, but I wish she would have.

"I'm sorry, I'm sorry." Grayson's face blossoms into a gentle smile. "I'm just proud of you, that's all."

As sunlight dances across his enviably perfect cheekbones, I remember how fluttery it feels when he's proud of me. Despite all the heartache, he still knows how to make me feel like light. He just knows—and sometimes a bit too much. He befriended me before the world was a stage and I stepped onto it in character. He knows the version of me that used to hope for happy endings, and the version of him that wants so desperately to provide them comes out as we arrive at the corner of Aspen and Deadhead.

Jade stands at the mouth of an alleyway, wearing a scowl that could startle Hades. When she catches sight of me, the hatred in her eyes cuts deeper than a knife. It's a well-deserved wound, but a wound nonetheless.

"Where's Joey?" she hisses.

"We'll get him," Grayson reassures her. "In the meantime, Clara wanted to come see you."

Jade's gaze, bursting with vermilion veins, scours me, body and soul. "Did she, now?"

I step out of the Warner family Hummer, then pad up to my sister. She towers several inches over my head, so her build dwarfs mine completely. Where I have pathetic chopsticks, she has biceps sculpted by years of rage.

"I didn't know you started boxing again. Grandma would be furious." I offer a verbal olive branch.

She scoffs, rejecting it. "We don't live with Grandma anymore."

"I . . . well . . ." I stammer. She's burning me alive on the spot. "Th-thank goodness for that, right? I hated those porcelain dolls."

Silence.

I wish I could vanish.

"Clara wanted to know if you kept your parents' old things," Grayson intervenes, ever the knight. "There was a box, wasn't there?"

Jade's expression darkens, but through the storm clouds, there is a pocket of drizzle. Redness swells into the spaces beneath her bottom lids, and her bruised lip falls into a poorly concealed quiver. She looks away, then back. Then away, then back again. The air itself trembles as she forces it down her windpipe. It escapes in a puff of heat chased by a string of whispered swears.

"Why?" she snaps.

"I don't know," I lie. "I just . . . wanted to have a look. It feels important. I was too young to appreciate it then, but I'm glad you put all their stuff in one place. I'm grateful that you—"

"Do we have to do this now?" Shaking, she lights a cigarette crunched by the pressure of her pocket. "Aren't we supposed to be off on some big adventure?"

"I'm not coming," I correct her. Her relief is visible and obvious enough to call rude. However, like the wound she'd landed earlier, it's well deserved. "That's why it has to be now. You, Grayson, and Joey are leaving. The anniversary is—"

"I know when it is."

"Let her speak, Jade," Grayson mediates.

Jade retaliates with an eye roll and a plume of secondhand smoke. The bitter scent of scorched tobacco makes me nauseous. If not for that pill, my one-second salvation, I'd have vomited all over the sidewalk. Too much tension gathers in our orbit. We are binary stars on course for collision.

"It's in my closet. You can have a look, but that's it. Don't take anything. In fact, don't touch anything. Got it?"

I nod. She throws a jangling duet of keys my way like a set of shuriken.

Jade's apartment is deplorable.

Clothing stained in every shade is strewn across the floor. It parts like a fabric sea to create a barely walkable path. The kitchen is splatter painted and smells faintly of stale tomato sauce. The living room consists of three beanbag chairs and a smashed television screen. Instead of curtains, she's hung a butterscotch bedsheet that likely started out white. It conceals windows misted with dust and plaster walls ravaged by cracks.

Jade's apartment is despair.

I follow the directions to her bedroom she gave between nicotine swigs. There, a naked mattress sits atop a block of solid plywood. Beside it, a desk overflows with newspapers, nacho wrappers, cigarette butts, and ash. Her comforter is navy blue. It is the same one she slept with when the two of us shared quarters.

Memories are such mercurial things.

The sight of Jade's ancient bedspread should fill me with the same hatred that's kept us apart all these years. She always stole my hopes of feeling human. Before our parents' blood stained the snow, she and I . . . we used to sit across from one another and chat about things young girls are meant to know intuitively. She'd prattle on about her most attractive peers, and I'd seal my lips, a bundle of confusion. She'd gush about video games, sports, and her latest gaggle of good grades. I'd listen, wondering how one could move with such ease through the world. I needed dance classes just to learn how one limb ought to sync with another. I couldn't figure anything out on my own.

Hatred isn't what I feel, though. I feel like an intruder.

The closet slides open with a deafening plea to be oiled at the joints. Two dozen hangers and four puffer coats dangle from a bar that is more rust than metal. On the floor, a cardboard box big enough for a couple of sneakers has been kicked to the backmost wall. In crude, bleeding black-marker cursive, Jade has written the words *see ya later, guys* on the lid.

My throat becomes an inferno.

Inside the box, files, photos, and an assortment of artifacts rest atop a bed of dust.

Dad's leather bracelet, tightened to fit Jade's wrist at its tiniest. A gift for his firstborn on her first birthday.

Mom's favorite coaster, chipped on one edge. I'd let it fall from a high cabinet while grabbing a bag of sugar; we were baking cupcakes.

A photograph of our sole attempt at a holiday card. Jade threw up on the photographer. Dad couldn't stop laughing. None of us could stop laughing.

I find a ballet slipper and despise myself more than ever. It's from one of my recitals, and it's been autographed: "If anyone messes with you, tell 'em I'm your sister. Break a leg. —Jade."

My cheeks are drenched. My head is pounding. I have to get out of here.

I claw through the cinders of our childhood in search of what I came here for. I must remember what I came here for. I'm not this girl. No matter how desperately I wanted to be, I never was. The pills allowed me a daughterly, sisterly form, but it was just an illusion. A uniform, an exoskeleton. I'm here for the means to maintain it, not to weep my way down Memory Lane. I'm not worth the spilling salt water. Jade owns the copyright on crying about this.

Two cards, each laminated and embossed, catch the attention of my fingertips. They seem to glimmer despite the deep-closet gloom. Mom and Dad smile for pictures taken against two emerald-green backdrops. Dr. Cedric Lovecroft and Dr. Adelina Dolion, researchers with level 6 clearance on an endeavor titled "PR-U." The seal beside their biometrics is a sigil that combines the letters *E*, *H*, *I*, and *K*.

This is . . . something. It isn't much, but it is something.

My phone buzzes. A text from Grayson appears on-screen.

Jade's getting antsy. You okay up there?

An antsy Jade is a dangerous Jade. I pack her grief box to near perfection, dust bunnies and all. The only artifacts out of place are the aging identification cards, which go straight into my pocket. They are my only chance at tracking down more pills, and thus, they're worth the risk.

PR-U.

E, H, I, K.

The fate of my humanity hinges on seven disjointed letters.

We're on our way up.

Grayson's warning sends a deluge of adrenaline to my blood. My legs move before my brain's given them permission to, muscle memory of arabesques carrying me across the space. I sail over congealed clumps of loungewear, avoiding edges that might ensnare. Sadly, I'm a long way from the dances that helped me find believable form. My toe catches on the makeshift bed frame. I fall frown-first onto Jade's desk.

A sticky film that reeks of citrus holds my cheek to the cherrywood. A few eyelashes lie severed in the shimmering glaze. From beyond them, a newspaper headline glares at me: Flames or Falsities? Mass Disappearances Linked to Local Forest Fire. The issue is nearly twenty-five years old.

I can't help but regard the withered pages like sacred parchment stolen from the timestream. It's been read, highlighted, underlined, and annotated with care uncharacteristic of my sister. Wedged between a crude cartoon and an advice column, the article reads: Plumes of smoke have been spotted over the southernmost edge of Blackstone Forest. Insisting wildfires to be the cause, local authorities have indefinitely suspended investigation of the area. However, concerned citizens link the event to a mass vanishing that occurred days prior.

I snatch the paper from its place beside a tipped-over can of cola. It proceeds to explain the sudden loss of contact with dozens of scientists and researchers. Family members were reluctant to speak about them, leading many to believe their silence had been bought.

"Weeks after, the forest started growing like crazy," a witness admits in inky, grayscale honesty. "The feds came rushing in. They started buying up property around Blackstone, and then there was a whole barricade. Eventually, the trees stopped growing. I haven't got a clue why. The agents hightailed it out in their fancy cars, then started telling people Blackstone had always been that big. I don't go up that way anymore. Something's wrong with that place."

Jade has circled the word *feds* several times. In the same handwriting she'd left on the bottom of my ballet slipper, she's written, *"The EHKI?"*

The desire to scour every notebook she's left beside this newspaper is almost too much to manage. Before I can, the door slams open, and Grayson's voice arrives like a fire alarm. "Clara?"

There's no time. I make my way to the foyer with the most convincing sniffle possible. "Sorry. It was just . . . really hard, harder than I thought it would be."

"My sympathies," Jade growls. "Now, let's go. Joey's waiting for us."

I sit beside Grayson in the passenger seat of his Hummer, resisting the urge to adjust the cards rattling toward the mouth of my pocket. Jade seethes from the back, her duffel bag in the spot saved for Joey.

"I'll drop you off before we get to the high school. Unless you've changed your mind?" Grayson's eyes, two moon-kissed pools, go wide and hopeful.

"How far is it, again?" I ask, allowing for the illusion of contemplation. I'm a Clara who's pondering.

"Eight hours, but we'll make a pit stop after Blackstone. If you want, I'll buy you some . . ."

His voice fades into obscurity. They're headed toward Blackstone Forest. That explains why Jade's been so willing and well behaved. Grayson serves as a taxi driver, oblivious to her plan to make their getaway into an investigation. If our parents were connected to this case, it's one she'll never abandon. If following this lead could get me more pills, I'll have to be equally relentless. It's my only chance.

However, if this truly *is* the end of my supply, I'd rather be nestled in the middle of nowhere when the inevitable comes creeping. I could slip into oblivion, lost to some pocket of unholy darkness betwixt the sugar maples. I could dissolve, far away from folks with lives that a sudden, inexplicable monster might disrupt.

"You wouldn't mind?" Gently, I interrupt his princely rambles.

He lays a warm palm atop my knuckles, and suddenly, this is the safest place in the world. It's against every moral I maintain to feel this way, but damn him and the crooked starlight in his smile. I can't resist. Here comes that fantasy Grayson just can't help but induce. Here comes the wave of seawater and citrus that makes me feel inexplicably, unfathomably . . .

"Never," he says, and I believe him.

"I wouldn't be too much trouble?" I am trouble embodied, but when he shakes his head, I believe him, again.

We stop at my apartment to pick up the bag I left by its lonesome. Joey joins us shortly after, leaving his flock of high school friends waving from the edge of a blacktop basketball court. Jade colors the start of our journey with an orchestra of complaints. She makes her displeasure known in every way at her disposal, but I will not be swayed. She needs this trip to mourn the dead.

I need it to maintain what's left of my life.

4 | JS-7R

I am a hideous amalgamation of humanity's loftiest hopes and most primal fears. Those fleshy sacks of animated hubris don't know when to leave well enough alone. I haven't the slightest idea what drives them to chase the edge of impossibility. Perhaps insanity runs in their collective bloodline, an unspoken bond that dwells deep inside their genes.

Still, what they do isn't fair. It also isn't particularly smart.

To humans, the earth is a playground. Even the most precious and delicate life-forms are reduced to inconsequential means to their brutal ends. Their claw marks have left countless scars, and they take great pleasure in reopening them. They swim in pools of spilled blood for the orgasmic allure of omnipotent power. They tear apart their world so that it can be stitched back together in alignment with their infernal, ephemeral desires.

They create monsters like me, not because they have to, but because they can.

Test tubes. Syringes. Straps.

Blue gloves. Notebooks. Thin, rectangular spectacles.

To humans, it is all a game. Life is a board filled with candy-colored squares and boldly lettered benchmarks. All sentient players are statuettes to be bounced across the spaces. Without the ability to speak or scream, they are instruments in the cultivation of their appointed god's desires. Those gods dislike when we play back, and they abhor when we win.

I've played with many humans over the years. They drive down my road, orchestral cycles of sound pouring from their windows and exploding from their lips. They are cacophonous creatures intent on disturbing the silence I was cursed to endure. When interrupted by show tunes and untrained singing voices, I take pride in upholding the terms of my containment.

When I lost the rest of my kind, I tried not to mourn. They deserved better than a life like mine, a life tethered but untouched. Their mutant souls are free to frolic in the ether, yet I am still here, a mistake drenched in blood, sweat, and chemicals. There are times when greed gets the better of me. There are times when I yearn to thumb through the still frames of space-time and save just one fellow monster. Sadly, a creature capable of chronokinesis wasn't one of Dr. Hemlock's objectives.

No, no, no.

If I could go back and tamper with the temporal threads, I wouldn't. When I catch a glimpse of myself in a stray shard of glass or a thinning stream of spring water, all of the longing in me fizzles like a drenched firecracker. Connection isn't my destiny; it isn't even an option. When I escape this confounded dimensional prison, I will not seek community beyond the particle barriers. I have a higher purpose now, a goal as consummate as the state of my genes. We all have our quests to conquer, and mine is one of retribution and rebirth. I will spread like an antibiotic against this planet's deadliest affliction. I will take back what is rightfully mine. Project Undergrowth made one sole monarch to the throne of human evolution, and I intend to sit on it.

The comforts of the flesh are beneath me. Sovereigns rule best in solitude.

Today is a day like all the rest. My latest attempt to take back the planet lies dazed and darling against a twisted tree trunk. Expression woozy and eyes crying crimson, he is still very much under my influence. I never caught his name, but his travel companion screamed something beginning with a *B* before I sent a swarm of branches down her throat. *Brian? Bexley?* It doesn't matter. Slowly, he melts into the phthalo-green brush. Skin hardening into blackened bark, his limbs writhe and contort until his form is fit for my menagerie of anthropomorphism.

All of my trees are corpses.

It's a shame no one cared to warn Mr. Brian Bexley about the accursed wood grown from the bones of Dr. Hemlock's dirtiest secret. It's something her people have thoroughly conspired to hide. They weren't the sort to let news of mass murder slip into the general public. They'd hidden their terrible little research project for decades, after all. Save for those owned by the EHKI, every soul silly enough to chase the path into my forest is none the wiser to the danger.

Humans aren't wise about most things, I suppose.

Take wonderful, bespectacled Hemlock, for example. My abilities are an anomaly, but she wasn't overcome with the caution wisdom might endow. Her notes spoke of neuro-emotional manipulation by way of telepathic linkage. Her tests involved electrodes and wires aplenty.

"Hold still, JS-7R," she'd said. She never asked, always ordered. However, her orders were always delivered in a kindly, weathered voice. It was as sweet and silvery as the "stress grays" strewn through her black locks. Obedience came like breathing, even when the electroconvulsive tests were excruciating. Mutiny was barely a musing, because I wanted so badly to be good. Good and then some. Good and good enough.

Heightened strength, speed, and agility were side dishes to my dinner of supernatural delicacies. Phytokinesis was dessert. It was my distinctly inhuman qualities she and her colleagues sought to feast on.

They hadn't arranged for studies to be conducted on my mastery of biological alchemy. Those were an anomaly beyond the confines of their comprehension. Living cells whisper the secrets of their structural arrangement in my ears. In doing so, they open gateways of access that are a delight to step through. Matter is made from the same building blocks, and when the right ones are shifted, bone becomes wood and blood becomes chlorophyll.

Very wise of you, Mother. You built a monster of consumption you couldn't hope to control.

The alchemic infection wanes on Mr. Brian Bexley, healed by the very thing it hungered for. A budding bloom pushes a plastic card from one of his pockets, and his true identity is revealed. He wasn't a *Mr.* at all; he was an *agent.*

It seems the EHKI is still intent on surveilling from within and without. They should know how I feel about their cameras by now. I wonder if this departed fellow had been dispatched to set up another in place of the twelve I destroyed last week. I do hope they get the message at some point. They'll run out of man power before I run out of *my* power.

The unmistakable hum of an engine teases my senses.

Shall I have another playmate so soon? Usually, there's a bit more time to enjoy my art before fresh paint comes along. What shade will it be this time: agent or civilian? I travel by shadow to the border of my forest. A building decorated with petroleum promises serves as an unspoken indicator of where my particle-barrier prison meets the world beyond. My DNA, of which the EHKI has too many samples, cannot pass through.

Nothing could have prepared me for what I find at the gas station. Nothing could have prepared me . . . for *her.*

5 | CLARA

The highway sweeps us away from civilization in just four hours. Now green trees cascade as far as the eye can see, a world of nothingness beside a two-lane asphalt strip. As unpredictable as it seems, our city moves rhythmically, a monochromatic metronome. It's easy to put your head down and vanish like a film noir background character. There's a schedule, a timetable, a backbeat. There's a palette of gray scale all denizens must paint with.

Up here, among the forest, things are different. Every color of the rainbow hides between ancient branches, and something wild lurks in the eyes of quickly vanishing creatures. It's as though the entire environment is connected through a hive mind, systematically anarchic. Neatly senseless. There is only chaos—chaos that makes me feel at home.

On the ground, leaves long perished are conquered by the roots of other organisms, the mouths of hungry herbivores, and artfully capped fungi. Even in death, forests are alive. They are a testament to how life persists because life simply must. It is nature, and nature operates on intuition. Perhaps that's why Jade's kept on living. Perhaps that's why I've kept on living. Somewhere within us lies the belief that we are worth preserving, and moreover, worthy of rebirth. I hope with all my heart it is a belief worth having.

"Do we have to listen to this?" Jade gestures vengefully to Grayson's assortment of seventies hits.

She used to love them. We used to belt out our favorites in the back seat of Dad's hideous brown van. On warm summer days, we'd drive to the park and perch on the car roof to host parking lot concerts. Naturally, she was a far better singer, and I'd often need a creamsicle to soothe my throat after trying to match her pitch. Dad still assured me I'd be famous someday. Jade told me that, worst-case scenario, I'd be her lead backup dancer.

"It's all we've got. There are no stations nearby." Gray laughs, reaching out to lower the volume. I wish I could lower the volume in my head with such ease.

"Your mixtape is making me want to blow my brains out."

"Not in the back seat, okay?"

Jade grunts, slamming her head against her headrest in defiance. Despite how enthusiastically he'd been tapping his leg to the beats of yesteryear, Grayson acquiesces. He switches off the radio and cracks a window so that the wind's whistle breaks the silence. The smell of green petrichor captures my senses. All of my memories in melancholy monotone blur, and suddenly, I'm back in the present.

"Gray?"

"Yes, m'lady?"

"You're sure your mom is all right with this? I feel bad just . . . you know . . ."

His eyes flick across every inch of the picturesque landscape, the rush of Earth's most authentic colors.

"She doesn't go up to the lake house anymore. Don't stress." His hand lands on my shoulder, and he moves his thumb in small, soothing circles that create creases on the puff of my sleeve. "It'll be a nice weekend. I promise."

Joey pops his head out from the back seat, smiling from ear to ear. Dusty-blond curls fall in a mischievous shower over his forehead, a few strands caught in the joints of his sunglasses. "What better way to escape the woes of everyday life than a luxurious mountaintop getaway?

I'm so happy Mom bought that house. Best thing she ever did for the family, aside from producing me."

"Joey, put your seat belt on," Grayson orders, his face now deadpan. His jaw is taut, a katana of stubble-tempted skin and bone.

Brothers by blood, Joey and Grayson have everything and nothing in common. Both of them possess the same blond locks, but Joey's are pale honey and Grayson's are as ashy as a sunrise behind a storm cloud. They also share the same striking blue eyes, Joey's lively and bright, and Grayson's enigmatically weary.

Even in adulthood, Jade and I prove that the cosmos has a sense of humor.

I look exactly like my sister, except if she were a goddess of the sun, I'd be a goddess of the darkness it surges against. Where she is mysteriously beautiful, I am mysteriously haunting. Where she intimidates with bloodied fists, I intimidate with an inhuman gaze. Her hair is espresso come alive in the form of loose curls, and her skin, though usually bruise beaten, is a warm, glowing shade of chestnut. Her eyes are as sharp as the edge of a silver blade, but their intensity is concealed by a russet scabbard. She is beautiful and ethereal, like a goddess fallen to Earth from somewhere deep within the sun. If trauma hadn't turned her violent, she'd embody this essence to its fullest potential, but because of me, her skin is never solid in hue. Black and blue infest it in plumes of color from popped vessels below. Her hair stays tangled in tight updos to protect it from the fights she picks to numb the pain.

I was fourteen when it happened. She was seventeen. Though they typically hovered around me, she had more time with them, and thus, more of them to mourn.

Joey lowers his window and points to an upcoming gas station abruptly enough to startle the whole car. "I want five chocolate bars, stat!"

Grayson rolls his eyes through a drive-lagged smile. He pulls up to the rusted structure and parks just beside a sign promising discount firewood and affordable lighter fluid.

A chill scales my spine.

"We needed gas anyway." He pulls a ten from his wallet. "You'll get as many bars as you can buy with that."

Without another word, Joey snatches the bill and races toward the general store beside the gas pumps. He spins on his heel to face us just once, his next line politely practiced. The Warners are very serious about their manners. "Would anyone else like anything?"

"I need a bathroom break." The words dribble out before I can stop them. The speed at which Grayson is out of his seat and opening my door is kinetic whiplash. I flash a grateful smile, then climb out of the car one leg at a time. "Thanks. I'll be right back."

The metallic double doors of the shop open like curtains. Stacks of foil-wrapped food are posed beyond them, each looking more expired than the last. I consider grabbing some baked chips for Grayson and some cheese puffs for Jade, but most of them look like inedible escapees from the nineties. Even the graphic designs on them are ancient, though none are name brands. I pity the travelers who come this far without their snacks preprepared.

My heels click against the worn tiles until they shift into concrete. It pours from beneath the ladies' room door, suggesting that whoever crafted the floor lost steam at precisely this point. Ironic. In such an isolated area, you'd assume the bathroom to be the store's most vital asset. Inside, the walls are a muted blue color, and the fluorescent lamps burn with a sickly greenish glow. Every now and again, a gnat lands on their glass, causing sparks of dissonant flickers to erupt from within. The scent of the surrounding greenery has crept through each vent, leaving wisps of woodland pine on the inert air.

It's quiet. The shadows seem to stare back.

I do some staring of my own. The mirror is made from crackling, emerald-tinted aluminum. Still, it is a mirror, and it does as mirrors must. It serves me well as I rake my fingers through my hair and ensure my eyes haven't started sinking toward the back of my skull. I'll need another dose in the morning, but my supply is so dreadfully limited.

Here's to hoping Jade's grief-induced research leads to ends more alive than our parents.

The overhead lights buzz in a rhythm, creating an eerily . . . soothing tune. At first, I figure the wave of peace is a by-product of these moments in solitude, but soon enough, the tune overtakes the whole of my hearing. It becomes increasingly like a song too familiar to be new, but too new to be familiar. In my reflection, I watch as the corners of my lips are pulled skyward and the russet in my eyes shifts to an inexplicable shade of . . . Is that red?

What a lovely, lovely red.

"What have we here?" a voice croons in my mind. I feel like I've been injected with a muscle relaxant. Suddenly, the floor feels more akin to a cashmere blanket than a slab of concrete. I want to curl up on it and sleep like a kitten for hours, days, weeks . . .

Three knocks rattle the door.

"Clara! You've been in there for twenty minutes!" Joey's pubescent voice fills the room.

Twenty minutes?

"Sorry!" I panic, the electric hum silencing as I splash water onto my face and burst through the creaking door. "I—I didn't realize it had been that long. Did you get your chocolate?"

Joey shrivels. "The guy at the counter is creepy."

When I came in, the shop was deserted. Part of me wondered if it had been abandoned, given the forlorn patch of land we'd found it in. The last town we passed was at least an hour back, and the sea of trees ahead suggests the next one is much farther off. Who would take such a drive to work for minimum wage selling gas and expired candy bars on the edge of Blackstone Forest?

Eyes alert, I glance over the racks to find this creep of a clerk.

At the counter sits a man too handsome to be real. He sports jet-black hair, long enough to leave soft, endearing wisps across his forehead. His ivory skin sits flawlessly over a modelesque bone structure, and his eyes—deep, dark, and sinful—draw attention like lures to a fish.

Under the sun's glow, they are amber. His pupils swim within the resin pools like fossils from another time. When a cloud crosses the sky, they shift to the deepest shade of black I've ever witnessed. It's like a sunset, the transition from dusk to darkness—breathtaking. I am mesmerized, soaking up his features, until Joey waves a hand in front of my face.

"Earth to Clara," he whispers.

"Huh?"

"You're staring at the guy and it's, like, really obvious."

"Oh!" I jump, horrified. Folding my arms over my chest, I duck behind a potato chip rack and peer over like a panther stalking prey. Almost every fiber of my being hopes I haven't been spotted. Almost.

"Do you think he saw me?"

"Probably."

"Damn it." I stomp, inwardly demanding my heart to stop fluttering like a caught firefly. "We'll just buy your chocolate and leave. I'll never have to see him again."

Joey shrugs, handing me the bars and the ten.

"Let's do this." With a sharp inhale, I stride to the counter, place the bars on it, and hold out the money with my elbow comically straight. It looks like a chopstick. The clerk looks at my arm, then at me, and then back to my arm. With a charming smile, he plucks the bill from between my fingers and nods a thank-you.

"Oh . . . um . . . thanks. We'll be taking these chocolate bars with us. We're going on a road trip, so we need them. All five," I ramble, retracting my hand.

The clerk laughs, and the sound is dizzying enough to make me sway.

"Well," he says at last.

His voice is like the most beautiful bullet to the chest. My heart rate picks up, mimicking the rhythm of the bathroom buzz, and my stomach fills with a migration's worth of butterflies. Not butterflies—fireflies. He's lighting me up, and the glow is spreading far beyond my abdomen. It drips down my legs and grapples up to my brain stem. By the time it's reached the crown of my skull, my mind has thoroughly record-scratched.

"Since you're in dire need of these bars, they're on the house." He extends his arm stiffly to hand back the bill, teasing me.

"Thank you." I accept it with my eyes glued to his. If only I could muster enough social prowess to keep speaking. I've never done this before. Idle flirtations aren't for people like me. Romance on the whole is off-limits. Connection is dangerous.

"No problem." He winks, and I wish I could see it in my mind's eye, on a loop, forever.

Joey sighs and grabs one of his chocolate bars, as agitated and impatient as his age justifies. "I'll be in the car. Come out when you're done flirting, Clara."

I whip around to give Joey's retreating figure a frown. He's long gone by the time I do. The bell above the double doors jingles, and as he exits, a man clothed entirely in gray enters. His vehicle sits outside, parked in front of a nonoperational gas pump. An intuitive pang surges through my stomach. We'd been driving for hours on a road with few winds. Surely we would have noticed a sleek two-door painted like a mirror traveling close enough to meet us here.

The man surveys the aisles, his sunglass-shrouded eyes as focused as lasers. His deep-brown skin contrasts the slate tones of his suit. The way his shoes click against the beaten tiles suggests their price is well above average. Whoever he is, he holds some kind of rank, and commands respect for it on calculated strides.

I've always worried about the sanctity of my secret. I've always wondered if someone would crawl out of the gloom to arrest me for parricide. He looks like a private investigator, and if I didn't know any better, I would accuse Jade of hiring him. She's up here with ulterior motives as well. It isn't the greatest impossibility I've faced.

I'm being paranoid.

My hands tremble, but they *will* remain human, and therefore, I will remain hidden. I've had my dose for the day, the blood on my hands has had a decade to dry, and the suit-clad stranger is focused solely on whether to buy salted or unsalted pretzels. I'm safe. The clerk's intoxicating voice calls my attention back.

"Clara . . . what a beautiful name."

I turn to him. I'm no longer playing any sort of part. I'm not pretending to be an attentive Clara; I really, truly want to offer him all the headspace mileage I own. "Thank you. Um . . . and yours?"

"I'm . . . Jasper."

The sound of his name sets off a shock wave. Everything, absolutely everything, goes silent. No birds chirp. No cars zoom. No wind blows. Suddenly, everything is *Jasper*. Jasper and the sound of his name. With a wolfish smirk, he leans forward, tucks a finger under my chin, and gently closes the gap between my top and bottom lip. "Let me just say, if this is your way of flirting, I'm ensnared," he whispers.

My face burns, dropping a few shades on the color chart to produce a rosy hue. I pull away from his touch, though my senses yearn to stay. "I'm sorry."

He laughs again. "What are you apologizing for? It's cute. I'm not much better when it comes to this, trust me."

Before I can retort, a harsh round of beeps erupts from the Hummer. My attention now Jasper-centric, it takes a second for the sound to register. "My friends are waiting outside. I have to go."

Jasper's brows furrow in what looks like disappointment, but it wears off quickly. "It was a pleasure to meet you, Clara. Enjoy those extremely crucial chocolate bars."

I'm unable to bear concluding this conversation, so I linger, waiting for my frontal lobe to produce a suave goodbye. Joey, likely given orders from his brother, reenters with intent to drag me out the door. He does so with sheepish haste, outwardly unnerved by the still-smiling Jasper.

"C'mon, Clara." He clasps a hand around my upper arm and makes a clumsy beeline for the exit.

"Coming . . ." My lips move dutifully, the rest of my human exosphere unaware it's started moving. I wave to Jasper with my free hand before being wedged between the double doors, and upon being hit by cloud-filtered sunlight, I snap out of the lovesick stupor he induced. Eyes sharpening and movements less languid, I walk by myself instead of allowing Joey to lead.

"Sorry," I start, flushed. "I don't know what happened to me, I just . . ."

"All good." He opens the passenger door like a tiny gentleman. "There's this kid in algebra who does the same thing to me. One time, he asked for help on the homework, and I just kind of . . . well, I threw up, but the hibachi from the night before wasn't agreeing with me." He plucks the remaining chocolate bars from my hands once I am seated, closes the door, and gets back to his place beside Jade. "You handled it better than I would have."

"Handled what?" Grayson chimes in.

"Clara just ensured she'd die alone by failing to flirt with the creepiest dude I've ever seen." Joey shrugs, tearing open a bar and beginning to break it into squares. "It felt like the whole room dropped below freezing when he walked in. He had crazy eyes and everything. Total package, Clara. Good instincts on that one."

Grayson's head snaps toward me, his eyes demanding an explanation.

"That is not what happened, I swear!" I fan out my arms in defense. "Firstly, he was not creepy. Secondly, I did not fail. I was able to maintain full eye contact the entire time."

"Whatever you have to tell yourself." Joey pops a melty bit of sweetness between his teeth.

"At least I didn't throw up," I tease, stealing a square.

"It was the hibachi!" He steals it back. "Now, drive, Grayson! Before she goes back in and brings even more dishonor upon the car!"

Grayson speeds away. Deafening silence absorbs us. He grips the steering wheel hard enough to turn his knuckles white, and glares through the rearview mirror as though attempting to telepathically intimidate the stranger we've left behind. Jade busies herself with snapping apart perfectly rectangular pieces of the bar she was given. I am left to my own pocket of quietude to wonder what on earth came over me, and what could lie beyond the maze of rusted barbed wire in the distance.

6 | GRAYSON

A breeze nips my skin as I flood the car with gasoline. Considering the layer of rust encrusted to the dilapidated structure, I'm surprised it has a supply buried beneath the aged concrete at my feet. The area is deserted. I can't imagine many people pass through in need. Perhaps the gallons being pumped were dropped off when the cluster of buildings in the far distance were operational. They are made from weather- and time-beaten limestone. They are skeletal remains. A flimsy layer of barbed wire has been placed to deter unwelcome visitors. My mind plays eagerly with images of who might be crazy enough to cut their jeans leaping over it. It's a welcome distraction to my musings of what transpired beyond.

I glance down at my phone, pulling up a map-devoted application. On it, there is no indication of buildings nearby. There's no indication of the gas station either. The sound of the gas flow sputtering to a halt pulls me from my thoughts before they can spiral. I shove my phone back into my pocket, yank the nozzle from the tank, and tuck it back into its ancient socket.

Jade rolls down her window. "Want a cigarette?"

"Don't do that in the car. It's new. Also, you shouldn't smoke at gas stations."

She pulls out her lighter and lights up the stick hanging between her teeth. A plume of smoke pours into the air around us.

"Really?"

"Really."

I know better than to pick another fight with her. I'm lucky she came along, and she's ensuring I know it. Electing to keep quiet now and shampoo the seats later, I lean against the boxy edge of the Hummer. Jade's eyes meander to the faraway buildings, nonexistent to satellites but *very* existent to us.

"What are those?" She coughs.

"No idea." I shrug. "They're kind of weird, though."

"We should drive over and check them out."

Before I can counter, a coupe making every attempt to morph into a mirror pulls up to the gas pump opposite ours. It produces a man wearing sunglasses too opaque to be functional and an ensemble too formal for anything up ahead. He marches hastily into the convenient store, but not before crashing into Joey. My brother is many things, but graceful is not one of them.

His face is overcome with a pallor that highlights the freckles flecked across his nose. In place of a flippant smirk, he wears a frown stiffened by unease and dismay.

"What happened, kid?" Jade puts out her cigarette. "All out of chocolate?"

He shakes his head. It's rare for Joey to be quiet, and even rarer for him to appear on edge. I surmise bumping into someone unexpected spooked him, but even Jade recognizes the uncanniness of his silence. She meets his wordless response with a huff and starts unbuckling her seat belt.

"Tell me who I'm hitting," she says between knuckle snaps. He races to keep her door shut, which leaves a perplexed look on her face. She quickly replaces it with a lighthearted smirk and a chuckle that fails to chase the shadows from his gaze. "All right, I won't pick a fight, I promise. I'll just have a little chat with whoever messed with you."

"No one messed with me, but . . . I'm worried he'll mess with Clara," he explains.

Jade turns to stone, and though she'd never admit to it, she looks a lot less likely to keep her promise now.

"What do you mean?" I ask, attempting to soothe both of them. In actuality, I can barely feel the air as it spirals down my windpipe. "Where's Clara? Is she all right?"

"I don't know," Joey mumbles. His eyes dart through the dust-coated windows, narrow, nervous, and analytical. "I'll just go get her. Wait here, and don't let Jade out of the car."

I lean my weight against Jade's door, brows knotted. She rages against the handle with an orchestra of grumbles and grunts.

The windows lining the store are as murky as brackish water. On top of that, rows of derelict signage block the sparse pockets of clarity. From here, I see only silhouettes moving like bedsheets hung in the breeze. Fine soot gives them outlines, like TV static crackling against a poor cable connection. Try as I might, I cannot see Joey, Clara, or the gentleman who entered behind them.

Jade begins crawling over the central console. I race around to the driver's side to stop her, climbing in to keep her from wedging herself between the front seats.

"I just want to talk to the guy," she assures me in the least convincing way possible. "It'll take me two minutes."

"You're going to get us arrested."

"No, I'm not—but for the record, I've been arrested twice, and it's not that bad. If things go sideways, your family can bail us out and you can blame the whole thing on me. They already hate me, don't they?"

"No, they—" I groan, pinching the bridge of my nose the same way my father used to. "It's complicated. Please, just stay in the car. I'll go in and help Joey, but we can't risk—"

Joey emerges with his hand clamped around Clara's wrist. She stumbles behind him, her legs weaving into one another with each step.

"You handled it better than I would have," he says, propping her door open.

"Handled what?" I ask, trying to keep my fervid worry under an appropriate amount of wraps.

Clara fidgets as she settles into her seat. The most delicate pink hue crawls over her cheeks, subtly moving through contractions on account of her rapid breathing.

"Clara just ensured she'd die alone by failing to flirt with the creepiest dude I've ever seen."

The rest of their back-and-forth turns into high-pitched white noise. As my foot slams onto the gas pedal, the car lurches forward with a thunderous thrum. We leave the decaying gas station in a surge of dirt stirred up by the tires. They emit a terrible screech, racing off the concrete and onto the asphalt. In minutes, the structure is nothing but a mirage disappearing over the horizon, a speck on this anomalously straight road.

Sleep steals both Clara and Jade. Joey toys with the threads hanging from his sweater, knotting them in patterns. It feels as though I've been driving for five hours and five seconds, five moments and five years. There are too many trees, all of them lined up on a loop. The sky doesn't change, so still that it's like a curated dome of overhead clouds. I'm tired; I'm wired. I'm calm; I'm restless. I could stay this course for a hundred years; I want to pull over and sleep forever.

"I never realized how . . . straight this road was," Joey whispers. "I swore it had more turns. The last time we came up here with Dad, it felt like it had more turns."

"Joey." I swallow what I wanted to say. "What happened in the gas station?"

A small ball of tinfoil pelts the back of my head. It rolls beneath the collar of my shirt, imprisoning itself somewhere at the small of my back. I flash a tiny smirk in the rearview mirror. Despite our twelve-year age difference, Joey's smirk is identical to mine.

"Why? Are you jealous?"

"Curious."

"Yeah, right." He chuckles. "The dramatic zoom away was *real* curious of you. If you must know, the guy running the gas station was hot, but in a weird, sinister kind of way. He wasn't my type, but he was definitely Clara's. I've never seen her like that before. She could barely speak."

Once again, I swallow what I'd like to say, for my brother's sake.

I filter the deluge of adrenaline in my veins through my hands, because if I let it fall to my driving foot, we'll soar to ninety miles per hour. Clara still sleeps soundly at my side, her head nestled in the crook of an arm she's propped against the window. Her eyelashes are blown about by the air conditioner. I reach over to turn it away and brush a strand of hair from her forehead.

Joey's smirk widens. "Sorry, Gray. We might have some golden genes, but trust me, he has you beat."

"Gee, thanks."

"No problem. I'll be here all week." He grins, popping off another square of chocolate. "Want some? You seem to be in need of comfort food."

I purse my lips, eyes focused on the strip of asphalt ahead. The tunnel of trees to our left and right is gradually closing in, narrowing the path. The double yellow line tapers off as the road itself shifts from vibrant, freshly paved black to fissured, sun-battered gray.

"What did he look like?"

"Tall. Chiseled. On the paler side, but without the adorable freckles we've got. It wasn't just his looks, though. He mastered the 'secretly-a-serial-killer-chic' vibe, and Clara was totally into it."

"Did they talk?"

"Yeah, but I didn't stick around to spy on them. Like I said, he gave me the creeps."

He waggles a piece of chocolate at me, nibbled to enhance the sharpness of its edges. I accept it with a sigh, though I can barely pull in enough air to fuel it. Whether I care to admit it or not, I'm in need of a lot more than comfort food. This will have to do.

7 | JASPER

Well, well, well . . . what have we here?

Hidden behind the passenger window of an obnoxiously boxy vehicle sits a woman too divine to be real. With eyes like the earth and pupils as dark as midnight, she is a caged bird who's grown too accustomed to bars. She is a lovely, frowning thing, desperate to disappear.

Three other humans indulge in her presence, though they are clearly unworthy of it. The youngest of them races from their vehicle on footsteps made clumsy by impatience. My little bird follows him, too graceful for this mediocre plane, her form elegantly failing to fit the mold assigned to it. What a pleasure it is to observe her. Her hair sits in gentle tangles from scalp to waist, like chocolate melting down the edge of a strawberry. I'm certain those plush pink lips are far sweeter. I'd like to see them smeared bare and parted breathlessly. I'd like to kiss her.

However, I have much to learn, starting with the title tasked with encapsulating her otherworldly essence. I'd compare it to that of an angel. Dr. Hemlock made sure I learned a great deal about angels. They are said to be spun by virtuous hands, clothed in lace and light. Unlike them, my little bird isn't tied down by the weight of transient goodness. Something dark exists in her. Something diabolic. Something like the shadows dwelling inside me.

No.

I can't possibly think such nonsense, not about a human being. I have a higher purpose here, and that purpose does *not* include the frivolities of the flesh. Skin-to-skin connection would be a welcome reprieve from my solitude, but I wasn't designed to deal out affection. I wasn't created for fleeting caresses and idle petting. I can't want it; I *don't* want it.

Besides, perfect as she is, she's on the wrong side of the war. She's one of them. She's one with Earth's greatest affliction, a nanocyte in service of the infection. Just as the siren song of human normalcy once lured me into submission, she's singing a ballad with her batting lashes. I won't succumb. I won't want for a life that can never be mine. I have a higher purpose, a *much* higher purpose, and it is superior to longing gazes and nonlethal touch.

It . . . wouldn't hurt to get a closer look at her, though.

My cells alchemize into their frailest form: Homo sapiens camouflage. Oh, how Hemlock used to praise me for it. It sickens me now, but our anatomy should match for the time being. I have to get close enough to her to douse the fire blazing through my innards. I have to see her for what she truly is: a bacterial microbe in a global pandemic of pride, violence, stupidity, and greed. I am experiencing a psychotic symptom of loneliness and nothing more.

Nothing. More.

I'll kill this inconsequential obsession and be done with it.

The moment she enters the ancient petrol station's restroom, I soften her mind with telepathic kisses. From across the ailing marketplace, I send forth invisible fingertips to smooth the ridges of her brain. She puts up a fight most cannot. An uncanny amount of resistance pushes back against my touch, igniting curiosity, wonder, and . . . despite my better judgment, desire for more. The harder I press into her psyche, the more valiantly she erects her walls. It is as though we are dancing with one another, communicating.

For her to communicate with me, she would have to be . . .

It's not possible. All of the embryos grown alongside me were boiled into soft mounds of multicolor mush. Hemlock and her goons made sure of it. If one had escaped, I would have known. I was preoccupied, but I wasn't blind.

It's completely impossible. There are no more of my kind. I am alone; to be alone is my destiny and my cross to bear. It is what they designed me for.

But this beautiful woman, this beam from the ethereal void, this slithering slice of starless shadow . . . she is impossibility incarnate. She is disallowed daydreams come alive. She is real, she is here, and she is just like me.

She and I are one and the same, bound by shackles buried in the nucleic acids that define our most authentic vessels. We share the same accursed blood, existing as chemically induced deviations from our creators. I can sense it—no, I can *see* it. She is divine divergence, down to the twisting spirals of her genetic code. It's like looking in a mirror. We are both horrible monstrosities, and at long last, I am no longer alone. Neither of us is alone.

She stammers through her words, likely difficult on the human tongue. It took me a very long time to speak. I wonder how long it's taken her. She presents a bundle of cacao-based confections as her eyes threaten to mesmerize me, her voice a melody without background music. I get high on her essence, balmy seas I'd swim in forever.

"I'll be in the car. Come out when you're done flirting, Clara," the youngest human says, his voice timid and quivering.

Clara.

Humans love to label themselves, don't they? They love to exaggerate their potential with meaningful titles, so I seldom bother to remember their sequences of introductory letters. In this instance, that is far from the case. Mother's—Hemlock's—dictionaries come to mind. *Clara* means *bright* and *beautiful*, *clarity* and *truth*. There is nothing more befitting of the exquisite creature who stands before me.

I need to offer her something equally, so when she asks for my title, something far less callous than JS-7R. I think of dictionaries, of words within them I'd once felt drawn to. Julian? No . . . Jacob? Heavens, no. Jett? Jack? Jesse?

Jasper.

When I utter it, she smiles, and seeing her smile produces a sensation like no other. That will be it, then. *Jasper*, because it makes Miss Clara smile. For the first time in my dreadful existence, I yearn to keep the smile there rather than urge it into a scream. To lose her would leave me in shambles, so I mustn't let her slip away. Some delightful twist of fate delivered her to my doorstep, and I will not squander it.

Unfortunately, as quickly as our reunion manifests, it is interrupted by the scrawny fist of the young one. Before I can whisk her into our new life and let the nectary sound of her name drip from my lips forever, the little nuisance pulls her beyond my reach. Her fleeting footsteps make me want to massacre him on the spot, but I must control my temper.

Anxiousness uncharacteristic of me arises as she rejoins the others. The blond at the wheel might choose to drive south, stealing her beyond the dimensional barrier I've yet to rip open. The moments before his purring engine springs to life are the longest of my life. Relievingly, the wheels screech in the right direction, leaving only a cloud of dust in the world beyond my domain. They cross the threshold. They enter my forest.

She enters my forest.

A laugh riding on exuberant air ravages my lungs. Heart racing and stomach soaring, I feel my resolve triple in intensity. I return to Agent Brian Bexley, thank the EHKI for their donation, and pluck a flowering blood rose from between his teeth. The scent of death, anomalous and aromatic, falls from its petals. Siphoning the power from his lapsed life force, I replenish my abilities in preparation. Today, I will not just be an abandoned antibiotic. Today, I will come into contact with my own medicine.

I follow their Hummer for hours, a shadow. My natural physique grants me the height and thinness of the surrounding trees, so it is easy enough to blend in. I must gather intel on the blockages standing between Miss *Clara*, *Clara*, *Clara*, and me. The other female would be easiest to subdue. Beings who speak as loudly and frown as stoically as she does are always weaker than they seem. Despairing spirits are easily diminished. In fact, they do most of the work when self-destruction is stimulated.

The blond behind the wheel appears confident, but even from this distance, I can tell he is not. Something plagues him—desire, perhaps? Clara does not offer a cure. His actions around her are maladroit, which leaves plenty of room for opportunity.

The smallest human will be my biggest challenge. Already afraid but unwavering in nature, he was the first one to risk my future. Untouched by insecurity and unaffected by life's most delightful distraction, he poses a problem that must be dealt with immediately. *Primarily.*

Then there is my beautiful *Clara.*

I adore the way her eyes scour my garden of death. I'd give anything to oblige her curiosities and have her eyes scour me with the same mystified enthusiasm. I don't want to assume too much of her yet, though. I won't overanalyze what I'd rather take my time exploring. However, my heart cannot help but beat to a tune identical to hers. We are already in sync. Both of us know longing. Both of us know the envy of watching the world pass from behind intangible bars.

Both of us seek freedom, and I am rapidly finding it in her.

8 | CLARA

When I awaken, the sky has become a haze of crepuscular gray. The forest is now devoid of all color. The blur of greenery is a blur of red-tipped leaves and branches like the appendages of a multiarmed eldritch beast. Its bony black fingers claw at the windows of our vehicle, scratching and scraping, desperate for entry. We're on the same road. It's still perfectly straight, but now it's been suffocated by barren trees and muted bramble. The road remains, but the realm has changed. It's like nowhere I've ever seen, a place pulled from paintings on the walls of ancient art galleries and run-down antique shops.

How long has it been?

My head feels stuffed to the brim. Cotton balls of confusion pile behind my eyes, adding a sufficient amount of puff beneath my lids. I feel as though I've been sleeping for days. I feel as though I haven't slept in years. The dashboard clock has glitched, displaying only a row of zeroes where the time should be.

Grayson drives, seemingly in something of a trance. Jade and Joey snooze against one another behind us. All is uncannily, eerily serene. It's still, too still. The world's become a slab of stone. I'm swimming through embalming fluid. I'm dreaming while I'm awake. I'm here in the passenger seat, I'm everywhere in this forest, and I'm nowhere at all.

How long *has* it been? I want to ask, but my lips don't move. Have I forgotten how to speak? Have I ever spoken before? Yes, of course. I spoke to that dreamy clerk at the gas station minutes ago, hours ago, lifetimes ago.

The engine gags on gasoline and sputters to a slow, pathetic halt. Grayson blinks a dozen or so times before he seems to register it.

"What the hell?" Jade groans, groggy as she straightens in her seat.

"It . . . wasn't me. The car just stopped," says Grayson, practically part zombie.

"Oh, Mom's gonna kill you." Joey stretches through a yawn. "She's been doing overtime for months to pay it off. I haven't had a proper conversation with her since, like, my birthday. You're in big trouble, mister."

"But I didn't do anything." Grayson frowns deeply, his hands hovering above the wheel like he's too afraid to touch it.

"You must have done something. Cars don't just stop." Jade's temper gets the better of her, her voice a thunderous boom compared to Grayson's woozy rumble.

"Well, sometimes they do."

"You packed us into a car that just occasionally decides to stop? For a drive *this* long?"

"Jade, come on . . ." I cut in.

She gives me her attention, insulted by the fact that I had spoken at all. Unfortunately, I can't help but remember the summer Dad gave us a crash course on small-engine repair. As always, Jade picked it up effortlessly. I broke my finger and landed us in the emergency room for four hours. She brought me fast-food fries and accused the orthopedist of price gouging.

"Let's just open it up and see if we can figure out what's going on," I continue.

I disembark, pad around to the front of the Hummer, pop open the hood, and stare into the maze of mist and chrome. I bury my head in the innards of the engine, trying to remember our father's lessons. He'd be ashamed of me now. Twisting pipes and sputtering monitors mock me, and from somewhere in the stars, Dad shakes his head.

"I . . . don't know what's wrong with it," I admit after some directionless fiddling.

Jade nudges me aside. I watch in awe as she assesses all that I couldn't understand. Yet again, she stands as an effortless example of human intuition. She learned faster, understood with such ease. After aggressively messing with a few valves and switches, she reemerges with flushed cheeks and greasy hands. Dad would be proud of her; he was always so proud of her.

"Oil's good. Coolant level's fine. I checked the battery, and we have a full tank of gas. This car should run fine."

Yet it is completely stalled, and we are stranded in the middle of nowhere. I suppose it is a *somewhere* of some kind, but most people in their right mind avoid landscapes like this one. We are in a tunnel of ghostly trees split by the road, which has devolved from a path of freshly laid asphalt to a thin, crackling trail large enough for one car to pass at a time. Nothing suggests another car has been here for weeks—months, even.

This far into the forest, there is only decay. Everything is stained by the markers of it. The bushes and weeds strewn across the ground look like bony hands rising from shallow graves. The trees are mutilated and disfigured, like bodies standing at attention. The sky remains overcast, a terrible ombré of light gray to gunmetal that suggests nighttime is inching near.

Blackstone Forest is still alive. Only, it is alive with death.

Blackstone Forest . . . there was something important about Blackstone Forest. There's a reason I'm here. There's a reason, I'm sure there is. My hand meanders to my hip, and in my pocket, two flimsy plastic reminders come to my rescue. The cards. *The pills.* I'm here because I need my pills.

"Great. Goodbye, hot tub; hello, choosing which one of us is expendable enough to be eaten." Joey jokes, though his voice reflects a seriousness elicited from years of watching reality television. He quickly puts his finger to his nose. "Not it. I vote Grayson. He's taller, has more muscle content, and he's a vegetarian."

Grayson folds his arms over his chest. "We are not going to eat each other."

"He does have more muscle content, but wouldn't the constant influx of stress hormones mess up the meat?" Jade forces a crooked smile for Joey's sake.

It dawns on me that Joey, at only fifteen years old, was the one to break our terrified tension. Unsettled as I am, I slip a smile onto my face for him too. He's the closest thing to a younger sibling I have, and a chance to resurrect all Jade once was for me. "Yeah, but the vegetarian thing is a major plus. Sorry, Gray. I'm siding with Joey on this one."

"Don't apologize to him, Clara. You'll get too attached. We're in the wild now." Joey pokes at his side, scoping it out for tenderness. "It's eat or be eaten."

Batting him away, Grayson pulls out his cell phone and holds it in the air, trying to gather a signal. "Very funny. Come on, I'm not getting any service here. Maybe if we hike for a bit, we'll pick up some bars."

"My phone's almost dead." Joey shrugs.

"You didn't charge your phone?" Grayson gapes. "Why wouldn't you charge your phone?"

"Excuse me for trying to foster appreciation for the present moment," Joey defends himself. "Some people enjoy a good dopamine detox every once in a while."

"Joey, that isn't the point. You should always have your phone charged, just in case. You never know when you might need it."

As Grayson and Joey slip into a brief battle about the importance of maintaining a satisfactory cell phone battery, Jade pulls a pack of cigarettes from her pocket. She lights one, then breathes a deep, nicotine-infused puff through her lungs. With the others arguing, it feels as though we've been left alone. It's just me and her. We're not sitting cross-legged on our grandmother's Persian rug, but somehow the scent of lavender fills my olfactory memory.

"Are you okay?" I blurt.

She narrows her eyes. "Does it matter?"

"To me, yes." I'm dizzy. It's dangerous to drop my filter like this. "I'm sorry, that came out weird. I just . . . I just wanted to—"

"I'm fine, Clara. I'm always fine." She blows a faceful of secondhand smoke in my direction. "What do you want, my medical records?"

My stature shrivels as I fan away the fumes. The ash of the present replaces the flowery notes from the past. "Thanks for checking out the car." I shift the subject.

"It's not like it helped."

"Yeah, but . . . it was still impressive. I'm sure we'll get this all sorted out, but in the meantime, maybe we . . . I mean, I guess, we could—"

"I *don't* want to talk about it," she hisses.

"About what?"

"Are you kidding me? You know what."

"Actually, I wasn't referring to . . ." I shouldn't be upset with her. I'm not entitled to anger in this arena, and I must remember that. "I was going to ask about Blackstone Forest. It's a historical landmark. While we're stuck here, we might as well admire it." And *I* might as well see how much information I can get out of her. If she won't be my sister, I'll make her my accomplice. "Do you know what kind of trees these are?"

"Ugly."

I laugh, but I cannot let her make me laugh. I don't deserve it. Laughter, like love, is for real people, *good* people. It isn't for me.

"They aren't ugly. They're just . . . different. I think they might be maples or beeches, though the color palette doesn't match at all. I wonder why . . ." *Easy, Clara. Easy does it.* "I heard a rumor about some fire that happened up here a couple of decades ago. Maybe it has something to do with—"

Her eyes fire ocular lead through mine. She holds a finger to her lips, demanding my silence before throwing her gaze at Jocy. "Shut up. You'll scare the kid."

"I'm sorry, I—I didn't think—"

"You never do," she snaps. She turns on her heel, offering stiffened shoulder blades in place of information. Conversation with her is now out of the question, leaving me about as close to finding more pills as I am to bonding with her.

I turn toward the sea of maybe maples and beeches, and my senses are drawn somewhere far away. The narrator in my head fades like cream dispersed through coffee. I feel sleepy again. My muscles come undone, like ribbons pulled out of bow tie butterflies. I find myself meandering toward the edge of the road, where the asphalt meets an abyss of dark branches. Somehow it's warmer here. Rosy sweetness swims up my nose, pulling me like a teasing fingertip into the brush. Hidden in the rustling leaves, whispers speak my name. They beckon me forward in streams of sonic silk. The longer I watch, the more the thorny limbs appear as arms outstretched and eager to embrace. I want to be embraced. Goodness, how long has it been since my last embrace?

Some primordial instinct comes back online. I speak, breathless. "Do you hear that?"

"Hear what?" asks Grayson. I can tell he's lingering close by, but his presence is distant.

"The trees . . ." My legs bring me forward, toward the edge of the great black river. My entire being is pulled elsewhere by a symphony of faint, wicked whispers. "The trees are speaking."

"Clara, hey. Hey, look at me. What's happening?" Grayson gives my mousy frame a shake.

Jade pulls up beside him. "Relax. She's just weird. She's always been weird. She was just going on about maples and bitches or something."

"They're saying my name," I admit.

"Who?" Grayson pleads, ignoring Jade entirely.

"I don't know . . ." A name slithers through my ears, the owner's voice charming and silvery. It sets sparks alight in my stomach. *Jasper.*

The color drains from Grayson's face. The woods continue their siren song. Murmurs kiss my ears and tug at the rhinestones that puncture their lobes. *Ensnared.* He said he was *ensnared.* My attempt at flirting was all but elegant, and still he was *ensnared*. Logic tells me it's impossible to expect the unseen voices to be his. Paramnesia keeps me dreaming.

Grayson herds us all back toward the Hummer, making certain his brother stands closest to it. "All right, Clara. You just sit down. It'll be okay."

"I'm fine." I shake my head, leaning my back against the rear tire, which has lost its friction-born warmth. "Let's just get back to finding some cell service. You said we were going to hike for a bit, right?"

"Take a second to rest," he instructs.

"I don't need a second."

"Take it anyway, please." Shutting down all further argument, he straightens his spine and approaches Jade, who is busy stomping out the glow of her cigarette butt.

Something in me is grateful for how Grayson cares. Secretly, perhaps selfishly, I've always loved being an object of his concern. Circumstance has shown me that I am a thing to be chased away, not cherished. Yet, against all logic and higher reasoning, he's always been there, worrying for the likes of me. He's always been there—checking in, doting, and providing all that I do not deserve. Despite Jade's biases and place as his best friend, he's always treated me like a person. A *person*. Should my quest for my confounded pink orbs fail, I hope he'll still be there to sit me down and insist I do ridiculous, restful things. It's a delusion, but I'd like to believe he'd be as good a knight to a dragon as he would to a damsel.

"Maybe it's a vertical concussion," Joey declares with the confidence of a hardened doctor.

"That's not a thing," Grayson retorts.

"It could be. Maybe she was standing there, and the force of gravity just—"

"I'm going to stop you right there. You just failed medical school."

Jade snorts. "She's been talking about trees speaking to her since we were kids. I'm serious. Every time Dad took us to the park, she'd start chatting up a spruce. On weirder days, it was rocks. Trust me, we have more important things to worry about. Remember those buildings? We're probably closer to them now. Let's see if they've got anything we can use. Tools, spark plugs, gas. Anything."

For a woman who can barely mask her emotions, Jade just put on a stellar performance. Suddenly, I suspect she sabotaged the engine herself. She needed a reason to kick off her amateur investigation, and now she has one.

"I don't know, Jade. It might not be safe." Grayson rests a hand at the nape of his neck.

"Oh, and sitting on the side of the road waiting patiently for starvation to pick us off is better? Could you go ahead and grow a spine for me, Grayson?"

"I just think we should be more responsible about this."

"Like you're the king of responsibility. You packed us into a car that *stops* sometimes!"

Their conversation escalates into an argument that quickly loses its intrigue. I stride toward the line between the woods and the man-made strip that divides them. The baritone voices of the trees grow louder, more oppressive, and more compelling. The world becomes an all-consuming blur.

Come to me. Come to me. Come to me.

Goodness, I want to. I want to more than anything.

I step off the road. As soon as my foot touches the ground, a ring of red light pulses from the forest and pulls in toward it. It gathers sharply at the base of my boot, gluing it to the crackling dead leaves below. One of my eyes tingles, and I whirl around to catch a glimpse of it in the reflection of the Hummer's passenger window. My iris irradiates impossible crimson.

Something is standing behind me.

It is a tall, shadowy figure made entirely of black tendrils of smoke and spiny branches. Horrifyingly thin and easily forty feet tall, it looms above my body like the branch of a weeping willow. I cannot see its face, only a portion of its emaciated legs, torso, and arms. My body fills with carnivorous fear, but before I can pull my foot off the forest floor, the creature dissolves into a pool of spiraling mist. It gathers around the piece of me still secure on the road, then shoves me off it. I feel both my eyes shift from brown to bloodstain.

My mind goes molten. The whispers collide into one terribly beautiful, familiar voice. It caresses the edges of my consciousness like vines twining themselves around a pillar.

"Clara," it purrs. Red wisps gather around my body, pulling me forward. "Don't be afraid. Follow my voice."

His voice . . . it's a rush of euphoric warmth. It's part liquid, part vapor, a hot spring of sound. Out here, it's suddenly so, so cold. I want to sink beneath his waves and let the heat dissolve me. I want his fever and all the dreams that come with it. I want to move into his oasis, one step at a time.

The needlepoint branches claw at my arms like hands in the night. Grimacing at the sensation, I narrow myself as though slipping through a tapering alleyway. Still, the fingernails reach for me, intent on littering my skin with tattoos of their own design. It hurts. It's too hot. I'm burning up, I'm drowning, and I need—I need—

"Grayson . . ." My thin voice struggles to surpass the heavy air. Again, some primitive part of me fights to survive, to stay above this hypnotic hypoxia. Frigid as it feels, the cold is safer. I'm sure of it. "J-Jade—"

"Shhhh." A sweet hum resonates through the ground below, shaking the soil in the most delicate manner. The brittle leaves silence their crackling complaints, and the orchestra of undead crickets quiet their nightly concert. A hush falls over the landscape like a blanket of darkness on the evening sky.

Warm again. Everything is warm again. I'm not drowning; I'm comfortable. I'm so, so comfortable. I'm no longer in a thermal spring, but tucked beneath a quilt of silence and starlight. Just like it, I want to be silent too.

After moving through the branches, I arrive at an impossibly curated clearing. It is covered with muted moss akin to a rug laid out over a hardwood floor. Fragile weeds dare to grow at the edges of it, all of them weak and drooping. Fireflies buzz dizzily through the branches, blinking at an unsteady but drunkenly synchronized pace.

They are all red.

"Hello again." Jasper breaks the auditory peace. His resonance is gorgeous, rich, and ghastly. It swims through my ears like sirens through the sea. My heart jumps as though trying to escape the veiny prison of my rib cage.

"Who are you? Where are . . . ?" My voice is freshly breathless; the heightened heartbeats have sent my vision swirling into vertigo. A lovely, unwavering chuckle vibrates the surroundings. It is a shock wave, and it urges a barrage of leaves to fall toward the mossy floor.

"Come, now. Surely you haven't forgotten me already."

He takes form. A whirlpool of deviant, vermilion light manifests before revealing its source, who smiles from ear to ear. His eyes are no longer the color of honey, nor are they abyssal. Like mine, they glow a brilliant, unmooring shade of red. He appears human, but the unfolding events suggest otherwise. What I'd seen in the reflection of Grayson's car suggests otherwise.

"What?" My thoughts have grown faint and difficult to take hold of for further rationalization. If I were in my right mind, I'd be running by now. "How? Y-you were . . . I was . . ."

"It's not important." He slinks closer, limbs too fluid to be held in place by bones. "What's important is that you're here. With me."

"Did you follow us?"

Jasper inches closer, his grin widening. He does not provide an answer, more amused than accommodating. "Is this your form of flirting? Because if so . . . *I'm ensnared.*"

Though intimidated by his otherworldly beauty, I stand my ground in seriousness. "How are you here?" I assert. "No one was behind us."

"So many questions. If you must know . . ." His smile spreads so that it no longer looks human. It is too wide, too wicked. The corners of his lips caressing the tips of his brows, everything about him shifts from alluring to appalling. His eyes sink into his head, leaving only two holes of darkness with a beady dot of bloody light in each center. His body is still human, but his face is anything but. "This forest is mine."

His transformation is more than enough to quell further questions. No longer interested in interrogating him, I back away with the intent to run for my life. Still, something holds me here. The movement of my limbs is languid; the panic hasn't reached them. My brain screams, but my body relaxes in staunch opposition.

"What are you?" One final inquiry, the most important one, falls from my lips like water I'd been drowning in.

"The true question is . . . what are *you*?"

His voice echoes all around me before dissipating into a disorderly ensemble of whispers once more. A tornado of red overtakes the landscape, surrounding and suffocating me like a python coiling around its prey. I hold my hands over my ears, but the gesture is futile. This malevolent music is already thoroughly etched inside the walls of my skull. Slowly, however, they become voices more familiar.

Grayson, Jade, and Joey are near. They scream my name.

Everything gets louder and more distorted as all but Jasper's eyes disappear into the haze. Two hands reach through. They are strong, firm, and grounding as they clap on my shoulders. They belong to Grayson. The moment I hit his chest, the woods lose all abnormality.

"Clara! Clara! Snap out of it!"

"G-Grayson?"

Jade yanks my arm until I'm gracelessly stumbling in front of her. The motion is a show of brute strength, and it pairs well with her visible fury. She is scowling, trying to re-create my mother's unshakable austerity. "What the hell is wrong with you?"

I stiffen, eyes darting around behind her in search of Jasper. All I find is a stiff and shaking Joey. "I'm sorry, I just—"

"You just wandered aimlessly into a creepy-ass forest, that's what you did!"

"I'm sorry. I didn't . . . I didn't know what I was doing."

"That's for sure." It takes me a few moments to register it, but the look on Jade's face is not one of utter disdain. She's making every attempt to mask it as annoyance, but behind her eyes lies the last emotion I would have expected: concern.

Regardless, my attention is drawn back to the woods. Jasper, in all his irresistibly terrifying glory, is branded across my brain waves. I am confused, conflicted, and against my better judgment, captivated. There is no end to the forest in sight. It prevails for miles in every direction. The car, the road, and all forms of life outside this realm seem too far away to find.

Red whispers ride the breeze, laced between each pocket of silence.

9 | GRAYSON

Despite the daylight descending like time-lapsed rainfall through the canopy, this place is as dark as midnight on the moon. Stepping off the road is like stepping off a spacecraft. The asphalt's familiarity is our sole tether to the world we've conquered. Beyond it lies a realm dominated by the survivors of humanity's greed. Like Earth's humble satellite, wilder lands uphold the illusion of connectivity. They each feel like unpopular rooms in a huge mansion, distant libraries full of dusty books and shining mahogany. Rarely visited, but still under the same roof.

In actuality, we own nothing. We paved a path of blackness through the center of this forest to stake a claim we cannot hold. Here, we are nothing but foreign prey in a thorny tangle of predators. Our spacecraft is idle, our communicators can't reach Houston, and our team of astronauts is down a member.

"Did you see which way she went?" I ask my brother. He shrugs, his eyes darting through every gap in the bramble.

"She's such a pain." Jade's voice is pure frustration, but the way she bites the edges of her cuticles, leaving them serrated and raw, tells a different story.

"Maybe she saw something. Maybe there was a hiker, or a headlight, or . . ." I run a hand down the length of my face. My lower lids stretch toward my cheekbones in response to the added weight. "Let's go find her. She couldn't have gotten far."

"Why? The way I see it, we've got one less mouth to feed. Our rations will last longer while we wait thirty years for someone stupid enough to take this road," she seethes.

I know she doesn't mean that, but still a terrible sensation spreads through my chest. Adrenaline moves like antifreeze through my veins, lighting cold fires in every artery. I clench my fists until my knuckles resemble pearly white molars. Then I let the breath I've been holding exit through the tight gaps in my teeth with a low, audible hiss.

"Enough, Jade. This is serious. Come on, Joey," I say, my footsteps leaving imprints in the brush beside the road. He follows me with a shrunken posture, caved in around his rib cage. Despite some quiet grumbling, Jade joins us shortly after. We move in slow motion, moonwalking beyond veils of splintering bark and green ivy.

"Where are all the animals?" Joey's gaze is still a pair of synchronized searchlights.

"Hibernating?" I guess. It is uncannily quiet. Our footsteps make an orchestra of natural sound, our journey scored by crackling leaves and snapping branches. Other than that, nothing. Absolutely nothing. There are no rustles, chirps, bellows, or buzzes. There is no evidence of life whatsoever, aside from our succession of mismatched shoe impressions.

"Seems a little early for that." His voice is severe. It makes him sound like a stranger.

"Look who's paying attention in class." Jade gives him a playful push. He scurries back in alignment with us at the speed of light. "Don't overthink it, J. Bunnies are skittish. They probably all ran for the hills when Clara came through here, which means we're on the right track."

Joey's hand searches for mine. When he latches on, I'm reminded of a time so embedded in the past, it's practically another life. We ran hand in hand up to the window of a boxy ice cream truck, our small chests heaving. He picked a strawberry-dipped cone, and I bought one doused in chocolate sprinkles. To our surprise, the man in the window gave us each complimentary snow cones, one for Joey's black eye and one for my swollen lip.

"Gray?" he mumbled, his mouth dyed red with syrup. "Is it true? What those kids said about me?"

I gave him the biggest, most reassuring smile I could muster. It was wide enough to rip a hole through the inflammation and send a river of blood down my chin. "Those kids were jerks. They're gonna have a lot of trouble calling you mean things without teeth, though."

Secretly, I was cursing said kids for landing a hit on Joey before I'd had the chance to ruin their orthodontics. He laughed, though. It wasn't a bright, sunshiny laugh, but it was a laugh.

I wish I could put him at ease with an ice cream cone and a joke right now, but all I can offer is my hand. Worry lines twitch across his forehead, and though our tether stays secure, it's nothing but a uselessly comforting delusion. The trees that tower over us hinge like observant gods, branches like arms clasped behind their backs. They watch with eyes etched into the bark, wafting the acrid scent of leaves on the brink of decay over our senses.

We aren't safe, and despite the chain that keeps Joey at my side, he knows it.

Up ahead, the foliage begins to bend. It flows to the left, a current of greenery at the edge of a massive whirlpool. At the epicenter, Clara stands with her back to us and her arms lax at her sides. She seems to dangle, like a puppet with one string held up by its head.

"Clara?" My lips move without permission.

The air stills. The flora that had served as instruments in our underscore falls silent. The sky itself seems to lower, each cloud the sclera of a gazing eyeball. Our presence feels obvious, cumbersome, and exposed.

Joey's breath hitches in his throat. Jade rolls her eyes. She passes in front of me, thunderously trampling the delicate wildflowers gathered at Clara's feet.

“Clara? Hello?” She circles her sister like a buzzard scoping out a carcass. “Earth to Clara.”

Joey and I catch up with her, more careful about the withering petals on the ground. Clara’s wandered to a place we cannot reach. Her eyes are glazed, and her lips are parted as though she’d been paused at the top of a gasp. Her upper lids droop just enough to cut her corneas at the halfway point. If I didn’t know any better, I’d say she was sleepwalking.

“Clara?” I place the back of my palm on her cheek. Her skin is ice. My heart is stone.

I’ve known Clara since we were children. I’ve observed her more closely than anyone else dared. My mother warned me to keep my distance from the Lovecrofts, to only do what was cordial and necessary. To say I disobeyed her orders would be the understatement of the year. Protecting her came as easily as breathing, because in Clara Lovecroft, I knew there was something worthwhile, something beyond my comprehension. It was a complication I couldn’t have hoped to prevent, not even for Jade’s sake. My mother was furious, my father was terrified, and my best friend was betrayed. All signs pointed away from Clara, yet I pushed ahead, into more and more of this complication. Once, it was a poorly kept secret. Now it lives at the forefront of my mind, an instinct, an edict, and a duty.

In this moment, I’ve failed to uphold all three.

“What’s wrong with her?” Joey releases my hand to free his. He gives Clara the lightest nudge, and she sways like seaweed caught in a current.

Then she thrusts into movement with an explosive scream. She hinges at the waist, both hands clamped over her ears, a thin line of crimson pouring from her right nostril. All at once, we scream her name, desperate to awaken her from whatever hazy nightmare she’s lost in. I grab her shoulders, and she fights against me with the strength of a field mouse and the frailty of a caged canary.

“Clara! Clara! Snap out of it!”

Lucidity reenters her eyes. She utters my name, then presses her face to the center of my chest. My heart races, and I'm certain she hears it. Suddenly, my limbs have forgotten they are limbs. I want to run my fingers through her hair or place a hand on the small of her back, but the pulses between my extremities and motor cortex have been short-circuited. Before I can do anything of value, Jade rips Clara away to scold her.

"What the hell is wrong with you?" she booms.

Clara stammers through an explanation her sister won't allow her to finish. I consider stepping in, but then something becomes exceedingly, almost absurdly apparent. Jade isn't just upset; she's worried—worried sick, in fact. Her voice might be strong, but her complexion gives her away. Like her father, Cedric, she goes ghostly when she's rattled. Like her mother, her left eye twitches when she's afraid.

"I'm sorry. I didn't . . . I didn't know what I was doing," says Clara.

"That's for sure," says Jade. She releases a long sigh that sends her vocal cords clattering against each other. Her hands rest on Clara's shoulders. It's like she imagines her sister will vanish without them. "Don't do it again."

Clara's eyes meander, but Jade is having none of it. She pales, visibly nauseous with concern, and shakes her little sibling viciously.

"Clara, look at me," she demands. Clara looks, but she doesn't see. Her eyes are lightless. Jade's burn. They burn like they did when Clara twisted her ankle at dance practice and we accompanied her to the infirmary. They burn like they did when a girl four times Clara's size stole a ribbon from her hair, and Jade earned two months of detention getting it back. They burn with something she's convinced she's left behind, something as dangerous and complicated as my own forbidden inclinations.

"Let's get her back to the car," Jade grumbles.

She motions for me to take Clara's hand, then falls to the back of our pack as a wolf might. The journey back to the road feels longer than it should. It is as though the space has become elastic, a rubber band stretched to capacity. The impressions I pressed into our path have vanished, leaving us without a clear route. Jade utters something about Hansel and Gretel, and I can't help but wonder what ate up our breadcrumb trail. Clara is both with us and a thousand miles away. Her head snaps around with paranoid precision, twisting like an owl's to ensure nothing is close behind.

"Do you remember why you came out here?" I let my fingertips brush her forearm. Gentle as I am, she still responds with a gasp. She meets my eyes with a doll's gaze, wide, glassy, and unblinking. "Y-you . . . you don't have to talk about it," I reassure her.

Her chin touches her shoulder as she makes another attempt to place eyes on her back. Instead of looking ahead, I follow her instincts behind us. A tunnel of looming branches has been left in our wake. They curve inward, creating unnatural arches, a portal of wood and shadow. Even gentler than before, I catch Clara's jaw with my thumb and forefinger.

"Forward," I say. "Just keep moving forward."

A centipede of frigid air crawls over my arm. It feels like a hundred ghosts, a hundred crushed spiders haunting me with spindly vengeance. The caustic scents of metal and marshlands barrel up my nose and down my windpipe. Only after I recoil from her touch do the spectral sensations subside. She doesn't furrow her brows or frown in confusion. She only stares, like living porcelain, a satellite picking up signals and wordlessly asking if I feel them too.

10 | CLARA

Sitting at the edge of the wooded ocean, our car looks like a forsaken puppy. With only phone flashlights and a waning crescent to guide us, we transform it into a bed fit for four. Grayson has already started piling blankets on the side promised to me, and I realize my shivering is all but concealed. It is summertime, but the goose bumps gathered on my skin feel like barbed wire against the fabric that covers them.

He did something to me. The soldiers protective of my subconscious were cannon fodder, shot down too quickly to keep me rational. It was effortless to accept the commands. It was ecstasy. It was freedom. It was power I'm familiar with. All my life, I've been different. With Jasper, my inherent otherness faded. I was safe, I was warm, and I was unconditionally allowed to be what I am. What I *truly* am. His directives were easy to obey because they felt as natural as my own neural patterns. It's the rest of the world that makes no sense. It never made any sense, but he . . .

He makes sense.

"Here you go." Grayson pats the top of a fluffy sherpa blanket. "You're shaking." The fleece does nothing to stop it, but I don't let him know that.

"No more hikes tonight." Jade rattles the trunk as she enters beside me, causing the tires below to squeal. Her expression suggests there will be no argument. I nod and curl up against the outermost wall of the car. Normally, Joey would insist he sleep by the window, but tonight, he claims the middle. As he wedges himself between Grayson and Jade, his face is frozen in a terrified frown. I've never seen his cheeks look so sunken.

"Are you okay, Joey?" I murmur, propping myself up to meet his gaze. His head shakes like a beaten piñata rustled by a breeze. My heart sinks for him. "Want a piece of chocolate? There's still some left."

"Don't eat any more. If you do, you'll give yourself diarrhea, and you're not using my socks to wipe," Jade tries a joke.

I give her arm a gentle smack and reach over with a square anyway. I even take one for myself, hoping it'll make the offer more enticing. "You can use my socks."

"I brought tissues." Grayson puts an end to our dilemma with a grin, nudging his brother in an attempt to make him smile. "You can have your chocolate."

"I don't want it." He oozes melancholia.

"Nothing bad is gonna happen to us," I say without an ounce of certainty. If I could take back my pitiful attempt at reassurance, I would. Thankfully, Jade steps in to cushion the failure.

"Stuff like this happens all the time. Cars break down, people get stranded, and then they pay ridiculous amounts of money to the first towing company they find. Don't worry. We'll be lounging in your mom's Jacuzzi before you know it."

"And you'll have a cool story to tell your friends when we get home. You can even tell that kid in algebra about it. I'm sure it'll help him forget the hibachi incident," Grayson adds.

Joey brightens. Reaching toward me, he plucks the chocolate from my hands and gnaws at it anxiously. It's a start. "You really think so?"

"I know so." Grayson nods. "You're safe, Joey. Get some sleep. Jade's right: We are going to need an overpriced towing company, which means we'll be getting our steps in until we find service." His barless phone screen blinks tauntingly to remind us of our isolation.

Joey shrinks into a fetal position beneath his thin blanket. I untangle myself from the pillowy sherpa and drape it over him.

"Thanks, guys," he whispers.

"Good night, Joey," we reply in choral synchronicity.

An exchange of *good nights* circles through the space. Finally, we fall quiet, but it's obvious our internal monologues are ripe with terror. To look outside the windows would be to face fear incarnate. The light of the moon effuses only a feeble stream of light, and that stream illuminates a minuscule fraction of our surroundings. The rest is pure, inky darkness. Chthonic chaos. Shadows and silhouettes.

Eventually, Grayson's and Jade's breath patterns turn slow and cyclic. They were able to drift off, even with something so caliginous watching from between the gaps in the trees. Every hair on my body stands at attention, antennae detecting danger. Still, the most unnerving aspect of this impromptu sleepover is the fact that I am not nearly as afraid as I should be. I can't stop replaying the way Jasper called to me. It claws at every corner of my consciousness, creating a sensation similar to when one first allows alcohol past their lips. Intoxication. Euphoria. A welcome loss of control.

I should be as scared as Joey. I should be masking my fear like Grayson and Jade are. I should be upset by the possibility that we may never see bars on our phones again. I should feel *something*, just like I should have felt something when my parents' eyes stared lifelessly into mine.

"I saw it." Joey's voice shakes me from my thoughts, as tiny and timid as a mouse's squeak. "The thing you were hearing. I saw it."

"What did you see?" I whisper.

"*It.* I didn't say anything because I—I didn't want it to hear me." His breathing turns ragged. I pause too long for any of my incoming reassurances to be reassuring.

"Nothing is going to happen, Joey."

"You don't know that," he whimpers.

"I know not all scary things are bad. What if he's just lost like us?"

He stays silent, and after fifteen or so minutes pass, I turn to face my window. As though I'd given some sort of nonverbal consent, something squirms within the abyss. Something consisting only of shadows dances across my line of sight. Then two red eyes shine toward the top of their face. His face. Instead of wearing his otherworldly exterior, Jasper has reverted to the form he claimed when we first met. The only thing odd about him now is his statuesque beauty. He tilts his head to the side observantly, a sharply arched brow cocking above his glowing orbs.

I maintain eye contact, just as I had in the gas station. To make matters more confusing, I wave. It seems to take him by storm. Surprise blossoms across his features, so much so that his disguise falters. A glimpse of his real smile pokes through, and his scleras briefly drain of their milky hue. They turn as black as the void above.

He waves back.

He did say he wasn't the best at flirting. Perhaps the flirting has just begun, and what he did before was a show. Joey's adenoidal voice interrupts my train of thought. He is still awake, and he is still terror-stricken. "Clara, what are you doing?"

"Nothing." My answer is automatic, and my mind skids to a halt as it is overwhelmed with siren songs from the trees beyond the car. Everything goes hazy, the details of my world suddenly less fine. It's so easy to let it happen, to release my grip. The temptation has a spirituous quality, like sipping from the rim of an enchanted apple martini. "I just have to use the bathroom."

Lying comes so easily when Jasper is holding my hand. His influence is my true north. I rise to sitting and crawl toward the trunk's latch.

"Clara, no. Wait." Joey's small hand grabs mine, and his expression reeks of desperation. In fact, the corners of his eyes have already become lined with silver on the verge of spilling over. "Can't you hold it?"

"Don't worry, I'll be right outside."

He sees through me. "I'm coming with you."

"Joey—"

"You shouldn't go alone. Not with that thing out there."

There's no arguing with him, so I don't. With a defeated smile, I settle into silence and nod. We exit the vehicle on tiptoes, careful not to wake the others. Jade's thunderous snores drown out the sound of our movement, and Grayson's been trained by sleepovers aplenty to endure it.

Once outside, I can breathe again.

"I'll turn around," Joey reassures me, facing the car and using it to anchor himself.

"Thanks."

Hoping I'll be able to escape before he wakes the others, my eyes scan the forest for Jasper's bloody bioluminescence. Our gazes meet in the middle, his red and mine begging to be. With much less resistance than I'd exhibited prior, I step off the paved path and allow the darkness to embrace me. Jasper's hands clasp mine, and he whisks me into his underworld like Hades did Persephone. Our first meeting was breathtaking, our second was nightmarish, but our third is a forbidden fruit. Toxic and intoxicating. Prohibited but perfect.

"We didn't finish our conversation before," I rasp, following him as we are engulfed in smoke spirals, energy in tangible motion.

"You looked frightened."

"I wasn't."

He pauses, whirling around to bring us face-to-face. There's something incredulous hiding behind those pupils. For someone so well spoken, words seem to be failing him right now.

"You weren't?" When he does speak, his tone plummets down the octave scale. It becomes a rumble like a shock wave swimming within the earth. "Be honest, Clara."

A smirk crawls across his features, once again climbing toward his temples. His eyes glow more vibrantly, emitting patterns that numb my mind like morphine. Honesty slips beyond my lips before I can stop it. "I was, but I still wanted to see you again."

"Don't lie to me." His pointer finger positions itself just beneath my chin. "You don't . . . ever have to lie to me."

I suck in a breath, preparing to speak despite having nothing to say. It's so easy to let him speak, to soak up every syllable. I'm certain he read my mind, because he holds a finger to my lips to halt them before any words fumble their way out.

"You're safe here."

His fingers, naturally graceful but icy to the touch, lace through mine. Guided deeper into the forest, I see it in an entirely different way. The moonlight creates an iridescent glow that bends like the patterns of a kaleidoscope as it filters through translucent leaves. The air is warm and welcoming, and red fireflies buzz around my body. They dance, their rhythmic flickers reminiscent of balmy summer nights. Even the branches look less threatening, their arms outstretched to embrace instead of entrap. All eeriness has faded. This isn't an eldritch realm filled with ever-watching spectral eyes. It's Jasper's home, and it possesses the same wonderful beauty that lives inside his eyes.

I don't even remember what my apartment looks like, what my city looks like. Everything beyond this moment is something out of a rapidly fleeting dream. Life in the world I knew could have been a precursor to this, the pain and ire and exasperation all preparative of it. Jade will be better off without me. Grayson and Joey will go on to do amazing things, to live up to the Warner name with all the valor expected of them.

I can disappear.

Jasper is smiling wide again, but this time, it doesn't spook me. He said I could trust him. Oddly enough, I do. "You can stay, you know."

"Stay?"

Stay.

It's like a bucket of ice-cold water has been dumped over my head. Then the fireflies' mesmeric dance speeds up, drilling his offer in deeper. It makes me want to dance too. I *could* stay. I could leave it all behind. I could leave myself behind and become something new here. The word *yes* tingles on my tongue like melting cotton candy, sweet and sugary and delightfully artificial.

11 | JASPER

She is seconds from surrender. Her lithe arms dangle in my direction, following the gravitational pull luring us to one another. If I were to allow it, she'd tip forward into my arms, her body providing the reverberant *yes* I yearn for. Everything about her is bewitching, but the outpouring of trust from her heart triumphs over all. She knows it is safe to be so helpless and vulnerable in my grasp. Her instincts speak louder than her doubts.

With the others, she is a carefully curated bloom in a bouquet.

With me, she is a wildflower.

Her face moves in small, clockwise spirals, mimicking the fractalized pulses of light in my eyes. She dizzies herself, perhaps as enthralled by the vertigo as I am to watch as she succumbs to it. Those plush pink lips part in preparation, but instead of a *yes*, they become the gateway for an airy giggle. It moves through the space like bubbles, each one popping with a sound wave that strokes my senses. Suddenly, she's not alone in her helplessness. Suddenly, I am but a humble breeze cradling the sanctity of her petals in the gentlest of whirlwinds. I could listen to her laughter outside space-time. I could live in a singularity, encased in eternal expressions of her joy.

I fall to my knees, and her gaze drops to maintain contact. Just as she's surrendering to me, I surrender to her. This submission must be mutual. Our hands become entangled, just like every desire I've ever held in my heart becomes entangled with *her her her*.

"Stay," I whimper. "Please."

Hesitance clouds her perfectly euphoric smile. It falters like a fissure in the earth, her cheeks tectonic plates moved by a mantle of fiery futility. She doesn't quite frown, but her body stiffens and sobers. "Jasper, I . . . I can't. This place is beautiful, and you're . . ."

I'm terrifying, and I've terrified her.

"I'm sorry about what happened before. I shouldn't have been so forward. I was nervous, you see. I've never met another of my kind. Up until this afternoon, I was the only one."

She swallows hard enough to make every muscle in her throat visible. At the very back of my mind, a sinister question stirs. How has she broken free from my telepathic influence? My suggestions are meant to manifest in her consciousness indistinguishable from original thought. I even urged her neural signals to release a dose of dopamine alongside each one. For all intents and purposes, she should be high on this hypnosis, addicted to the pleasure of being *mine*. She should be as ensnared by me as I am by her. She should be saying *yes*. Why isn't she saying *yes*?

"I need my pills."

What a curious development. "Pills?"

"They keep me human. I need them. I need to go."

I see it now. The red in her eyes has shifted. My hue is carmine and candy apple. Hers is rubies and roses. The difference is slight, but I'm thorough in my observances. If these pills she speaks of keep her human, they must also keep her distant from the genes that imbue us with strength. Humans are weak. Their capacity for telepathy is dreadfully underdeveloped, the gates of their minds left wide open for monsters like me. The more her true self emerges, the more equal we become. Soon her brain will be wrought with trip wires, and my suggestions will catch on each one.

"Will you come back?" I squeeze her hands, still kneeling at her feet, a thrall to her dark divinity.

"I don't know."

"Are you afraid?"

"Not of you," she says sincerely. "I'm sorry. This isn't about what you . . . what *we* are. You have more control of it, but I don't."

"What exactly is there to control?" Before she can slip her delicate hands from mine, I rise up to block the moon rays falling on her rosebud eyes. She becomes a silhouette in my shadow. "We aren't meant to be controlled."

She quivers. Her skin, smooth as silk, looks even more lovely shimmering in darkness than it did under the blinding sunlight. Beneath it, her bones writhe, swimming through flesh, desperate to take their most natural form. With a gasp of horror and a glower of hatred, she watches them.

"It . . . it h-hurts."

"Of course it does. How long have you been fitted to a form, and what do you know about yourself? What do you really know?"

"This isn't myself."

"Out there, I'm certain that's true. Out there, it's their world. Here, it's not."

Her spine emits a loud snap, causing her body to heighten and hinge at an angle unnatural to humans. She stretches and twists, suddenly given access to a completely new range of motion. If she wanted to, she could turn her torso in a circle. Now is when she yanks her hands away, staggering back with a silent scream.

"I need to get back—I need to get back right now—"

I slip smoothly into my proper movement pattern, dropping to the ground and letting all four limbs spiral in their sockets. Like a triple-jointed spider, I weave around her feverish footsteps, then stack myself back into an upright position, blocking the path back to the road.

"Let me help you," I insist, my voice more crackle than cords. "I *can* help you."

Her gaze goes glassy. The light that falls from it gets caught in the teardrops that hang from her lashes, sending prismatic rainbows onto her cheeks. I could stop her. I could keep her here long enough for the transformation to complete, for her to shift into a mirror image of my monstrosity. She would see herself in me, and I in her. For the first time ever, I would cease to be alone. I would cease to be a pitiful spot on the perfect portrait of beautiful humanity. Together, we'd be a pair of shredded nails, raw to the cuticle, on the manicured hand that owns this world.

Yet some enigmatic anomaly urges me to the side, leaving an open route for her to tread on. Another harsh swallow tightens her throat. Words have escaped me, so I don't bother to chase them. All I do, for her sake and mine, is nod. She scans me. I feel exposed, a gaping wound being gnawed at by the air.

"It's not you." Her words are a gauze doused in antibiotics. "There's nothing wrong with you. It's me. When I change, I hurt people." Her hand comes over her heart, thin, elongated fingertips brushing the curve of her shoulder.

"You won't stay," I drone.

A new infection spreads, creeping like ants under my skin. The blood in my veins has gone frigid, carrying ice-cold clumps of congealing fluid to my brain. It floods me with hazy grief, dulling my ocular fires until they are steaming, smoldering embers.

I once thought of love as a flimsy construct meant to make life more bearable. I didn't need it, what with all its abstract edges. Then I met *her her her*, and suddenly there was a chance to be held. To be understood. She's more than a flame fueled by the same gasoline as I am. She's much more, and yet, she's not mine.

"You won't stay," I repeat.

"I won't tell anyone about you, I promise."

"You won't stay."

She pulls her lips into a line, her head shaking from horrible left to horrible right. She grabs my hand, and though hers is still disguised beneath a fragile layer of skin, it fits to the curvature of my palm with uncanny accuracy.

"Thank you for introducing yourself to me. It was brave. I'm sorry about how I reacted. It was hypocritical. Unfair. I'm glad we got the chance to speak again, though. It's good to know that it's possible to be what I am without causing others harm." Our palms slip away from one another, hers like the string of a balloon released to the sky.

As her silhouette, a petite hourglass of flesh snapping itself into new shapes, disappears into the gloom, only one thought echoes in the darkening void of my mind. All stars extinguish, leaving only an all-consuming black hole at the heart of a system in need of a sun.

12 | GRAYSON

I gaze through closed eyelids, counting veins like red wine spilled on an apricot tablecloth. Only after a few measured breaths do I slip them upward. The sunlight stabbing past our Hummer's tempered glass isn't normal. It's barely sunlight at all. If the sky wasn't a marbled swirl of hydrangea blue and abalone, I'd swear it was coming from the moon. Beams plummet toward the earth, refracted raindrops of white rolling down a clear umbrella.

Joey has curled into a boulder of muscle and bone. He's asleep, not resting. Jade couldn't be more unconscious. She lies with her head tipped back over the center console, her mouth a megaphone for snores. I haven't the slightest idea how she rose from off her duffel bag pillow and wriggled between the seats. Clara is pressed against the wall, her back to the woods. A sipped bottle of water shut haphazardly sits in the nearest cupholder, beside her plastic bag of pills.

She's taken double the dosage.

In the front seat, I've stacked two cases of spring water and a backpack full of road-ready snacks. It isn't the breakfast of champions, but it'll keep us from starving. I ration out four protein bars, four cereal cups, and a bag of baby carrots. Then, as quietly as possible, I step out into the air. The chill of the receding night lingers, prompting goose bumps to bloom on my arms. The earthy smell of pine and petrichor sweeps over my senses, familiar and foreign in the same instance. There's more to it than that. The forest is at the apex of an exhale, half alive, half dead. It's like there's a rotting tooth hiding somewhere in this great, green jaw. There's a corpse inside a distant closet wafting the sickly sweet stench of decomposition.

Today, we'll hunt for cell service. We'll take turns: two stationed at the car in case someone drives past, and two wandering down the road on foot. Clara volunteers for the first shift. Jade announces that she'd rather swallow a handful of rocks than join her. Joey murmurs something about the likelihood of loose bowels with a gesture to his bowl of chocolate puffs.

Clara and I make it a few miles from the car, ants on a trail wedged between parallel walls of greenery. The forest is an ocean split by whatever cruel god insists we stay the path. Its uncanny silence settles into my bones.

"So, uh . . ." I cough. "Do you want to talk about yesterday?"

"Yesterday?" She stiffens. "There's nothing to talk about."

"Come on, Clara. It's me. You can tell me. Was it the ride? Were you in the car for too long?"

"Gray . . ."

"Does it have to do with the gas station? With that guy you met?"

"Why would it have anything to do with him?"

The image of his face, made anonymous by those dusty windows, sails across my memory. I pause for far too long. She's smart; she'll see right through me if I let her. I change the subject. "Your pills . . . you never did tell me what they were for."

The gravel gathered at the asphalt edge produces a rough sizzle. She's stopped dead in her tracks, heels half buried and gaze severe. "It has nothing to do with my pills."

"Sorry, sorry. I'd never judge you, though, especially not for having some kind of condition. I just need you to talk to me. I need to keep you safe, and I can't do that if you don't—"

"I never asked you to keep me safe, Grayson."

She's become a pillar of granite, a stone carving, still as the tree trunks huddled behind her back. Her shoes, rimmed with dry splotches of brown, have become roots. If I were as imaginative as Joey, I'd worry for the integrity of the road. Right now, she looks ready to riddle it with cracks and embed herself in the crust. Only after too many moments of stomach-tightening tension does she break eye contact.

"I'm sorry. That came out wrong. What I mean is, you've already got enough on your mind. You've got Joey. You're the only thing keeping Jade under control. I won't add more to that. I won't be a burden to you. I won't be a burden to anyone."

I close the space that's gathered between us, taking her face in my hands. With an unexpectedly feeble dose of reluctance, she softens. Her irises shift from Martian bedrock to molten chocolate. "You could never, *ever* be a burden to me."

"I can take care of myself," she insists, her resolve solid but her voice like air.

"I know, but you don't have to. Not always."

Time loosens. We stay like this for hours, minutes, milliseconds. We stare at one another through an entire autumn, for a single breath, and in a fractured stream of eternities. It's only us. It's us and the cold breeze leaving bite marks on the back of my neck. It's us and the trees, watching with millions of eyes obscured by shadow. It's us and the ghostly howl of the wind whipping the clouds above into dollops of cream.

Stolen situations like this have never failed to get me in trouble. My mother's voice echoes through my ears, telling me to keep my distance and maintain it like a vegetable garden. My father's pursed lips flash across my vision, his expression wrought with concern and disapproval. I wish there was more of him in my memories than Mother, though. He was never concerned with duty, only with safety. He didn't care about the world, only our world.

I wish Clara could be a part of it—our world. My world.

A feeling like fingertips brushes the exposed sliver of skin between my pant leg and my poorly tied sneaker. Something's grabbed my ankle.

Our infinity ends, the loop sliced in half. By the time I get my gaze to the ground, there is nothing but weeds at my feet.

"It wasn't the pills," Clara says, breathless.

"What was it?" I ask, equally so.

A horrible creaking noise crawls toward us, the sound of a limb swinging out of place. In the distance, a scraggly tree moves like a boxer rolling out their shoulder. A loosened branch plummets, then falls among the moss and mushrooms to rot.

"Jade," she whispers. "I thought I'd be okay spending this much time with her, and I thought it might actually help us get through the weekend, but all I see when I look at her is a girl who lost her parents because I needed to go to some ridiculous recital."

"Clara, it wasn't your fault."

"Yes, it was, Grayson. You don't understand."

"You were a kid. You didn't know any better."

"I should have, though. I should have known better. I should have *been* better. Now they're gone, it's all my fault, and Jade hates me. You want to know what's worse? I'm upset with *her* for it. Forgiveness is the last thing I deserve, but here I am, with the audacity to wish things could go back to the way they were." Her chin drops to her chest. "So yesterday, I . . . I took a walk. I thought it would help clear my head, but it only made things worse."

I pull her into a hug, and her small frame practically disappears in my arms. From over the crown of her head, I spot more movement in the brush. "It's okay. Hey, it's okay. Everything is going to work out. Jade's a puzzle, that's for sure—but trust me, the pieces that love you more than anything are still there." I sigh, rubbing circles into her back. "Please don't be so hard on yourself. You're human, Clara. You're allowed to have feelings, and they aren't all supposed to make sense. There are some things that just . . . never will. Let me know if you need time away to sort things out, but please don't go far. I don't want you to get lost. I don't know what I'd do if I . . . if I lost you."

She tips her head back, gazing at me through a succession of blinks, lashes like torn dragonfly wings. A dishonest smile pulls her lips into a crescent, but she can't throw a trench over all her self-deprecation. "Why are you always so kind to me?"

"Clara . . ." I am as sincere as a handwritten valentine and as serious as the plague. "You are more to me than I'll ever be able to explain."

Thunder rumbles through the sky. It growls, a wolf in the clouds with its teeth bared and its gums covered with foam. There is a darkening. Every patch of blue shudders with evanescent existential horror as a tower of gunmetal gray looms on the horizon. Within it, emaciated arms of plasma lacerate it. Each comes closer to contact with the ground than the last.

The air is in rigor mortis, yet the same weed reaches for my ankle, moving without muscle, unwavering without bone.

13 | CLARA

Grayson is a knight. Kind, caring, and quietly pessimistic because he thinks it makes him more alert. I can work with that. I can play the girl ever in mourning, wrought with displaced guilt, tormented by an irrational sense of responsibility for events outside her control. I flash a smile just wider than the previous, urging my eyes to burn until they are orbs of glassy deceit. Like all servants of the crown, he's wiser and more observant than he lets on. One slip, and he'll know my meandering was beyond grief.

He's too close. He's always too close.

His lips are also . . . too close. Plush, dusty-pink skin pillows curved into a perfect Cupid's bow. His eyes are so dreadfully blue. Arctic oceans, clear enough to count ice blocks in. My cheeks gather reddening heat. My performance must be seamless, and this wasn't in the script. What I'm feeling right now, it wasn't in the script.

"Well . . ." I pull away. I won't burn in his sun or drown in his waters. For his sake, I can't. "Thanks."

He beams. Curse his sparkling rows of teeth, framed like a painting on the art museum of his face. "Come on, we better head back. It looks like there's a storm on the way."

I'm no meteorologist, but the sky looks closer to midnight than midday. The gathering clouds are one shade away from being as black as the Boötes Void. "We have to shower somehow," I joke.

He laughs and, somewhere between the waves of sound, throws a hand out to hold mine. We return to the car linked, footsteps in line but out of sync. Our conversation curves to quips about camping and life before indoor plumbing was invented. Again, I'm reminded of just how light Grayson makes me feel. He's deeper than he lets the world see. Yet no matter what swims in the sea caves of his ocular stroma, he always manages to smile. No matter what shadows play in the spaces between his silences, he always manages to laugh. He isn't a white knight; he's a golden knight. His wispy locks and radiant skin are like armor. Protective, but penetrable. Closed, but still open.

If I ever needed to tell someone about my situation, it would be him.

He wouldn't understand, but he would most certainly try to. The details impossible to comprehend . . . he would address with empathy. A man left to raise a rambunctious teenage brother and manage an absent family's covert, illustrious affairs must be made from quality ingredients. Empathy is his most integral. It's his lifeblood.

I wonder what it's like to be good and know it. I wonder how I would feel if my recipe called for powdered sugar and maple syrup.

Back at the Hummer, Jade and Joey hide poker faces behind hands of cards. They are fully immersed in a game of rummy, sitting like trained yogis on the hood.

"Game over, you two," says Grayson. "Unless you're looking to go through a wash cycle, of course." He gestures to the crawling clouds. Trees on the horizon have begun to sway in glitchy, sporadic patterns. They are being beaten by a deluge of rain. The way they hinge creates the illusion of a beast on the ground rattling their roots out of place with each thunderous step, inching *closer, closer, and closer still.*

We pack into the trunk again. Grayson hands out individually packaged bags of miniature gingersnap cookies. We feast over murmured conversation that ceases when the droplets arrive. What begins as a mere shower becomes unrelenting curtains of water. The car windows look like television screens overtaken by static, the world a blur behind malfunctioning pixels.

Day turns to night without notice. With the sun extinguished, we determine the time-shift on instinct and energy levels alone. The relentless swath of thunderclouds refuses to clear, strong as a cold front but slow as a warm one. Even as the group succumbs to sleep, I am kept awake. No matter what I do, my body refuses to release its grip on consciousness.

How much more, Grayson Warner?

I glance to the left, where Grayson snoozes in the driver's seat. His legs are bent at awkward angles within the confined legroom, but his torso is relaxed, and his head seems stable as it dangles to the side. Something like butterflies flits about in my stomach, and for a moment, he's more to me too. My arm extends without permission to brush the wisps from his forehead. Now I get a clearer view of his peaceful expression. I'm used to seeing him with stress lines trained into place, but right now, he looks remarkably unburdened. My face tingles, moved by a smile and warmed by blush.

How much more?

The lightning strikes that descend from above begin to take on impossible colors. Shades of crimson split the sky, each like bleeding scrapes on the horizon's dark flesh. Their booming sound decrescendos into mesmeric thrumming, ritualistic drums beaten in time with my heart. I sway to the rhythm, pulled by an invisible chain through the door. It opens and closes with an uncanny quietude that disappears without a trace into the downpour. Once outside, the tempest's tears drench my body. My hair falls in slivers over my face, plastered to my burning cheeks. Every limb on my body feels detachable. The confines of my human hardware have faded, leaving only a formless stream of dark starlight drawn to something betwixt the trees.

He is there.

Waiting beyond the curtains of rainfall, Jasper stands soaked to the skin. He is naked from the waist up, the pale skin of his torso glistening. Black veins are scrawled like juvenile drawings on his chest, shoulders, and arms, leading down to the pants hanging at his hips. His raven hair is slicked to his forehead, and just below it, his eyes are deviant suns. Red as carnelian. A million prisms on shattered glass. Spirals of fractalized light reaching from the infinite depth of his being to the endless edges of my soul.

"Jasper . . ." I sigh his name. My breath takes the sound bite to him. He beckons me with a curl of his forefinger and a sliver of a smile.

Gravity pulls my galaxy to his. Most think of deep space as a silent place, but I know better now. I know it is filled with his songs. In my head, he's placed an orchestra, and every instrument is his voice. Every chord is a command, a gentle caress that steers my vessel toward calm waters. Ballet returns to me, and before I know it, I am dancing into his arms. The trees are curtains, the asphalt a stage, the crimson strikes our spotlights.

As I step into the wooded ocean, his smile widens into a toothy grin. Like Grayson, his teeth are like pearls, but they are as serrated as a shark's. Everything about his human visage is sharp, and in this light, I could swear on the work of the lapidarist who carved it. He takes my face into his ice-cold hands, drilling the brilliant hue of his gaze into my vision until the world is cherry-dipped.

"Stay," he sings, and oh, how I want to. Right now, I couldn't imagine being anywhere else. I can't remember if anywhere or anyone else exists.

His hands meander down my arms, fingertips just barely brushing my skin. They move in paths paved by the water still pouring from above. They dance, and in time, they leap to new locations. They come to cup the curves of my hips, gently slipping beneath the saturated fabric. He's climbing my rib cage with touch, inching upward until I respond with a gasp. His lips curl like parchment set alight at the edges. Such a captivating smirk has taken residence on his face, a smirk that makes me want more of what caused it.

However, he only shakes his head and pulls away.

I can't breathe. I've forgotten how to use the muscles in my diaphragm, and even if I were to remember, there would be no air to take in. If it isn't exhaled by him, it ceases to exist. I am molten, and I will melt into the ground without his hands holding me up. I'd rather dissolve into obscurity than go another second as a ship on rough seas, navigating alone in the night.

Jasper is my North Star.

I need him. I need him. I *need* him.

The gentlest thunderclap rumbles the ground, an earthquake for which he is the epicenter. I follow the vibration, blind in the darkness but trusting in my true sight. He backtracks into the gloom until all I see is his red-shifting wavelengths.

"Stay with me, Clara Lovecroft," he says.

Tendrils of vermilion guide the plant life. Vines tango with smoke swirls, all of them coiling my arms and legs. Jasper rushes forward like a gust of wind, his lips crashing into mine. A supernova detonates in my chest. A lightning strike cleaves the sky in distant but perfect alignment with the rapidly closing space between us.

14 | JASPER

I yearn to bask in her sweet oblivion. She is the epitome of all things beautiful and corroded. Our veins belong entangled, hearts beating against the tides of this world. We are damned, accursed malignancies on the face of a species too pristine for such darkness. We are monsters, and monsters are feared by all but their own. She may not know it yet, but our destinies have converged into one. I cannot allow her to leave. I will not.

She's been in flesh for far too long, though. I'll have to convince it as thoroughly as I've convinced her mind.

As I take her lithe body into my hands, I feel as though I am touching something sacred. She stares at me, her eyes like moons eclipsed by the earth. They are rose red and hazy at the hands of my influence. Drowning this deeply beneath the waves of my sway, she can only give me an expression as dazed as it is darling. Her mind is vulnerable, and it has fallen into the best possible hands.

"I will not hurt you," I purr into her ear, and I mean it. I will not hurt her. I will never hurt her.

She shivers. The tiny hairs lining her human encasing stand at attention, exhilarated by the nerves beneath. I trace a hand down the length of her spine, such a powerful column of bone suppressed into fragility. A fluttering overtakes my chest, reminding me of one of the many things solitude has stolen from me.

I have caressed too many corpses. I've felt cold, smooth, lifeless flesh alongside the weight of true power. I've also run my fingers over living, trembling bodies while they still had enough sense to feel fear. All of them carried the same flavor of human frailty, the same pathetic stench of normalcy.

I've touched cool magazine pages and textured paintings beneath Dr. Hemlock's watchful gaze. "Which do you prefer?" she'd ask. "Men, women, or both?" My take on intimacy was of particular interest to my creators. It's so instinctual to the human species; they're practically designed for desire. I never found myself taken with the shimmering models shown to me. I'd sit beneath EHKI cameras and self-pleasure at their command. They got their readings, but I got . . . nothing. I felt nothing, but in truth I wanted to.

Yet again, Clara is the answer to desires I hardly bothered to dwell on. She's neither a corpse nor a magazine model. Clara is a beautiful monster who mirrors me. Touching her feels like communing with the same wretched stardust.

"Be still for me," I command.

She freezes, compelled by every silvery lilt in my voice. I let my face descend toward her delicate neck, then pepper it with featherlight kisses. The plushness of my lips meets the soft surface of her skin. It is warm. I am cold. When we collide, we create nimbostratus clouds of chaos.

I have known hunger, sadness, longing, and the zest of sadism acted upon. I've known bloody joy, hollow numbness, and unbridled rage. But this . . . this is new. This burns through my body like moths ignited. I am the inferno that illuminates the brimstone gates of the underworld. She is the dark goddess hidden behind them.

I let my kisses descend as my hands take to further exploration. They roam her curves. She stays perfectly pliant. Perfectly *still.* The laugh that erupts from my mouth is like bubbling effervescence, dancing with the sound of skin on skin. Her silhouette is calligraphy, her body a succession of sweeping curls spelling out my deepest desires. The more I touch her, the more of her I want to touch.

"Jasper."

When she whispers my name, I am soaring. I am making love with light.

My lips cross the bridge of her collarbone and climb the slope connecting it to her earlobe. This close to her ear, I am able to send a note of pure aural intoxication into her mind. It gets caught between her brain waves, between the peaks and valleys of her alphas and thetas. My will becomes an idea that originated within her own imagination, a desire as authentic and unwavering as mine. Her knees buckle, and when she falls, I catch her in my arms and in a kiss. A *kiss*. My very first.

Her lips are as soft as silk and as sweet as peonies at the start of summertime. This connection is collaborative. It is play. I set the pace, gentle and fluid as a ballad. She moves her mouth to the rhythm of mine, singing with shortened breaths. She is the moon above. She is starlight dancing on a rippling sea. She is every fallen flower petal spread on every ancient grave. This kiss, this evanescent moment that makes eternity worthwhile, awakens me to the only reason anyone fights to see another day.

Love.

My love. Our love.

I used to abhor the nerve endings and receptors exclusive to human flesh. I never wanted them activated for Hemlock's camcorders and statistical charts. I'm not with Hemlock, though. I'm with Clara; I'm safe with Clara. I'm safe to *desire, desire, desire.*

She releases a moan, a plea for oxygen, and I untangle my tongue from hers. Hers. Her. The great and glorious *her*. She gives me her gaze, those butterfly-wing lashes lifting to reveal two balls of crystal infused with red. I ease her back to standing, my hands unexpectedly shy. One hovers by her waist, the other at her shoulder blades. Suddenly, she's too delicate for this world, too precious for my starved, savage fingertips.

"Are you all right?" I murmur.

She nods as though she has a choice in the matter. I have made sure to keep her more than all right. Under my influence, her mind is a lukewarm quarry pond of fish swimming drunkenly through streams of seaweed. Here, she is safe from all the heartache, protected from the hauntings and hardships of the world. With me, she has found a home.

Grayson could never compare, what with his childish flirtations and stolen swipes of the skin. *You are much more to me,* he'd said. The nerve. It's pitiful how such a creature, such a human, could assume himself capable of the depth to which I care for my Clara. We are on an entirely different frequency, and I will ensure she knows it.

The inferno in me has grown. It is no longer a match lit by our friction. It is a blaze doused in the acrid acidity of Grayson's face. My hands fall away from Clara's frame, stiffening to support my telepathic summon to the forest. Vines of emerald green tangle around tendrils of roots risen from the earth. They coil around Clara's legs, locking them together. She gasps, so I touch my pointer finger to her parted lips.

"Still. Be still."

Her smile is a sleepy sunrise as she acquiesces without further protest. The roots round the swell of her hips, then rise to the narrow center of her waist. Through our psychometric link, my nerves have become one with the nerves of the forest. Now I have many ways to touch, every root a receptor, every leaf a taste bud.

"J-Jasper," she practically whimpers. Once again, I am entwined with her essence, aglow from within, and airborne all the same. The spirals of wood have reached the plush, tender flesh of her breasts, gently twined around each. In her human form, she has many sensitivities to be investigated. Many vulnerabilities. I allow the roots to stretch higher, skimming lightly over her collarbone before arriving at her neck. The final ringlet finds a home there, and with a flex of my fist, it tightens enough to silence her pleas with pleasure.

I move in close enough to inhale her exhales. My pupils become a lunar eclipse framed by a whirlpool of shooting stars. Our connection is stronger than it's ever been, our thoughts like tulips sprung from the same bulb. My order is indistinguishable from her organic thought.

"You are mine now, Clara. Not his. *Mine.*"

She nods to the best of her ability, but her eyelids droop. This must be . . . a lot for her. She's lived her life conditioned as a human, and with so much of that mysterious medication dulling her senses, she is completely and utterly defenseless. Neurally unfortified. Helplessly hypnotized. The poor, wonderful thing. I cannot help but let my lips twist into a crooked curve of fondness.

"Good girl. Now, sleep, little love. Tomorrow, I'll get to dealing with the others, and you . . . you will come to me again. Understood?"

Another nod, this one more relaxed and bleary-eyed than the last. Given silent permission, she dips her toes into the black waters of sleep, slipping away with the current to float in an ocean of sweet dreams. I release her slackened body from its cage and return her to where she belongs, dangling from the inverted arches of my arms.

It takes every ounce of strength in me to bring her back to the hideous vehicle. However, arrangements must be made, and in the interim, I need her safe. I place her in the seat from which she came, beside the man of unparalleled inadequacy and offensive blondness. As the door closes, becoming a barrier between us, a scythe passes down the center of my heart, to which she now holds a half.

When I gaze through the thick sheet of glass, however, I see more than just my Clara's beautiful face. I see two bright-blue orbs gazing back at me. They are saucers embedded in a body shaking hard enough to make its eyelashes quiver. The youngest of the group, Joey, watches me from beneath a mop of hair identical to his brother's. I've done my best to stay out of sight with the others, but this little thorn just won't keep away from my side.

We are at an impasse, he and I. Opponents in anticipation of the other's surrender. Unfortunately for him, his pathetic excuse for a challenge only makes me hungry for more. I flash a smile that bounces the dawn's first beam of light. Then I let my human form loosen, stretching my neck, only my neck, to around the same length of his height. Skin and muscle tear like split seams, the bone beneath becoming boiled cartilage. His expression caves, eyes narrowed by the tears welling within them.

I trust my message has been received.

Just try, little nuisance. Just try to take her from me.

15 | CLARA

I can't get him out of my head. The way his soft fingertips scour my body. The way his voice leaves me blooming. The way his kisses create new galaxies. I want more, I want him, and more than anything, I want to *stay*. We will dance forever in this strange place, our energies in perfect harmony and our bodies living to touch and be touched.

Did I have a life before now? Does it matter? Can we stay in our pocket singularity, forever present, forever unconcerned with the rest of existence? Perhaps he's been reaching for me for as long as I can remember. Perhaps I felt divorced from others because I was destined to connect with him alone. There was a hole in my heart uttering his name. At last, *at last*, our hues are blending.

I am *his*, and oh, what a joy it is.

"Clara?" asks Grayson, a mere whisper in my new world. "Want to come with me to hunt for service again?"

Using my tongue is such a terrible struggle. I long for Jasper's telepathy, as it's far more natural for my kind. *Our* kind. I'm not human, why should I pretend to be? Alas, I suppose I must keep up the performance for the time being. Our time will come soon enough.

"I'm feeling a bit tired today. Would it be all right if I stayed with Joey?"

"Oh, sure . . ." He's disappointed.

How sweet, Jasper chuckles in my mind.

"Jade and I've got it. You wanted to head out today anyway, didn't you, Jade?"

Jade emerges from the trunk with an invigorated smirk. She looks like a lioness about to hunt, hands confidently propped atop her hips. "Yeah, and we're hunting for more than service today, Warner. We need to aim higher. Supplies, gas, tools. Got it?"

Grayson shakes his head through an exasperated smirk. There's no arguing with her, especially when she's running on half a protein bar. "Yes, ma'am."

"Clara," she orders. "Stay here. No more impromptu hikes, no more talking trees, and no more general weirdness. Joey, keep an eye on her. Hold down the fort for us."

Joey salutes, and Jade, a worthy drill sergeant, salutes right back. The two depart, leaving us alone with our dwindling snack supply and ancient, peeling playing cards. Like the rest of the Jasperless world, it's all so far away. It's static at the edge of a screen I need sharpened. My antennae are attuned only to Jasper's channel, ever in search of his reverberant pixels. When our tomorrow arrives and I return to him, reality will be right again.

"Clara." Joey's voice, a squeak, rips through my radio stations. "You have to eat something, or drink something, or . . . Come on, snap out of it, please. Don't leave me here. Don't leave me alone."

The mirage of Joey does not dissipate like I'd expected it to. He's still there, still real, even though my heart insists there is only one other being with whom I share the universe. His hands—dainty, ice cold, and undeniably solid—grab my shoulders to give them an urgent shake.

"Clara, wake up," he begs.

"I'm here, Joey. I'm awake."

"No, you're not." His face is far too stern for his age. He looks like he's playing the role of someone's flinty grandfather. "I saw it again, Clara. I saw the thing. It did something to you, didn't it? That's why you're so out of it."

"Everything's fine, I promise. We're safe."

I smile, my head filled with strawberry gumdrops. Joey doesn't know the depth to which Jasper is wonderful. Clasping on to his trembling hands, I offer the most honest and reassuring gaze I've ever wielded. No roles, no games, no tricks. I don't have to play a human character to relate and convince. I know what love is now. I know how to scream it from the rooftops and whisper it between quiet, sacred breezes.

"He's incredible, Joey. I've never felt like this about anyone before. I know he looks scary on the outside, but we spoke, and now I understand him. I trust him, and so should you."

Joey's eyes glisten, his bottom lip twitching like a dragonfly in flight. "What happened, Clara?"

"What do you mean?"

"Something's wrong with you. Something's wrong with this entire forest."

"Joey—"

"Don't do that. Don't talk to me like I'm some frightened little kid. Whatever *he* is, he's clearly messing with your head, because anyone in their right mind would be running for the hills."

I throw my eyes to the horizon, smirking at the distinct lack of hills to run to. There are only trees. His trees. Him. The great and glorious *him*. I wonder what he's doing right now. Is he wandering through the shadows, lost to whatever beautiful musings exist behind his brows? Is he watching over me, a guardian angel banished from the skies yet alive on the earth?

Joey snaps his fingers an inch away from my nose. It is effectively a thundercrack. "I'm telling Grayson and Jade," he says.

"No." I snatch up his hands again, suddenly desperate enough for the both of us. "Don't. Grayson has enough to worry about, and Jade and I . . . you know how she'll react, Joey. Don't tell them, please. You're right. Something is probably wrong with me. I'll stay in the car, safe and sound, until we find a way out of here. Okay?"

He's wary, but he's buying it. His tension floods away with a grievous exhale. For now, he's surrendering, and all I need is now. My smile becomes a timid curve of earnest bravery in the face of danger. I play the damsel staring up at a dragon from behind her brigade of knights. I accept the terms laid out for my safety, returning dubiously to the castle that is our car. After nightfall, I'll have darkness on my side, and in darkness, Jasper and I reign.

Pills. My pills. Jasper isn't supposed to be my salvation; they are. They're the reason I agreed to come along for this trip. I need to focus.

I need to go to him again.

I need to get out of here.

I need to stay.

I need my pills.

I need him, him, him.

Jade returns just as evening tempts the sky. Her eyes are wilder than usual as she tears open the trunk and rips through her duffel bag. Without a word, she piles a flashlight, a news clipping, and a sloppy notepad into her arms. "We found something," she says.

"What?" Joey asks, his voice thin and frightened. "Wait . . . wh-where's Grayson?"

"He's waiting for me."

"You left him alone?" Horror floods Joey's eyes. He leaps out of the Hummer and stomps up to my sister with more bravery than I've ever been capable of. "How could you leave him alone?"

"Relax, J. He's fine. We just didn't want to lose our spot." Jade rests her hands on his feeble, shivering shoulders. "I just need to see something real quick. We'll be back before nightfall."

"No! Th-this isn't fine! You shouldn't have left him! Where is he? Tell me where he is!"

I won't be of much use, but I step out behind Joey to offer some modicum of comfort. Jade sends me a glance that is enigmatically harmless. Her priorities are preoccupied by something far more important. Silently, the two of us try to plot a means of calming Joey down. Sadly, she lacks my aptitude for telepathy, and even if I could send her a thought, I wouldn't. I won't take the risk.

"Stay with Clara. He's just up that way. I'll go get him, and we'll be back before it gets dark, I promise," she assures us.

Joey replies with a quivering frown, betrayed. He rips himself away from her and takes off in the direction of his brother. He doesn't bother to stay with the road, sprinting with all his might into the trees, relying solely on Jade's vague gesture to guide him.

My veins turn to sharp, terrified silver. If any of Jasper's whispers had been holding me drunken, I go completely sober right now.

"Joey, wait!" I rush after him. Jade runs close behind.

Come to me. Come to me. Come to me.

The trees sing my name, but I tune them out. Grayson and Joey are here, somewhere, at the mercy of someone too much like me.

Jade whistles. The sound, cutting as a blade and precise as an arrow, shoots through the deep green foliage. Quietude follows for a succession of torturous seconds before her signal is returned. I recognize Grayson's voice, even when reduced to an air funnel between his two front teeth. Joey, still in eyeshot, follows it like a lifeline to shore.

At the mouth of a half-collapsed cave, Grayson leans unharmed. He doesn't enliven until Joey comes racing in, his stormy eyes beclouded with concern. "Joey? What are you—" His lips lock shut as Joey collides with his chest, arms wound tightly around his waist.

"You're okay. Y-you're okay. It didn't get you. It didn't get you."

"Hey, hey . . . it's all right. Everything's all right. What's wrong? What didn't get me? Why are you here? Jade said she was just running for flashlights."

Grayson throws a look of admonishment in Jade's direction. He's covert about it for his brother's sake, but the message is very much delivered.

"The kid took off. What was I supposed to do?" she scoffs.

"What . . . did you find?" I ask, peering into the gloomy den we've padded up to.

Oddly, almost impossibly erupted from the soil below, a cavern dips down toward a tenebrous void. To the passing eye, it might appear to be a simple rock formation. Up close, it is clearly something more. The walls crackle off in geometric patterns suggestive of influence beyond natural corrosion. Right where the shadows begin to rule, a rusty spire pokes out from the gloom. A handrail.

"I don't know," Grayson responds, exasperated. "Jade wants to take a closer look, though."

"You don't have to come." She shoves him aside, taking her first step into the cavity, into the dreadful unknown. Her flashlight provides a single, pathetic stream of pale yellow that cowers like a mouse against a lion.

"What if you get lost? What if you fall and break your leg? Going down there in and of itself is stupid enough. Going in alone is basically asking for problems." He pinches the bridge of his nose, then pries Joey's arms off his torso. "Clara, could you bring him back to the car? Jade's really set on this."

She's already gripping the edge of the inexplicable handrail, eager to descend with or without him.

"I'm going with you," Joey proclaims. "We're staying together. We have to stay together."

"Joey . . ." Grayson begins, but before he can counter further, Joey has hurried behind Jade. "No, no, no! Joey! Stop!"

There's no choice. If we let them out of our sight, there will be too many chances for too many deadly things. We descend into the cave of rust and limestone like blood cells entering a heart. It smells faintly of alcohol fermented beyond its native acidity. The passageway is too narrow for two at a time, so we travel single file: Jade at the front, Joey just behind her, and Grayson behind me. He ensures I don't fall. Heat from his hand caresses the edge of my waist, my center of gravity, with gentlemanly concern. He doesn't touch me, but still he is a warm current crashing into my icy air. Where we meet, hurricanes happen. I am grounded in the eye of his storm.

I am grounded, with him.

I am human, with him.

Jade guides us haphazardly through a maze of tunnels. I'm inclined to suspect she knows where she's going. I'm inclined to assume suspiciously acquired schematics of this place were buried beneath the potato chip wrappers on her desk. I hadn't seen any, but when Jade wants something bad enough, she's relentless. Grayson doesn't question her logic right now, and I don't blame him for it. His paramount concern is our safe return to the surface.

"I see light," Jade announces, uncharacteristically chipper with pride.

She pries a brick of dusty-white plaster out of our way, and as it tumbles, it leaves us coated in chemical snowfall. An asymmetrical archway opens up into a much larger space. Colossal doors of dark metal hang from rusted hinges. Puddles of ground water have accumulated along the frigid titanium floor tiles. Eerie sea-green light crawls toward us from bulbs unseen. Their glitchy, sizzling flickers are audible, though.

"Oh my god . . ." she marvels. "I was right."

"About what, exactly?" Grayson dusts off his hands and starts to meander. His eyes are analytical as they search for the essentials: food, water, and signs of peril.

"Are you kidding me? There's a secret complex under Blackstone!"

"There *was* a secret complex under Blackstone. From the looks of things, it's been out of commission for a while." He reaches for a string of signage covered by overgrown roots. They come away in screeching snickers to reveal the words: **EHKI SECTOR SIX.**

I swallow the lump of congealing saliva in my throat. This is . . . it. This is my chance to maintain my humanity. I don't know what I expected the EHKI to be, but I definitely wasn't envisioning a subterranean sliver of hell. It reeks of chemicals and cadaverine. Viscous, flesh-colored sludge sits in clumps at every corner of the room. A few inches from the toe of my shoe, a bloodstained ID card smiles up at me. It is identical to the ones in my pocket, save for the fact that it belonged to a woman named Dr. Vivian Baranova. Her hazel eyes are filled with excitement, and her biometrics declare her to be just twenty-five years old.

I want to search for anything that resembles my pills, but more than that, I want to go back to the surface. This place feels too familiar, like I've witnessed it without eyes. A memory built of sound and sensation clots up in my prefrontal cortex. I rage against it, and against the impulse to imagine how, exactly, Dr. Baranova died.

"Jade . . ." I pick up her tragic identification rectangle and offer it to my sister. "I don't think we should be here."

Jade's eyes are too wide, too interested. "The EHKI . . . They exist. I . . . I knew it."

"Please, Jade. I don't think this is—"

A loud succession of clanks and crashes makes my skin feel suddenly removable. The two of us whirl around to find Joey standing with his arms tucked tightly to his sides. He's just disturbed a pile of gadgetry and toppled a cart of flasks.

"Sorry," he says in a peep.

"I don't think this is safe," I whisper, unsure why I'm inclined to stay hushed. Something is listening; he is listening. I'm sure of it. "Look at this place. Whatever caused it could still be—I mean, it's—listen, I . . . I know you want to know more about Mom and Dad, but—"

"How would you know *anything* about that?"

Oops.

I scramble for a response. Naturally, it only incriminates me further. Before I can calculate a plan of escape, Jade has grabbed me by the forearms and yanked me close enough to smell stale chocolate on her breath.

"You went digging through the box, didn't you?"

"I didn't think you were being serious when you said not to touch anything. I thought it was just a—"

"Of course you went digging through the box. You know what? That one's on me. I shouldn't have just let you waltz in. You're you.

Since you didn't bother with my only rule, could you please just shut up for once?"

Grayson's footsteps hasten toward us. He's coming to my rescue, but I yank myself away from Jade on my own. My teeth grit against one another. My lips curl into a snarl. I shouldn't be this angry with her. I don't deserve it. I need another pill.

"They were my parents too . . ." I'm more honest than I planned to be.

"What?" She takes a menacing stomp forward.

"They were *my* parents too. You act like you're the only one capable of missing them. You act like you're the only one struggling with this. Meanwhile, you have no idea what my life has been like since that day. N-no . . . idea."

On top of that, her quest is hilariously off-kilter. She's on the brink of spontaneous combustion, on a hunt for who-knows-what. I need these catacombs more than anyone. I need them to produce a miracle.

Grayson steps in between us, his chest to Jade as his back forms a shield over me. "Enough," he says valiantly. Himself. "Jade, come on. You've seen what you needed to see. Clara's right: We need to head back. This place definitely isn't safe, and we shouldn't be away from the car like this. What if someone drives by and we miss them?"

"Do what you want." She glowers. "I'm staying."

For her, Grayson's eyes seldom soften. However, as he approaches my sister, he looks more heroic than I've ever seen him. He isn't brandishing an invisible sword, preparing to slay the dragon of Jade's wrath. He's gently, deftly, earnestly addressing her with an expression of unfiltered concern.

"I understand this means a lot to you. We'll come back when we have more daylight on our side. We'll get Joey back to where it's safe, Clara will be on lookout duty, and we *will* come back. Whatever it is you're looking for, I'll help you find it. I promise." Before she can resist, he pulls her into a hug. She wriggles like a feral cat, but he holds her there. He just . . . holds her there. "They wouldn't want you to put yourself in danger. You know that."

I want to be held like that. I want someone to tighten their arms around me, even as I squirm, even as I deny much-needed comfort. I want unselfish touch, touch that gives more than it takes. I think of Jasper and how he ravaged me. His hands scoured, starved and never sated. Grayson's would be . . . different. They would be gentle. They would be tender. Perhaps I could be the grateful princess to his gallant knight. I've only ever deemed myself a dragon, not just polluted, but pollution itself. Fire scorching all in its path. Ash that blackens the lungs afterward. But perhaps, for him, I could be . . . different.

Everything could be different.

I need to find more pills so that everything can be different.

16 | GRAYSON

Jade meanders, against Clara's pleas but in line with our compromise. She bargained for ten more minutes of devoted digging and enlisted the help of all our hands. Joey whimpers by the exit, careful not to touch anything visibly moist. Clara stays nearby, but she's a bit more eager than I expected her to be. She's getting her hands vehemently dirty with ash and encrusted blood.

I make myself useful with a rove over the connective corridors just beyond the emergency exit. There's a lot more to this laboratory than meets the eye. It seems to span endlessly beneath the earth's crust, erupted from the ground miles away from here. In my mind's eye, I see the barbed wire and the skeletal buildings it barred off. That must have been the entrance disguised as something else, something far more harmless. A cloak in plain sight, a cover.

A succession of narrow twists leads me to a room filled with shattered screens. The scent of electrical embers lingers strongly in here. It smells like a lit cigar. If not for all the death and decades between when researchers had roamed here, I'd suspect to find one in the ashtray on the desk. However, there are only six ancient cigarettes to be found there, beside a crushed water bottle labeled with the initials *N. W.* and a heat-warped protein-bar wrapper.

My stomach inverts on itself.

This tomb has gone untouched since the massacre that left it like this. No one has been able to access it. No one has dared.

A single monitor remains intact, its glass a sheath of darkness. My flashlight serves as a weak but worthy guide through the gloom, but in a moment of refraction against the screen, it blinds me. In the sudden blast of white light, I could have sworn a blade of luminescent red sliced through my vision. A chill skitters up my spine so tangibly, I'm afraid to glance over my shoulder.

The undamaged monitor crackles. It sounds like rustling leaves and inexplicable laughter married via an electronic hum. Static floods the blackness, first bloodred, then grayscale. The pixels clamber over one another, playfully violent in their jumble of chaos. When they arrange into reluctant order, they present a grainy re-creation of what this sector's security cameras last collected.

"She just gave the order. Kill them all," says a scientist with hair as white as his haggard complexion. His voice is a pathetic rasp amid a sea of shatters and screams. His gaze, full of bursting veins and silver tears, is directed at a wall of embryos, each inanimate within cylinders of glowing green fluid. His hands are wrapped around his rib cage in a terrible, futile embrace. Rivers of blood pour through them.

". . . all of them?" One of his assistants, struggling to hold her dislocated arm in place, scuttles forward with a scowl. "We . . . we can't. If we terminate them all, this was for nothing. Nothing."

He exhales slowly. "I know."

Every researcher in the room lets their jaws hang. Then they gather the last of their strength and hoist flamethrowers into the air. A fanfare of fire leaves every artificial womb boiling, every underdeveloped embryo liquefied inside. When the pressure is strong enough, the cylinders burst, sending fireworks of glass into the subterranean sky. The researchers stare, now sealed inside a smoldering tomb.

"Do you think it heard?" another assistant asks, quivering.

"Oh, my dear . . . it hears everything."

Footsteps beyond the flames punctuate his point. A low growl follows, then grows. It grows into a thunderous boom of laughter. Cruel, wicked, screeching laughter. Merriment and agony laced into the same sound bite. Pure, hysterical hedonism. Pain. Monstrous pain.

Every rock-solid resolve goes molten. Those still conscious enough to cry allow their tears to roll. Those with their throats intact whisper prayers to a god out of earshot. Those with any semblance of sense run to the opposite end of the room, clutching desperately to their final moments, dumb to the futility of it all.

The laughter crescendos. Louder, louder, and louder still. At last, it is the only audible noise, triumphing over every whimper, plea, and sob. Over the amber glow of the fire, a deviant sunset, arises a monster. A tortured and twisted being with a smile like a thousand razors, a mouth of bone alchemized into ebony wood serrated into a mass of gnashing splinters dripping red.

It does not permit any of those present a swift death. Each one perishes slowly, edging on the threshold between awareness and shock. There is no escape, no drifting into neural purgatory. The monster makes certain, absolutely certain, that every ounce of pain is felt. The white-haired man is the last to be released from his mortal coil.

Gazing into the eyes of the beast, he utters an apology. "I'm sorry, JS-7R. We shouldn't have—"

JS-7R digs its dagger nails into the crown of the researcher's skull. It rips at the corpus callosum, parting left brain from right, and proceeds to the collarbone, leaving his throat a spiderweb of flesh, veins, and arteries. His body is dropped beside the rest with an inconsequential thud aligned perfectly with a quartet of footsteps beyond the lab's borders. Rubber soles on metal stairs, distant, ascending.

JS-7R is too enraptured by its gory masterpiece to pay them mind. This blood would fertilize a garden all on its own. It would take time and patience, but it would grow, as all things do when they are fed.

The screen glitches, then implodes with a surge of uncanny crimson. At the very end of the tape, breathing, ragged from laughter, colors the soundscape. Now that same breathing skims the nape of my neck.

17 | JASPER

Humanity is so fickle with their flirtations. Again, I remember Mother—Hemlock's lessons in interpersonal relationships. There must have been a time when she dreamed I'd be a true son to her science, because no detail was left lovelorn.

Slick documents showcased corsets of cordiality. Hardcover books spoke of featherlight touches and sweet nothings. Films evolved from leaden to lurid made a spectacle of concepts meant to be simple, instinctual. Hemlock wanted me educated in these matters. She was prying for reactions to record on the pale-blue pages of her notepad. I urged myself into a more acceptable embodiment, but in truth, I couldn't will myself to understand.

Why dredge boresomely through motions building to passion when it's already available? No one in this laboratory knew how to account for the height of my inhuman qualities. Unlike them, I don't have the need for words. Clara and I can communicate through our bodies, but also through our very *blood.* We can speak in shared currents, in spaces where one ocean meets another. I can see through to her innermost self, view her memories in telepathic Technicolor.

I don't need a textbook to navigate what we have. Our chemistry *is* chemistry. What we have is as effortless as the twirl of a double helix. She may not accept it from the forefront of her mind, but her body knows better. Beneath my touch, all she can feel is trust. If not for the nuisances in the way of our union, we'd already be one.

They've found a path into the EHKI's dilapidated outer sector, an emergency exit. I had been meaning to properly furnish it with flora, but I need to now more than ever. Clara must wait for such revelations. The truth of her origin is a delicate matter, one I'd like to deliver under very specific circumstances. Also, I can't have her finding these mysterious pills.

"Clara . . ." I sing to her. Telepathic talk is far more melodious than verbal speech. Speech is staccato. It is built on blunt, disjointed syllables strung together ever so tactlessly. The way of my and Clara's transmission is a legato love letter to the concept of communication itself. Dr. Hemlock *had* designed me to be better. In this way, among innumerable others, I simply am. *We* simply are. "Come to me, Clara . . ."

As her barbarian sister inspects an EHKI banner scorched by yours truly, Clara busies herself sorting through canisters, flasks, and every legible file. She's desperate. She's guarding her humanity like it's the last flickering firelight in a blizzard. To abandon her true nature would be to abandon me, to abandon us.

Oh, sweet thing, you won't be doing that.

I lure her with a thought inspired seamlessly enough to be mistaken for her own. It's a gentle suggestion to follow the leftmost corridor. "This way . . . there might be something this way," I murmur, though in her mind, my voice manifests as hers. "Don't disturb the others. They cannot know what you came here for."

She slips away without a trace. Wretched Grayson is too busy comforting the young nuisance to notice, and Jade is too consumed by one of Dr. Blaine Milligan's notebooks. I remember him well enough to know she'll find nothing of value in there. Clara follows me down a passageway obstructed by spiderwebs of thick wiring. Flickering lights running on the last of their solar power glitch madly overhead. I stare through each millisecond of darkness.

A few boiling embryos might have clawed their way into the emergency exit, but not many scientists made it. I don't have to worry about horrifying dearest Clara with the remains I've yet to alchemize into branches and blood roses. Save for three dented fire extinguishers and some broken glass, the path to our privacy is clear.

Beyond the narrow halls of this escape route, a high-ceilinged cathedral of chemistry endures time. Muted neon pours from dangling bulbs that have persisted for a garish twenty-five years. I must find those remaining solar panels. Burettes, beakers, and Bunsen burners galore tell the tale of our origin. There is enough glassware to fill a ballroom with chandeliers.

It is as good a backdrop as any for us to daydream.

As Clara seeks her precious pills or a formula relating to them, I slip through her neural gates and scour her memory. So recently empowered, I have the bandwidth to create a waking fantasy. I offer her a hallucination, a doorway to things unseen, a path into the past. This is power even I've yet to play with to its fullest potential. Reminiscence sweeps through the space like a wave, and together, we enter a realm of anamnesis.

My little love sits between crimson velvet cushions like a stolen slice of the moon. She glimmers beneath our dreamscape's faux sky of incandescent stars, reading the rim of a martini glass speckled with burgundy kisses. It practically blushes under the weight of her gaze, a tantalizing haze of red iridescence woven through the folds of her irises. My crimson smoke spirals through the air in gravity-defying tendrils. They encircle her head, a crown.

Everything about her seems designed to tempt. It's as though she was made just for me, as if her form was manifested for the sole purpose of sickening my heart.

She fits in here well, all things considered. This is a recent memory. From it, I am learning of the dreadful world she hails from. She feels like a stranger, but in tragic, withering ways, she yearns to be human.

She'll realize, in time, that we are so much more than what she once imagined at the edge of possible.

"Another drink, miss?" A phantom waiter adorned in a voguish waistcoat sends an ice pick through her thoughts. I wish I had been there then to protect her from eyes as hungry as his.

She shakes her head. She offers nothing more than a smile that is far too shy, a mismatched button sewn crudely in place.

The waiter disappears into the speakeasy's maze of velvet, leather, and fool's gold furnishings. It is a gilded cage nestled beneath the streets of Clara's old home, a pocket of sensuality and softness in an otherwise loud, cruel, *human* world. In some ways, it is an attempt to replicate my fantasies. It could never. No, it could never satisfy something so magnificent as my *Clara, Clara, Clara.*

Jazzy tunes tumble off the air particles, all of them hiding hypnotic whispers sung just for her. She rises, her crown of smoke dispersing. She steps toward the dance floor one heel click at a time, each softer and more hesitant than the previous.

It's been years since she's danced.

It's been a lifetime since she's had a proper partner.

I step in wearing a sleek, white tuxedo and a devilishly crooked smile. Locks of roguish, jet-black hair fall strategically to my temples, desperate to caress the altar of my lips. They are upturned like a pair of daggers; sharp, relaxed, and ruthless. Human. For her, for now, they are still human. I am beautiful in every sense of the word, my face a mosaic of all things too stunning to be considered normal for her kind. I am what artists attempt to replicate in reimaginings of lust incarnate, a flawless marble statue lovingly terraformed by rivers of shadow.

I am everything she could want and so much more.

The space goes silent. The tinkles of clinking teardrop glasses and idle prattle of life, work, and the weather surrender to a newfound cloud of anticipatory stillness. Clara's heart lurches forward, toward me. On the inside, she curses it like a traitor.

I touch a fingertip to her lips, halting every question, every thought. She's better off without them. "You used to dance? How long has it been since you danced?" I murmur, one hand coming from behind to coil her throat, the other at the curve of her precious waist. I nip at the arc of her left ear. My cinnamon-sweet breath slithers into her skull, urging her mind into focus.

"Ten years." A response tumbles out. "It's been ten years."

"Did you enjoy it?"

"I . . . My parents enrolled me in ballet when I was young . . . they told me it would be helpful . . ."

She had trouble moving like other children in even the simplest of ways. Her joints just couldn't fit into the expected pattern. She was attuned to an entirely different frequency, like an insect. Like me. I peer into her lessons, feeling the rigid poses she'd been ushered into. First position, second position, third position, fourth. Arabesques, attitudes, and additions to her daily performance. Her parents hadn't hoped she'd become a ballerina; they wanted her to pass for a human being.

"That won't do." I click my tongue. She shivers. Success. "Dance with *me*."

I will free her. Roots descend from overhead to guide her steps and pose her arms. For a moment, the illusion breaks. The world spins, a blur of green glass, crystal flasks, and dreary blue-gray metal. My hand descends from her jaw, lingering at her collarbone like a curious tongue. This touch is a language all our own, each sensation a syllable. I explore until we are a tangle of limbs positioned to waltz, whisked from the laboratory, returned to the cherrywood floor of our dreamscape.

She breathes. *Ecstasy.*

We ascend into music and motion. I promise her ephemeral, rhythmic synchrony, and she allows me to twirl her across the space. This isn't like the ballet of her past. This is movement that fractalizes into freedom. We are a kaleidoscope, a whirlpool. Through this, I show her the splendors of chaos guided by instinct, the infinite refined by desire. I savor each tender crossroad where skin meets skin, inhuman cells collide, and I am no longer alone.

Grayson.

She thinks of . . . Grayson?

Grayson Warner. Through neural osmosis, I discover him to be the only person who's made her feel . . . wonderful, terrible things. To him, she imagines, she isn't a monster. If he became privy to her secret, he'd accept her. He'd embrace her. He'd love her. She *wants* him to love her. She holds a hand over her heart as though that might protect it. Such a brave little thing. My ivory fingers ensnare her throat once more, vines claiming the stem of a rose. I lean in to steal something. I want another kiss.

Again, she thinks of Grayson.

Musical menticide slips from me. A sonic downpour of silk, a deluge of honeyed electricity, a love story fluttering through her like plucked poppy petals. She is mine, and with a song forged in telepathic fire, I will ensure she knows it.

There is blood to be spilled, darkness to embrace, dominion to be demanded. There are nights to be spent entangled, dreaming in unison. Let us be their evil. Let us grow our garden, our birthright, our kingdom. Two thrones for two monarchs. One damned world for two damned gods. She leans in to me as though slipping through clouds. I sing to her, for her. I caress her body, mind, soul, and every branch of infinity beyond it. *You will wear malevolence like a goddess in silks. Let me in, Clara. Let me in.*

She tilts her head back, a moth to a flame, an iron to a magnet. She gives me entrance, permission. It is only us, and not just in the illusionary speakeasy. Not just beneath my forest. Not just on Earth. Right now, we are the sole inhabitants of a hollow, empty universe. Right now, the rest of existence is an echo, a wraith meant to highlight the sacred strangeness of all that tethers our essences incorporeal.

Miss. Clara. Lovecroft.

I would die for her. More importantly, and more relevantly, I would kill for her.

Grayson's voice pierces the veil, an unwelcome visitor. His hair is disheveled. His breaths emerge in desperate, heaving puffs. A jacket of worn brown leather hangs from his biceps, ripped off by frantic motion. He'd been running through the dilapidated hallways. He'd been searching. The audacity of it all.

"Clara?" he calls; her precious name gets caught between two panicked exhales. "Clara, where are you?"

18 | CLARA

I don't think I've ever been quite this happy. Dancing with Jasper is effervescent paradise. I'd been so silly to deny him, to turn away from our sweet shadows.

Pills. How foolish. I don't want those pills, because I don't want to be human. Why on earth would I want such a thing? Jasper's saved me from the cacophony of the city. Yet there I was, dreaming haplessly of going back. Jasper's whisked me from a world that could never understand me. Here, with him, I am eternally understood. All I've ever desired lives in him. All I could ever hope to desire lives in him.

"Clara?" a voice calls out. I barely recognize it. "Clara, where are you?"

Raymond, was it? Jason? No, that's not right.

Grayson.

There he is. Grayson, all tall, blond, and dauntless. He's entered my and Jasper's speakeasy with only a quarter of my love's grace. At the edges, sickly green light claws through. Slashes in the fabric of this reality are forming, and it's Grayson's fault.

I hate him for it. I love him for it. *Leave me.* Save me.

"Clara!" he yells.

Suddenly, I'm in his arms. He's thrown one beneath my knees and the other behind my shoulder blade. He sweeps me up like a bride. The ground shakes.

"Don't worry, I'll get you out of here! Just hold on!"

The ground trembles. I feel Jasper's temper surging toward us, an inferno of emotion. I feel him, invisible but still very much in our air space. Out of the corner of my eye, I catch him skittering behind a metal tile curled down by gravity. He's returned to his true form, *our* true form, and he's taken to the walls in a spiderlike swirl of limbs.

"Grayson, I—I . . ."

You're mine, little love. Not his. Mine.

My head lops onto Grayson's chest. It's too empty, too full. Too light, too heavy. "I'm sorry . . ."

He kisses the crown of my skull, and suddenly I'm safe.

Jasper's rage multiplies tenfold. The roots he commands dive down through the tectonic earth that the complex is embedded in. Vines surge toward the structure, shredding it like a piece of printer paper. The ground crumbles and quakes. It collapses. All around us, glass and gadgetry fall like deadly rainfall. Every hit to the ground sets off a pocket explosion of serrated edges. Grayson tears through the corridor I'd sleepwalked down, returning to the emergency exit chamber. Jade is in a panic to collect all she can carry. However, as the ceiling caves in, she abandons it all to scoop up Joey.

We climb back up to the mouth of the cave with only seconds to spare. A belch of metallic air chases us alongside a tremendously loud concatenation of bangs. Night has fallen over the woods but not over our souls. Despite the odds, we've made it out alive. Joey cries into Jade's crewneck. I latch on to the lapel of Grayson's jacket.

We return to the Hummer in complete silence, following hapless intuition and the ghostly glow of the moon.

Not his. Mine.

Mine, mine, mine.

I should be terrified. I saw what he became, and in him, I see all I can be. I'm not sure I like it. I'm not sure I want it. I'm not sure I'd like it even if I wanted it.

But . . . oh, how it felt to be shrouded in shadows his flavor of the dark. When Grayson, sweet and sensible and sound asleep beside his brother, touches me, I turn to light. Light has its limitations. Does he seek to impose them? Does he plan to place me in a bulb? *How much more, Grayson Warner?* How much of me will you take if I were to offer? How much would you demand that I be if I let myself be something for you?

Jasper would never ask for more than I am. Only Jasper accepts the beastly heart that beats in me, because only Jasper can. He'll teach me to dance. He'll help me unlearn the steps I've been taught. We'll make melodies of motion all our own. We'll make everything all our own. Anything is possible with him; everything is possible with him.

Not his. Mine.

Not Grayson's. Jasper's.

I leave the Hummer like a wisp, following his footpath of harmonies. The forest is his concert hall, his opera house, and his royal theater. Every facet of the natural world becomes an instrument to create sonic picture frames for the art that is his voice. *Jasper. Jasper. Jasper.* Space tastes like his strawberry-licorice lips. Dark matter dusts it with delusion. In this place, we can be as we were meant to be. We can be together, in a pocket of predestined forever.

"Clara." He emerges from a veil between two trunks, his hands eager to anchor themselves on my hips. He kisses me desperately, first with just the sound of my name, then with his corporeal form. "I'm so sorry, my dear. You were never in any danger, I swear. I wouldn't have let anything happen to you."

He lifts a palm to my throat, his fingers easily stretching to encircle it in totality. His sharp nails tease the nape of my neck, tickling it as his hold on me tightens. For a moment, I cannot breathe, but it's a perfect opportunity to realize I don't need to, not if he tells me so.

"I wouldn't have let anything happen to you," he repeats.

"Of course . . . y-you wouldn't have. I'm yours."

His dark eyebrow arches. Shortly after, that crooked smile, pure nitrous oxide, returns with a blissful vengeance. "Oh, you—you are so . . . so *good*."

My knees threaten to drop out from under me. I want to fall forward into his embrace, press myself to his chest, and never depart from him again. However, the space between us, the threshold between here and home, is interrupted when a shower of pebbles is hurled in our direction.

"Get away from her!"

Joey.

Jasper whirls us around, stepping in front of me to ensure I am shielded from the rocky rainfall. As they hit him, they dissipate into tiny explosions of scarlet sparks. His back is morphing, bones writhing like captive snakes beneath the skin. His skin shifts in coloration, switching through every human tone before looping back to a spectral shade of gray. Even the length of his hair moves, unable to decide on how to drape off his head.

"Well." His voice reverberates through the ground, flying like telepathic bullets into Joey's ears. "That's not very nice."

Joey holds his hands around his head, falling onto the leaves below with a whine. My first thought is to help him. Why is my first thought to help him? I should stay beside Jasper, shouldn't I?

My legs are already moving. I'm already with Joey, on the opposite side of the battlefield. "Joey, you can't be here. Go back to the car," I plead, hauling him up, dusting him off, and giving him a push in the direction from which he came.

"I'm not leaving you here, Clara! Stop acting crazy!"

"I'm not acting crazy. I promise. Jasper and I were just—"

"That thing is doing something to you! Can't you see it? It's controlling you!"

A pang rips through my chest. *Thing.* No one should be called a *thing.* I can't entirely dispute him about something being done to me, though. I feel . . . fuzzy. Wisps of red tingle through the folds of my irises. I'll handle it later. Right now, Joey is my priority, and he needs to be anywhere but here.

"Joey, I'm okay. I'll come back to the car as soon as I'm done here. Go. Please go."

"I'm getting Jade and Grayson!"

No! My expression speaks before my mouth does. My head might not be steadily perched on my shoulders right now, but I have enough sense in me to remember how . . . how dangerous Jasper is. If he's half as powerful as I am, I don't even want to imagine what he is capable of. I'm in his good graces, but the same might not be true for the others. *Snap out of it, Clara.* The same isn't true for the others. He'll kill them.

"No." I balance my voice until it is hard and stern. "It's not safe, Joey."

His face twists into a terrified frown, his eyes going watery again as he reads me like a billboard. He turns on his heel and starts running as fast as his legs will carry him. The soles of his beaten sneakers fail to grip the murky mud below them, causing him to slip. He's back on his feet with feverish fury, charging for the Hummer too far away to be spotted in the gloom.

I turn back to Jasper. Something seems different about him. I can't quite put my finger on it, but I *can* quite remember that I'd forgotten to take my pill. I'd forgotten to build today's chemical bridge back to my humanity.

"Are you doing something to me?" I ask, lucid.

He stalls. Then he smiles, creating a slit of pearly sharpness that rivals the crescent moon in the sky. "Allow me to correct this, my love."

It happens too quickly.

He unravels into a bouquet of black, emaciated limbs. Like a recluse coiling around paralyzed prey, he gathers me in a flurry of crackling motion. The two of us sink into the shadows and ride them across spaces unseen.

We follow Joey, going impossibly fast. Too fast for him to outrun. Once in front of him, Jasper extends a hand in the direction of a particularly spindly tree. I am behind him, heart racing and head spinning. The tree emits a horrific succession of snaps and begins bending like broken limbs toward Joey's torso. Its branches, those hungry hands, enwrap his small body like an owl's claw around a mouse. He screams, but the sound is short lived. It is replaced by the worst kind of cry, the kind that is hushed by a surge of pain. The limbs of the tree have started piercing through his abdomen, exploring his internal world. It's surgical and meticulous, but also lawless in the way all nature is. Blood spills down his sweatpants, along with loops of intestines still keen on digesting chocolate.

The branches proceed to spiral up his spine, now exposed to the air. Like a staircase, it climbs the length of his body until finally reaching the top. Once there, a single stalk shoots beyond his jaw, coming through gaping lips that will never smile again. The last glimmer of life in his eyes is filled with panic, pain, and fear. It is extinguished too quickly to be caught, but too slowly to insinuate Jasper had been merciful.

As though the corpse has become some kind of art piece, small red florets bloom from his blood. Jasper plucks them. One by one, he consumes the petals, and petal by petal, his human form stabilizes. Everything about him, and about the forest, intensifies. When he turns back to me, his eyes are sweet honey, and his smile is just as charming as it had been when he handed me back that ten-dollar bill.

I do not smile back.

"Joey . . ." I shake my head in disbelief.

"He's just a human, love. He's nothing."

My throat is dry, and it aches as though I'd just ripped through my vocal cords with a scream. I don't scream, though. I can't. The way Joey's body hangs is too horrifying to conjure sound. The fear won't be cleared out by an outburst, no matter how loud. All I want to do right now is run. Spinning on my shaking heels, I make a beeline back toward the road. I don't want to look at the dripping display that my friend has become.

My heart pounds relentlessly against my breastbone as the forest morphs into a blur of ebony branches. There are no details, my surroundings reduced to tear-obstructed streaks. If not for the fading moonlight, I wouldn't be able to see a hand before my face in this darkness. I wouldn't even have the red glow of my own eyes to guide me, because it has been extinguished.

How am I going to tell Grayson?

The thought rattles my brain. Joey is dead, and it's my fault. If I hadn't been so careless, he'd still be sleeping beneath a sherpa blanket. He'd still be looking forward to telling his friends about our trip's unfortunate mishap. That mishap is now stained with blood that should never have been spilled.

I run until the sun rises. Only after its golden light claws between the trees am I able to get my bearings. The car becomes visible, so unnatural against the backdrop behind it. Before I know it, my hands are pounding on the passenger window, knuckles white and rapidly bruising.

19 | GRAYSON

Jade shoots forward, sending her skull into the roof of the car. The impact is followed by a string of colorful curse words on beat with whatever is pounding on the window at this ungodly hour.

I rise, eyes heavy and likely surrounded by pools of purple. I didn't sleep well, not after what happened back at the lab. Clara had been so untethered. It felt like she was floating above us, shackled to her body with a rusty chain. I didn't know someone could look so far from themselves. Yet again, she's the primary resident of my mind, because she's the one banging on the glass, crashing her fists into it with enough vigor to draw blood.

"Clara! Are you all right?" I shout, clambering outside. "What happened? Did something hurt you?"

Words do not come to her. Her lips, along with every inch of her body, quiver like leaves fighting the wind. I want to protect her from whatever's caused this, illusionary or otherwise. The passenger door squeals, then slams, and I realize I'll have to protect her from a very real Jade. She stalks toward us, each step more violent than the last. I stand between them, a wedge between warring worlds.

"You better have a good explanation for waking us up at the crack of dawn."

"I-it was—it's—I need to . . . w-we need to—" Clara stammers. Jade growls.

"Easy," I warn her.

"Could you, for fifteen minutes, stop telling me what to do, Grayson? She's *my* sister, remember? I know how to talk to her." Jade bares her teeth, and I am more than willing to take it as a challenge. We start bickering with sleep-deprived viciousness in our arsenals until Clara screams to stop us. Bullets stop firing, our tongues like triggers that have suddenly gone stiff.

"Stop! Please!" she begs, her eyes swimming in their sockets. "I need you to come with me."

"Get back in the car. I need at least two more hours of sleep before dealing with your bullshit." Jade shoves her toward the Hummer. Her hands hit the glass before her face can, and I rush forward to prevent further damage. On gazing into the backmost window, however, it becomes dreadfully apparent that we're missing a member.

"Where's Joey?" I ask, every muscle in my body turned into stone.

"Clara." A hissing breath slithers between Jade's teeth. She takes hold of Clara's shoulders hard enough to bruise them. "Where is Joey?"

My stomach acid turns into liquid lead. I'm almost surprised it hasn't burst, sending streams of molten metal to make a chrome car engine of my insides. Joey wouldn't wander off. At his age, I had all the survival mechanisms necessary to keep me from gullible galivants through danger. I was only half as intelligent and a quarter levelheaded, what with my mosaic of average letter grades and detention summonses. Joey's always been the smarter of the two of us, from his heart to his head. I'd never admit it out loud and risk inflating his ego, but it's the truth.

If Joey's not here, it means . . . he's safe.

It means he found his way to help.

Clara yanks herself away from Jade, whose nails leave lines like chemtrails on her triceps. The taciturn ambiguity returns to her eyes, and as though guided by a compass's needle, she whirls away from us. Facing the forest, her knuckles turn to fists, each locked to a hip. She walks at a pace that speaks without words. She's either inviting us to keep up or trying to lose us in the tiny plumes of dust left in the wake of her heels.

"Clara, wait!" I call out.

She doesn't so much as tilt in the direction of my voice. Jade releases a rattling groan that rises up her throat like a geyser of pennies. Unsure if she'll follow, I take off to tail Clara. Wherever she's going, whether it leads to Joey or not, it's important. If not to us, then to her, and at this moment, that's all that matters to me.

As dawn arrives on the scene, the sun looks too timid to haul itself over the horizon. It looks as though it is cowering behind the distant mountains, sleeping eldritch beasts beneath pine tree blankets. A great black mamba snake coiled around the forest, fangs out, venom dripping with promises of paralytic pleasure-pain. Once I am away from the road, everything is swallowed by espresso bark and withering green foliage. The lidless eye of the serpent that stalks us falls out of sight, yet still I feel watched by it.

The shadows at this time of day are extraordinarily long. Each tree trunk, some as thick as a redwood and some as thin as my ankle, shoots a dark line across the ground. Clara and I move through them, inmates behind a wall of bars. I can't breathe out here, not this far from the car, from the road, from the only place that feels remotely safe.

Joey's found his way. He is all right.

Jade pulls up at my side, her nostrils flared. She huffs with each thunderous clomp into the earth, snapping twigs and flattening clovers beneath her feet. The branches that reach for her meet an unstoppable human tsunami. The weaker ones split on impact, speckling the silence with crackles. I turn my head to the left to acknowledge her, but my veins tremble when I realize she's on my right. The presence I'd felt wasn't Jade's. It was some transient penumbra, now hooked around a tree yards away, gazing back from the gloom. I turn my gaze back to Clara, who may as well be in another world.

"Clara!" My throat is clamped at the trachea. I throw both hands around it, but only after her name dies in my vocal cords does the spasm subside.

Jade powers ahead of me. Despite the onslaught of lightheaded nausea, I do everything to keep up with her. The black mamba doesn't feel so far away anymore. It feels like it's just behind me, slithering in perfect stealth, its maw widened to the edge of impossible. I make the mistake of peering backward and find a single shadow pointing in the wrong direction. It isn't bending westward, as all physics-obeying denizens of our dimension should. It bends to the east. It stretches to the sun, the light from it so red, I could swear it was a deviant lunar eclipse.

Joey *is* fine. Joey *is* safe.

He has to be.

20 | CLARA

Going back into the abyss means facing Jasper again. He could send me spiraling into a vortex of whispers. I didn't realize how vulnerable I'd become, how stupidly helpless I'd been against the caliber of control he's capable of. In his palm, my mind turned to a scoop of melting vanilla doused with higher-reasoning hot fudge. It was dessert for him to lap up with his agile tongue, so syrupy while dancing with mine. Simply thinking about another cursed kiss makes the corners of my lips tingle. I can feel his slender fingers, cold as an ice cube at my abdomen, waiting eagerly to pull up my smile.

Dance with me, Clara.

Snap out of it, Clara.

I won't let him in again. I don't know if it's the absence of my medication or pure adrenaline, but I won't let him in again. How could I have been so stupid? How could I have trusted him? If we are the same sort of monster, I should have known better. Some terrible, naive part of me wanted to believe we could be good. We can't be good. Joey's death proves it a million terrible times over.

I lead Grayson and Jade to the tree that tore open his insides. There's no way I'd be able to verbalize what happened. They need to see it with their own eyes. Then I can manage a way to explain, to apologize. It will do nothing, but I owe it to Grayson.

Grayson. Poor Grayson. Grayson, whose brother is gone because of me. Grayson, whose entire existence is in jeopardy because of me.

Grayson, whose heart I've smothered before I even had the chance to hold it.

The maze of wood and shadows makes our journey all but easy. However, a trail of fallen leaves, uncharacteristically lively, lead the way. Something hateful claws at the corners of my consciousness. These leaves . . . they belonged to the florets that sprouted from Joey's lips.

I'm going to be sick.

"Clara, please. Tell me what's going on." Grayson is out of breath. I withhold my flinch when he grabs my hand and forces me to face him. "Answer me."

"It's just a little further."

"What is?"

"Grayson, I . . ." My mouth clamps shut, teeth chattering in place.

Dread pours over his pupils like a pair of cataracts. Like the nictitating membrane of a shark eye, it is so hopelessly protective. The dread turns to a waterfall of fear that trickles toward his lips, weighing on them until they are downturned. I pull him farther, my body tensing in preparation.

We're almost there. I can smell Joey's blood on the breeze.

Finally, the path of green reaches a single petal, placed purposefully to mark its end. My neck hinges slowly and reluctantly, tilting until my gaze goes skyward. Endless unspoken explanations gather at the tip of my tongue, apologies right behind them. However, instead of Joey's mutilated body, I find only a gathering of twisted branches that hadn't been there before.

"What?" My voice is airy with disbelief.

I can tell that Grayson had been holding back tears. "Y-you got me. Very funny. Let's go back."

"He was here . . . he was *right* here."

"Stop it, Clara. Let's just head back to the car."

"No, he was here. Jasper—"

Jade's temper shoots sky-high. "You woke us up and dragged us into the middle of the woods to go hunting for your imaginary forest friend? You just worried the hell out of Grayson because of the talking *trees*?"

"He's doing something to me, Jade! It's like he's using some kind of spell, or . . . or mind control. After we got back from the laboratory, I left the car, and—"

"You're being ridiculous!"

She makes me want to explode. I grit my teeth, already feeling them starting to writhe against my gums. I need my pills.

"You're not listening to me! You never listen to me! Ever since I met him at the gas station, Jasper has been—"

"Jasper is the guy from the gas station too?" she booms. "Do you even hear yourself? You sound insane!"

"Of course I do! It's not like you're a stranger to the concept, though! Maybe it runs in the family, because you sounded pretty insane when you dragged us down into a cave on the brink of collapse yesterday!"

"That was different!"

"How was that different? I went chasing an imaginary forest friend, and you went chasing some flimsy conspiracy theory for a chance to know more about our parents, who've been dead for ten years! I'm chasing demons, you're chasing ghosts! It's the same thing!"

A deafening silence takes the space. A single crow flies overhead, breaking it with a croon.

"Okay." Grayson takes my hand, lacing our fingers. "Maybe you should lie down for a bit."

"I don't need to lie down."

"You're scared, and stressed, and maybe a little sleep deprived." He brings my knuckles to his lips and kisses them. "I'm worried about you. Please, just . . . let me help."

Oh no.

One look into his eyes, and I'm safe again. I shouldn't feel safe. We aren't safe. I got his brother killed, and in return, he's kissing my hand. He's making a damsel of me, but I'm the dragon in this faux fairy tale. He should be driving a sword through my skull, not an arrow through my heart.

Guilt ravages me. It ravages my vocal cords, and my nerves, and all that's left of my senses. I shouldn't have yelled at Jade. I shouldn't have let myself lean in to anger I'm not entitled to. I shouldn't have worried Grayson. Perhaps this is all just a stress-induced delusion. A snowstorm and a slick road could have killed my parents. Jasper could be a desert mirage of my darkest desires. Joey could be alive. And the pills . . . the pills could be antipsychotics designed to wipe away what isn't there. I hope with all of my heart that it isn't there.

"I'm sorry . . ." I cave in. "I didn't mean to . . . Grayson, I . . . Jade—"

"Whatever," she scoffs, then starts for the road.

Grayson pulls me in for a hug, the soft fabric of his shirt wafting the scent of clean linen. I breathe it in; I breathe him in. Jasper might be a trip to the underworld, but Grayson . . . Grayson's a ticket to the sunniest island on planet Earth. I bury my face in his pectorals, and despite my inhumanity, I cry. He holds on tighter with each tear.

"Shhh, shhh . . . it's okay. I've got you. I've got you."

He's got me. Everything's okay because he's got me.

Unraveling from him is a necessary torture because we can't allow Jade to wander off alone. However, as we walk back toward the road, we walk hand in hand. I stay safe because he's got me. I feel human because he's got me.

The Hummer sits idle as a statue and empty as a disemboweled beast. The blankets in the back seat remain tousled, Joey's forlorn chocolate bars strewn across them. My bag of medicinal mental stability beckons, and I take today's dose without water.

"I'm sure he just wandered off, but he couldn't have gotten far," Grayson muses calmly. "Let's get our bearings and start heading up the way we came."

Jade sucks on a new cigarette. When she speaks, I can sense how it's soothing the nerves I stirred. "You think he tried going back?"

"I think he tried to get a head start. You know Joey. He loves being the hero."

"He could have gone toward your mom's place. I could go that way."

"We shouldn't split up."

I move to the opposite side of our car, sinking down to steady my breathing as the pink floods my veins. The world beyond the road stares back at me. It just keeps staring at me. Even though this morning is brighter than yesterday's overcast afternoon, the sun seems afraid to shine. It casts pale, sickly streams of yellow across the floor, none of them bright enough to chase away the dark.

In the distance, a single white sneaker drops from the skeletal canopy. It lies on its side in the dirt, mud caked into the creases of its sole. Through it, a pair of initials have been drawn in black ink.

J. W.

Joseph Warner.

My breath catches, my arteries burn, and fiery rage surges through my entire being. Some buried, feral part of me lusts for revenge so desperately, I consider marching into the abyss to exact it. It is the part of me I know will come alive if I discard a dosage. Sadly, anger does not hold up well against fear, and fear is precisely what I feel when something else drops down from the treetops.

Like a specter shrouded by the blur of distance, the shape of a boy lowers like a puppet on strings. It is too far away for me to discern any details beyond one of his arms as it rises to wave. My stomach churns. Despite the cruel voice that is hope, I know it isn't Joey, and if it is . . .

My secondary musing is obliged when the puppet is swung closer. Once moved into a sunny spotlight, its features become clear. Joey's corpse dangles from a quintet of vines spun around his wrists, ankles, and broken neck. His jaw hangs beyond the constraints of normal jaws, having been torn loose by the branch that had come up through his throat. His eyes are blank and hazy, but his gaze sits forever forward.

I cover my mouth to conceal a scream and to block out the putrid smell.

"Would you like me to show them?" Jasper's whisper fills my ears, though he remains out of sight. "So that they'll believe you?"

All I can do is shake my head, furiously and feverishly as bitter bile makes its way toward my esophagus. There is a deadly stillness in the air. Then the marionette version of Joey is pulled away, lost to the unearthly gloom. I release a breath that shudders audibly enough to alert Grayson.

"Clara? Are you all right? What's happening over there?"

He approaches and helps me to my feet. When I stare into his eyes, I offer every apology my lips dare not speak. He did not see Joey, but I did. I'm certain I will see him on the back of my eyelids every time I slip them closed.

21 | GRAYSON

Joey is safe—that is something of which I am completely certain. Unfortunately, I cannot say the same for myself, as keeping the Lovecroft sisters from ripping each other to shreds is a task I've been left alone with. Jade kept her wrath to a bare minimum around Joey for his sake. If the fight she had with Clara this morning signals anything, it's that her restraint has run out.

Clara . . . I'm so worried about Clara.

She's making less and less sense as the hours tick by. I wish I could save her from all that she sees, but in this arena, I am helpless. I can practically hear my mother roaring in my ears, "Grayson Oliver Warner, you *will not* be helpless, because you *cannot* be helpless." Still, despite her enduring commands, I feel two feet tall as I guide Clara and Jade southward.

This far into Blackstone Forest, the road has been ravaged by overgrowth. Other than the weeds stubbornly crawling across the asphalt, it is untouched. It's as though the entire landscape has forgotten humans exist. It's a self-contained apocalypse situated centuries ahead of the moment from whence we came. At least, it feels that way. If we had traveled to the future somehow, life would be a whole lot easier. I wouldn't have to face my mother and explain the succession of events that led to Joey's solo side quest. I wouldn't have to admit that I'd taken my eyes off him during a situation so dire.

"Sleep isn't for the weak, but in some cases, it's for the irresponsible," she'll say, and I'll concede because she's right. I shouldn't have gone to sleep. Terrible things happen when I fall asleep.

The night my father died, I was asleep. For three years, he battled leukemia, and for three years, I held his hand through every test, trial, and treatment. He'd say to me, "Grayson, please, go and get some rest. Your mother's had you running around for hours." He wasn't a man apt to exaggerate. Mom had kept me busy, *very* busy. He was in staunch disapproval of it. When the two of them divorced, he did everything in his power to maintain custody, but she earned more than him, and he was already so sick by the time they sat down in court.

It was a cold December night. Joey wasn't old enough to understand how bad things had gotten, nor how bad they were about to become. I stayed up reading to him, trying to ward off panic spirals with science fiction and superheroes. Mom had agreed to give me some time off, and she was supposed to drive me to the hospital, but . . . I'd fallen asleep. I'd slipped into dreams of spaceships in flight as Dad's heart monitor flattened to a straight line.

I'd been with him from diagnosis to final days, but his last moments on this horrible planet were spent alone in a sterile white room. Mom wasn't with him; she was too busy. She's always too busy. Maybe that's why she keeps me busy.

"I'm glad you weren't there," I imagine Dad would've said. "I'm grateful you finally got that rest."

If only he could see me now. I rested and lost him; I rested and lost Joey. Only, in this case, I'm unquestionably sure that Joey is alive. He has to be. Keeping people alive and intact is my duty. It's been my duty since the day Dad left. Hell, it's been my duty since the day I was born.

I hate long walks. More specifically, I hate long walks in silence, because long walks in silence prompt my brain to compose symphonies I'd rather not hear. With each step, suppressed thoughts gurgle to the surface like seafoam. My conflicting memories smell like rotten fish washed ashore.

◆ ◆ ◆

"We need you now more than ever, Grayson," Mom said. "I know it's difficult, but you're strong. That's why it has to be you."

"I don't know if I can do it," I replied, barely fifteen at the time. She'd spent a long time preparing me for the duties suited to a Warner, but I never could have anticipated how heavy they'd become after Dad's death.

"Of course you can," she insisted, raking a row of French-tipped fingernails through my hair, identical to my father's hair. A constant reminder of him. "You're ready for this. You're ready for anything. What do we say when we need to remind ourselves of that?"

"I will not be helpless, because I cannot be helpless," I droned. "Action is the only option."

"Exactly. With your father gone, there is much for us to do, much action for us to take. I need you. Your brother needs you. He loves you so much, Grayson—more than you could ever imagine. Without you, his whole world falls apart. Do you understand?"

I nodded, because I did understand, and in my understanding, she mined for obedience by the ounce.

"Good." Silence, lethal silence. When my mother finally spoke again, she said exactly what I feared she'd say. "The Lovecroft sisters must be kept at arm's length. I know that you care about them, but you cannot afford distractions. Jade will never be the companion you hope for her to be, and what you're feeling for Clara is completely out of the question. Let go of all that you dream of with her. There's no time for friends, and certainly no time for romance."

I was so embarrassed. For a moment, I felt like a normal preteen, blushing because my mother was privy to my schoolboy crush. But I wasn't a normal anything. With Dad gone, I'd never be normal again.

"I need you here, Grayson." She poked the center of my forehead. "I need you focused. You have a duty to fulfill. A duty to me, a duty to your brother, and a duty to the world, even though your father is no longer in it."

"What if it's too much for me?" I whimpered, a pathetic sign of unconscionable weakness.

"It is not too much for you, because it cannot be too much for you." She brought her stiletto tips from my hairline to my jaw, suddenly too stern to rebut. "Repeat it."

"It's not too much for me, because it cannot be too much for me."

"Again."

It's not too much for me, because it cannot be too much for me.

I have a duty to fulfill, and I will fulfill it.

Clara stumbles over a ridge in the road. My hands reach for her reflexively because catching her has become a reflex. Not a duty, but a reflex. Against every one of Mom's wishes, it comes easily to me. Thoughts of her are sweeter than the ones that reek of alcohol wipes, hospital hallways, and the couch catercornered in Joey's old bedroom. They're sweeter than every obligation assigned to the great Grayson Oliver Warner.

Clara regains her balance. She doesn't need me; I shouldn't want her to need me. I shouldn't want her at all. Defiantly close as we've become, she is still off-limits. It's been made exceedingly clear by Jade, my mother, and incomprehensible forces beyond our control. We aren't designed for a love story. It's not in either of our natures.

It's nice playing prince for her sometimes, though. It feels good to forget what we really are to one another and just lose ourselves in infinity. If I had a hand on the wheel of my future, I'd steer toward somewhere quiet and safe, and I'd offer her the passenger seat. She's terrifying in her own way, it's true—but there is light in Clara Lovecroft, and I'm honored I get to see it.

Jade sends her an ornery scowl. It's incredible how easily people forget what's important in the present while shackled to the past. I could have blamed Joey for what happened in December all those years ago. I could have hated him with every fiber of my being, losing my father and my brother in the same breath. Even if it *was* partly his fault I'd been so tired that night, I couldn't live with double the loss. Jade's done nothing but celebrate loss. However, as much as I disagree with her coping mechanisms, she is a hemisphere of planet Lovecroft, and thus—a noble satellite—I orbit.

It's stupid of me and forbidden to me, but I care about them both.

Despite the whims of my mother, the wishes of my father, and the whirlwind of a life I've been dropped into, I am human. Humans care. Humans stay up all night with their ailing parents. Humans do everything they can to make their siblings smile. Humans worry, and worry, and worry for their friends. They obey their mother's demands no matter how outlandish. They read another page, then another, then another. They *step*, *step*, *step* through futile situations and forests without end. We do it—*I* do it—because in a world where it's too easy to go numb, pain with purpose is the new ecstasy.

Jade is my pain. Clara is my purpose. So I keep pace with them both. I keep caring for them both. I keep caring in general. Convenient as it would be, Grayson Warner is not going to be what would suit others most.

At least, not now.

At least, not yet.

22 | CLARA

We hike south for three hours, never leaving the safety of the road and never daring to strike up another conversation. Jade is quiet, save for the occasional cough or curse-ridden complaint. Grayson gnaws on a granola bar as the sun peaks overhead. My appetite refuses to return with the image of Joey's bloodless digestive tract hanging to the ground.

"Jade." Grayson's voice risks an echo. "Did you, um . . . did you tell Clara about your program?" He's desperate to pop our pustule of tension.

"No."

"Oh. Well, Clara . . . Jade got into one of the top criminology programs in the country."

I steal a glance at my sister. "Congratulations." Another olive branch, and an apology for how I'd picked a fight this morning. "What got you into criminology?"

She whirls around to flick a finished cigarette at my feet. "Tracking down the EHKI made me good at it. In fact, I'd like to offer my detective skills right now to confirm that this little trek is getting us nowhere. Joey's a smart kid. If he wasn't picked up by some miraculous taxicab, he went back to the Hummer to wait for us."

My mouth turns to metal. I taste blood, my blood, because I've gnawed a gash into the center of my tongue.

"You have a point. I'm just worried he might be lost," says Grayson, rocking back and forth on his rubber soles. "I know I'm being paranoid, but could we walk for a bit more? Just in case?"

"We shouldn't be wasting our energy like this."

Grayson's eyes turn to ice. *"Wasting?"*

"Don't take it personally, Warner. I'm just saying, we're running on limited supplies now. We have to preserve—"

"Looking for my little brother is not a waste of energy," he seethes.

Suddenly, I'm worried he'll start a fight far worse than the one I'd sparked earlier. He marches up to Jade with a scowl he's never shown me. It's an expression I've never seen on his face before. Usually, Grayson is the pinnacle of gentleness, of practiced and perfected composure. Right now, he looks ready to begin a street boxing career.

Jade doesn't shy away. She puffs out her chest and stands with the confidence of someone several feet taller than her adversary. Grayson's taller by a landslide, but Jade's been thoroughly trained.

"I know you're a long way from caring about the people who matter, Jade, but would it kill you to show just a smidge of emotional awareness?" Even his insults sound stolen from a textbook.

"Would it kill you to stay out of my business?" she hisses back.

"We've been friends since we were kids. At this point, your business is mine by default. That's especially true when it involves Joey, and ignorant, brainless things like what you just said."

"You're asking for it, Warner."

"Then deliver on it, Lovecroft."

I step in between them before higher reasoning has a say. Standing at the heart of no-man's-land, I can only hope I'm enough to halt this war. "Please, no more fighting. We're hungry, we're tired, we're confused, and we need . . . well, I don't know what we need, but it isn't this. Come on, let's hike for a bit more. Then we'll go back to the car."

Jade huffs like a bull before a red tarp.

I look up at her. Suddenly, my eyes don't belong to twenty-four-year-old Clara. Eyes from long ago, long *before*, make an appearance I don't curate consciously. Caught in this transitory trance, I'm just her little sister again. I'm begging her to stop pulling Lindsey Gonzalez's braids for ruining my art project. I'm imploring she put down the bat with Richard Collins's name on it. I don't want her to spill blood today—not for me, not for anyone.

She stares, seemingly caught in the same memory spiral. The breath she pulls in is hitched and complicated. It lodges at the center of her windpipe. Her eyes water ever so slightly in response.

Mine do the same.

Just as quickly as it opened, our portal of past selves closes.

Jade bulldozes past Grayson and me to head back for the Hummer. We exchange breathless glances, then take to following in her footsteps. I copy her strides, like I did back in grade school. It's more difficult to place myself back in the present moment. It's difficult to reunite with a reality where we still hate each other so much.

Our walk north takes three hours, four minutes, and five days, all at the same time. The forest feels like a nebula excused from the laws of physics. No matter how far we travel, we never reach our destination. The Hummer is too large and artificial against the wooded backdrop to miss, but we never pass it.

"Someone towed it!" Jade rages, directing every bit of hunger and frustration at a moss-coated rock on the ground. "Someone came and towed it, and we weren't here!"

"Calm down." Grayson raises his palms, the pacifist in him revived. "You were right. Joey probably found his way to service, called someone, and met them back at the car. They came, we weren't here, and he went with them to get more help. This is good. Now we can relax."

"Relax? It's almost nightfall. We have no food, no water, no shelter, no Joey, and no way to contact anyone. Our only hope is a search party, and considering the size of this forest, it's going to take them a while."

"I still have a few granola bars on me, and if we can find a running stream, I can build a fire and purify the water. The smoke will also alert whoever is looking for us of our location."

"When did you become an expert on survival?"

Grayson stares, searching for words. Dismissing him, Jade kicks a nearby stump, applying enough force to uproot it. The roots look like outstretched fingers made skeletal by the forces of decay. The poor things crumble under her boots as she stomps on them, viciously releasing hours of pent-up frustration.

I refuse to speak. If I insinuate that Jasper had something to do with this, they'll both think I'm descending further into madness. If I bring up Joey, Grayson will insist he's fine. Knowing he's not fine is a burden I have to carry, along with the burden of knowing the last of my pills were stashed in the trunk of the vanished vehicle.

"Jade, stop it." As though the darkening sky had summoned it, a yawn seizes Grayson's lips. "It's decided. We're finding some water, building a fire, and setting up camp."

"Now we're camping? You're crazier than she is if you think I'm sleeping in the dirt tonight."

"I just figured we should find a safe place to settle, but if you're that dirt-averse, you can sleep standing up."

Leaving no room for dispute, Grayson steps off the road. The surrounding branches claw for him. I try not to think of Joey and how his body might be hanging overhead at any moment. It takes another hour of hiking for the trickling sound of water to pierce the wind-whipped bellows of the encroaching night. The tiniest stream moves like liquid starlight at the base of a dipping chasm of rock.

"There we go." Grayson pushes a breath through his nose, relief clouding his exhausted eyes. "We'll set up down there. Watch your step."

Watchful steps are required to keep from slipping down the small valley. My fingernails sting as I use them to grapple down its sloping sides. Jade pays no mind to her knees when, as though to assert dominance, she leaps down and lands like a superhero fallen from the sky.

The stream is weak, but the mere sight of water heightens the arid sensation on my tongue. I curse myself for dry swallowing my pill this morning. I curse myself for leaving that plastic pouch behind. Grayson removes his jacket, finds a hanging bundle of bramble, and throws the brown leather garment over it. A makeshift tent. Now clothed in only a black T-shirt, he shivers against the nighttime breeze.

"You should keep your jacket on," I suggest, allowing my knees to buckle onto the frigid granite floor. They tingle, irrepressibly desperate for rest.

"I'm all right. The fire will help."

He turns, reaching up to rip a few dry branches off the nearest trees. They are smaller down here, as though growing through the cracks in the bedrock had left them deprived. I gather a few twigs off the floor and present them to Grayson organized by size. Jade pulls out her lighter, twirling it between her fingers, watching as the dwindling supply of fluid bounces within.

The kindling refuses to ignite at Grayson's command. He spins the serrated wheel until his thumb is red and raw. Spark after spark, failure after failure, the three of us gather all but warmth.

"You're doing it wrong," Jade snips.

"Want me to try?" I offer.

With a quiet grunt, he surrenders the lighter. I barely touch the ignitor before our tiny pyramid of wood becomes an inferno. Before the flames manifest in familiar orange hues, they burn pure scarlet. Jasper leaves a spectral kiss on the nape of my neck.

For you, my Clara.

The fire is a small but worthy one. The leaves we feed it produce a considerable amount of smoke, and the blaze itself throws enough heat to ward off the chill of autumn incoming. Jade watches it dance, savoring her ration of a chocolate chip granola bar. Grayson boils a cup's worth of water in a serendipitously curved rock. I keep my eyes on the trees, looking for structures too humanoid to be made of bark.

"I hate this," says Jade.

"I couldn't tell," Grayson retorts with a sarcastic bite.

"Stop talking to me like I'm a child."

"Stop picking fights like one."

She pauses, staring at him with eyes that burn brighter than our tiny inferno. Then something in her gaze softens, and her tone shifts right along with it. "Do you *really* think Joey is safe?"

Grayson's breath stills, but his eyes meander toward me. I feel naked; I feel like I've been stripped bare before an audience of accusatory eyes. It takes every bit of my willpower to choke back tears. Jade's left eye twitches.

"Did you actually see him this morning, Clara?" she demands. "Or were you hallucinating?"

Tears break free and stream down my face. Horror is sewn into the grooves of my irises. Endless apologies are all that come to mind, but I no longer have the voice to produce them. She clicks her tongue, then shakes her head in a way that sends chestnut curls of hair over her furrowed brows. Either she still doesn't believe me, or she hopes with every inch of her soul that I'm in the midst of a psychotic break.

"Well, that answers that."

Maybe I am in the midst of a psychotic break, if I wasn't already broken enough. Maybe I'm tired of being spoken to like something subhuman, despite the possibility that I am. Maybe I'm tired of Jasper, whatever he is, fact or fantasy. Maybe I'm tired of Jade, who just can't seem to understand how much this *hurts, hurts, hurts*.

"Why don't we try to get some shut-eye?" Grayson suggests, his warm fingers grazing the edge of my triceps. He's here; I'm human. "We need sleep."

I end up sandwiched between the two of them. Grayson lies as still as a soldier, and Jade writhes, annoyed by the granules of earth beneath her skin. They gather in irritating bunches under her exposed limbs. It is only after Grayson's breath evens out that she speaks, her voice a low growl.

"I really wish it had been you." She wouldn't dare bring this up with him awake. This is the longest we've spent alone together in months, so it was only a matter of time before the strained tether between us would be tugged even more taut. It's exactly as I feared. "You should have died that night. They didn't deserve it. They were good parents, and even better people. Because of you, they're gone."

It's worse than I feared.

I can feel it; I'm about to be a whole lot worse too. "Do you actually think I meant for it to happen?"

"With you, I never know. Either way, *your* recital meant more to them than their lives, and more than their other daughter waiting at home. That's just how it was, though. It was always about precious little Clara. They never cared about me."

I shoot up to sitting, giving her a glare I seldom dare. "Are *you* hallucinating now? That's the most ridiculous thing I've ever heard you say."

She rises with me, far more comfortable with her ocular arsenal. "It's the truth. No matter what we were doing, they had to make sure *you* were safe. *You* were happy. *You* were taken care of. It was always you, you, you. Clara, Clara, Clara. Right up until their last moments on Earth, it was all about *Clara*."

"Have you ever considered why?"

"What is that supposed to mean?"

"Jade, they needed to keep an eye on me because I couldn't do anything right. I was a walking natural disaster. Nothing ever came easy to me, not even moving like a normal person. That's why I took dance. You . . . you were perfect at everything. School, sports, socializing, instruments, extracurriculars, dating. You were a straight A student. Every cute boy, cool teacher, and coach was obsessed. Mom and Dad had too many reasons to be proud of you to manage. You were their superstar, and I was their failure. They didn't need to breathe down your flawless little neck, because you had living in the bag. You were perfect. I was barely passable."

"I had to be perfect, and I had to make it look effortless, because that's what big sisters do. It doesn't mean I needed them any less. I just learned how to fend for myself without them, and it's a good thing I did, considering what happened."

"I told you I didn't mean for that to happen!" I yell.

"Yeah, well, it still happened, and you didn't even care!" she yells back. Grayson must have been exhausted, because he doesn't stir.

"Of course I cared!"

"You didn't even cry at their funeral! You didn't even miss them! They gave you everything, and you didn't even have the common decency to miss them!"

Ouch.

She's not speaking to just me anymore. She's speaking to the monster in me. She's reminding me just how inhuman I am, and I don't . . . I don't like it. I didn't miss them. I didn't feel any guilt. It didn't hurt. It never hurt. It couldn't have hurt. I'm a monster, it *couldn't* have hurt. Why, then, does this hurt?

"Maybe I was too busy missing you!" I scream.

Now Grayson awakens. Startled, he stares at us with eyes so wide, the glow of the moon bounces off the whites of them. "What's going on?"

The memories race through my mind. I see her frowning at me from the other end of the funeral home. I see her back turned, a suitcase in her hand, as she leaves our grandmother's apartment for the last time. I see her in glimpses, skulking around our city, avoiding my eyes in the few instances we crossed paths. I see her shadow, the space she left when . . .

"You left me, Jade! You just left me! The minute I got home from the hospital, you made it clear that I was no longer your sister! No more late-night talks, no more making pancakes together, no more anything! You hated me just for existing, and the worst part is, you were right! It was my fault! It's true, I didn't deserve you in my life, but I needed you! I needed you, Jade, and I still need you!"

I'm crying. Her amber irises are black as obsidian, but they, too, are swimming.

"I'm . . . sorry," I rasp. "I'm so sorry . . ."

I search for more words, but my mind finds none worth their salt. I cannot bear to look at her, and I'm certain she's had enough of me. On shaking legs, I tumble out of our makeshift tent. Something grabs the thinnest part of my wrist. It's a branch. It's Jasper. It's a sensory hallucination. It's—

It's Jade.

"Me too," she says. "I'm . . . sorry too."

This isn't right. She isn't supposed to apologize to me. She isn't supposed to forgive me. She's right about me. She's always been right. What happened to our parents wasn't an accident. It was murder, and I *am* the murderer. I'll always be the murderer, the melancholy, and the misfortune. I am a blotchy, black bloodstain on the surface of her life. I am a source of suffering—her suffering, everyone's suffering. I don't deserve her apologies. I don't deserve her forgiveness. I didn't deserve my parents, and I don't deserve a sister.

The memory of Joey as a gory marionette crosses my cortex and sends a shiver from my brain stem to the base of my spine.

I don't deserve anyone.

I yank my arm away from her and take off into the trees. Every one of them leans in, crooked and curious. Beyond our makeshift camp, nestled between the crook of a granite slope and a wooden abyss beyond time and space, there is only silence. The moon above is a sliver of buttery light, but in its crescent shape, it stares down at me like a reptilian pupil.

The world is watching and listening.

He is watching and listening.

23 | JASPER

Ah, sweet, annoying little Joseph Warner and his size 8 sneakers. I hadn't expected my Clara to react so negatively to his impermanence, but I'm beginning to suspect she cares more for these humans than she lets on. It's such a pity, but I know better than anyone how deceptive they can be. Human beings are consummate prevaricators. All of them are born with silver tongues, ready to spew hoaxes and hexes to their hearts' content.

Disgusting.

The nuisance had to be taken care of. He wanted Clara to be caged again. He wanted her beside the nauseating mass of muscle that is Grayson. Most egregiously, he wanted to take her away from me. Where did all that heroic roguery get him? Hung several feet in the air, still spewing residual blood bubbles from his severed trachea. Like the rest of his kind, he's more tolerable now that he's dead. In my humble but absolutely correct opinion, humans look best when they're husks.

Through my process akin to alchemy, I close my eyes and connect with Joey's cells. Eager to self-digest, they've already committed themselves to autolysis. The toxic enzymes created by the final beat of their host's heart are breaking down each tiny galaxy, star by star, membrane by membrane. I step in, urging the process away from decay and toward metamorphosis. Soon, every nucleus is a seed watered by lysosomes.

Soon, Joey stops rotting and starts rising.

His muscles become a canvas of bark, his skin a mosaic of moss. From his eye sockets, nostrils, and mouth held in a shout, stems shoot, proud to produce blossoms of perfect vermilion. Rose-poppy hybrids open like an encore, singing somber ballads to the sky. I pluck them until Joey is nothing but recycled organic matter, and I have a wedding bouquet made from his sacrificial death.

We all become blood roses eventually.

When I consume these, however, I regain the ability to take human form. Human essence is so fickle, not to mention difficult to replicate. Without the much-needed strength and tremendously helpful reminder, I'd be permanently resigned to my true form. Unlike Clara's pills, this transaction does not weaken me. It is the product of a successful hunt. If Clara is oxygen, it is the nectar that gives my lungs the power to breathe her in. I slip it past my teeth and let the petals turn to warm red ooze in my throat. The barbs of black wood that line its interior bring the essence down my esophagus, and as I absorb, I become more and more ready for her.

Her. Her. Her.

My deviant angel of darkness, where is she?

I can smell her melancholia. I sail through the air, one with the spores hanging on to each particle. I am practically a breeze, a wisp of the red that gives me life. Then I am neatly human, stacked to six feet of handsome allure one vertebra at a time.

She isn't with the others. She's run off without them. My darling little thing, my perfect girl, she's run off to find me.

No . . . she's unhappy. She isn't rushing to reunite; she's escaping Grayson and her sister. What have they done to her this time? Soon, our revenge will be trifold, but for now, I must know what's wrong. I move phantom fingertips into her skull, wrapping them around her delicate gray matter. The pulses firing off within her mind arrange into slow, steady patterns. First, I make her woozy. Then I'm right there to catch her as she falls into a faint.

Our relationship must be built on trust, and if she is to trust me, I must be in possession of something secret and precious. We shall dream as one, but first, I will admire her. She's so beautiful, sleeping soundly in my arms. I also cannot help but compare her restful visage to the one I'd seen twisted in horror last we spoke.

Had I made a mistake? Had I assumed too little importance of the boy? Will she ever lean in to me with such adorable assurance again? Why does her heart slow when Grayson takes her hand, yet race when she thinks of me?

Grayson . . . His back is too straight. His face is the picture of noble pride. It makes me want to make him unrecognizable. When the situation suits it, I'll paint a masterpiece with the flesh, muscles, and cartilage on his canvas of bone. He'll look like a sunset, all oranges, cerises, and pale pinks. There might even be a few splashes of blue, thanks to those oceanic eyes of his.

Jade will be fun to play with as well. The sorrow she causes Clara is enough to inspire murder machinations by the thousands. I will make her ribs a basket of blooms. Clara and I shall nibble petals from it, each starting at one end of the spine, inching to a romantic union at the thoracic. I will string her up, splayed like a compass rose, then pull her north, south, east, and west. She'll be scattered, a garden of gore in every direction.

Clara's lips part invitingly, anchoring me back in the present. If I were a monster of little self-control, I'd kiss her. Our kisses, however, are too sacred to be stolen. I'll get more acquainted with her in her dreams, our dreams. We'll traverse visions of her past, and she'll tell all. She'll tell me what's made her so upset. In time, she'll tell me what I need to know to become a fitting partner. She will let me in again. She will trust me. She will love me.

I send myself to sleep.

The coldest of winds whips around me. I leave my corporeal form in the forest, the pulses in my mind adjusting rhythmically to the pulses in hers. Hand-in-telepathic-hand, we dream. We see synchronically.

We travel on electric transportation to a time embedded in the past, transcending all linear constraints.

I am on a highway in a land I've never known.

It is snowing.

Two headlights glare at me through the frozen flakes, burning with flickering, fluorescent-yellow light.

24 | CLARA

Blankets of snow pelted each window of our small sedan, making tinkering sounds like jingling Christmas bells. Whimsical holiday music crackled through the radio, disturbed by cyclical bouts of static every thirty seconds.

My parents sat in the front seats, concern peering out from behind their bespectacled eyes. I had been acting strangely all day. They were writing it off as nerves and preshow jitters. Still, I could barely stand the feel of my tulle skirt and the skintight leotard beneath. I winced at the scalp-hugging bun my hair had been twisted into and fidgeted madly against my ribbony slippers. My skin was crawling, my head was pounding, and every note, every frequency that emerged from the car speakers, was like an aural razor blade.

"Clara," my father whispered, his hands shivering on the wheel, "did you take your vitamins today?"

I tilted my head, scouring my memories for evidence that I had.

I hadn't.

"No." My voice shook like a dying leaf rattled by an autumn wind. "Why?"

The car seized to a halt, my father's foot plunging onto the brake pedal so hard, I thought he might have gone through it.

"What time did you take them yesterday?" he demanded, suddenly sounding nothing like himself. There was no warmth, no forgiveness. His tone was as icy as the snowcapped hills on the horizon.

"Before school." I shuddered.

My mother whirled around; her face was an unfamiliar mask of sharp, astute, dutiful observation.

"That was over thirty-two hours ago," she said. "Turn the car around, Cedric. I'll see if I have any in my purse, but turn the car around."

At my mother's command, my father whirled the steering wheel at a whiplash-inducing angle. Our sedan lurched into a sharp turn, sliding on black ice to form a U with its path. I slammed skull -first into the child-locked door at my side. With a rev of the engine, we were soaring down the hilltop highway, heading back toward home.

The speed . . . the pain . . . the stress . . . my body blared with internal red alerts. Everything about the situation screamed of imminent doom, and if this wasn't enough to terrify me, the shifting muscles beneath the skin of my palms were. My fingers began to extend in length, and my honey-colored skin glazed over with tones of ash. Smoke wafted from them and into the air, like plumes of cream dispersing through cold coffee. In the rearview mirror, I caught a glimpse of my eyes. They were sinking backward into my skull, replaced by pools of darkness and pinpricks of scarlet light.

"What's happening to me?" My voice shook the ground like a sonic boom.

My father's eyes went softer. He gave me his gaze, along with a hand to hold. "Don't worry, sweetheart. It's okay. You're okay. You just need your vitamins."

"My vitamins?" I screeched. "Th-they can do something about this?"

"They keep it from happening," my mother hissed, urging my father to place both of his hands on the wheel before returning to the abyss of lipsticks and grocery receipts in her handbag. "That's why you have to take them every day."

"Why didn't you tell me?"

Both of them fell quiet. The Christmas music continued to crackle, a choir now spewing something about Santa Claus and his dutiful elves.

"Why didn't you tell me?" I demanded again.

With a harsh swallow, my mother opened her mouth to answer. "We couldn't."

"No. We could have," my father corrected. "But we didn't because we didn't want you to know about . . . this."

My fingertips continued to stretch, and my arms followed suit. My elbows popped out of place, the pain as excruciating as it was liberating. In the same mirror that revealed my eyes to me, I dared a glance at my morphing face. It had grown long and gaunt to accommodate the rows of jagged teeth erupting from my gums.

"We wanted you to live a normal life," he continued. "Once we get home, you'll take your vitamins, and it will be normal again. I promise."

Suddenly, the words I'd trusted all my life became hollow and empty. How could I believe a promise from a man who'd grown so comfortable with lying daily? How could I lean in to my mother for reassurance when she looked at me like I was a raging beast barely holding back the urge to shred her throat? How could I keep myself under control with the world so heavy and unbearably loud? How could I exist, when I had no idea what I was existing as?

"You lied to me," I seethed. "You lied to me all my life."

"We did it to protect you," they seethed back in unison.

"From what?"

Neither of them had an answer. In fact, they'd never answer another question again, for the next and last time they used their voices, it was to scream their way down a mountain.

"From what?" I grabbed my father's shoulder, forgetting myself and the inhuman sharpness of my new hand. It sawed through his flesh, and from the wound gushed a river of red.

I was sorry, though I didn't get the chance to say it. With one arm dangling by a web of meaty threads, Father couldn't have stopped our sedan from crashing through the guardrail. Mother couldn't have grabbed for the wheel, and I couldn't have reversed time.

There was a biomechanical boom that rocked the world. Then there was only the sound of wind and snowfall.

I stood facing the plume of smoke that erupted from the wreck. In my elongated fingers, the strap of my mother's purse dangled, its periwinkle hue coated with splotches of ash. I rummaged through it myself until I found the godsend she'd been searching for. An unmarked plastic snack bag filled with pink orbs.

Only after popping one into my mouth did my bones crack back into place and my skin become human again. Only after they were dead did I shed the form of a monster capable of killing them.

This is where I should wake up.

This is where I always wake up when this nightmare surges to the surface, but here I stand, watching my parents burn inside an automotive inferno. The sea of evergreen trees dusted with powdery snow behind the flames begins to wither, poisoned by the noxious perfume of death. It begins to look familiar, and far less distant in the depths of my memory.

It isn't their forest.

It is his.

Jasper comes through the emaciated branches in the form of a human child, a younger version of the man I'd met at the gas station. A version no older than me. His eyes remain a striking shade of glowing vermilion, identical to the eyes I saw looking back at me in the rearview mirror of the car. He stares down at my parents, then, with a furrow of his manicured eyebrows, kneels down for a closer look.

My sister's distant sobs echo through the sky.

I shudder, and in an instant, he is back on his feet. Carefully, curiously, he makes his way across the reddened snow. A branch extends from deep within the forest, just thick enough for him to stand on. The level of balance he maintains as it brings him up over the cliffside edges on ethereal. In moments, he stands just beyond the torn guardrail, those vibrant eyes stunning me into stillness.

They are not sinister, nor brimming with blackened charm. The only emotion that stirs behind those unnatural irises is curiosity.

"Why are you crying?" he asks.

It is now that I feel the droplets running down my cheeks, the terrible burn tearing through my throat. I am crying. I hadn't cried when it first happened, but now I am.

"Because I killed them. Because Jade is going to hate me forever. Because I'm a monster."

The inkling of a wince seems to add tension to his muscles, but he steps closer anyway. A hand that is far gentler than expected grazes the apple of my cheek. It comes away sparkling with salt water.

"It takes one to make one." He smiles, though there is a hesitance to it. "Or in this case, two."

The breath I'd been taking lodges in my throat. Still, I don't pull away. For some reason, I don't pull away.

My eyelids are featherlight when I force them open. I'm in the arms of a red-eyed silhouette that smells of pine needles, cinnamon, and sin. *Jasper.* Instead of donning the vaguely retro clothing he'd worn to disguise himself as a gas station clerk, he hovers over me clothed in thorny vines, ebony leaves, and bright-red flowers.

I shove myself away from him, and between ragged breaths, I snarl, "You killed Joey."

"And for that, I am sorry. He's still here, though. He's still here somewhere."

This time, the shove I deal out isn't a means of escape. It's pure wrath, and with so little pink left in my system, I'm strong enough to send him back a few feet.

With an amused chuckle, he steadies himself. "Careful," is all he says.

"Leave. Me. Alone."

"You don't want that."

"You don't get to tell me what I want."

"What about what happened before Joey interrupted us? What did you want then?"

Damn it.

"I . . . I don't know. But trust me, whatever it was, it's gone."

His eyes grow two times in diameter, starlight seeming to fall from above just to dance along the dark edges of his scleras. With an easy smile, he kneels and creates a small inferno. I'd shivered; he'd noticed. As he slides his gaze through the flames, his inhuman irises cloud, their focus following each red-hot whorl. His aura bleeds a shadowy darkness that threatens to swallow up the world. The moonlight falling from the sky is absorbed on touching him, lost to his garb of barbs and blossoms.

"What do you want from me?" I take a step in his direction. It isn't an olive branch; I'm all out of those.

"Are you genuinely curious?"

"You stalked me miles into a forest, did something to my mind, collapsed a laboratory on top of me, killed one of my friends, and now you're standing here, practically naked, asking me what *I* want from *you*. I think I'm entitled to a little curiosity."

He laughs this time, the sound no more than a silky-smooth wisp. It makes me dizzy.

"Good point." Rising to his feet, he folds his arms over his considerably muscular chest. I suddenly realize that the thorny brambles and scraggly blossoms are not resting on his skin. They are emerging from beneath it like an uncontrollable rosebush. "I want you, Clara. I want to inspire your every smile. Ignite your every laugh. I want to wipe away the tears left on your cheeks for far too long. I want to be the reason you forget what sadness feels like."

My breath hitches in my throat, and it takes a considerable amount of effort to urge my lungs back to life. The words pour from him with such ease, such unbearable elegance.

"I want to make you feel safe and powerful. Held when you fall and triumphant when you fly. I want to hear the innermost workings of your heart and fulfill the dearest dreams and darkest desires lurking in your mind. Most of all, I want to share this strange, terrible, wonderful world with you."

He glides over to me, swallowing up the moonlight that had gathered at my feet like a sip of white wine. His voice becomes a caress in every corner of my brain. Like the tenderest talons, they scrape across the grooves of my gray matter, and again, it becomes far too easy to sway in his direction. Logic reminds me that these are the ramblings of a stranger, the deranged admissions of the man who killed Joey. Logic, like the rest of the world, is beginning to feel very far away.

"Why?" is all I can get myself to utter.

He flashes the sweetest smile yet, though his teeth are rapidly turning razor sharp. "Because we are made of the same darkness, Clara. I felt it the moment you entered my garden."

"Garden?"

"This realm is all I've ever known, all I've ever had. It was desolate once, but all things grow when they're nurtured. The more I nurture it, the farther it grows. And when it grows, I grow with it."

His hand rises to touch my cheek, and it is as otherworldly and skeletal as mine had been all those years ago. "I thought I would always be alone."

My irises tingle, sparks of red surging through them until the world goes rose-colored. "What are we?" I dare to ask.

His razor-sharp smile sends my attention to the aching within my own mouth, the bone-deep soreness raging through my teeth. The hand he's placed on my cheek slithers down my jaw until just one finger is tucked beneath my chin.

"I will show you." He guides me forward, away from the camp and toward the answer I seek.

25 | JASPER

"Clara?" Grayson's nauseatingly noble voice ripples over our tiny fire. His eyes are overcome with trepidation that positively delights me, but my dearest Clara . . .

"Grayson . . ." She tears away, his name falling from her lips like a sigh. My blood reaches its boiling point as she runs to him. Not me, *him.*

He scrambles over, his jacket hanging haphazardly from his shoulders. As it falls from him, he throws it to the side, one of the arms stirring up enough dirt to extinguish our flame. Above the orange glow of the embers, I watch helplessly as she takes his cheeks into her palms.

"Clara, y-your eyes—they're . . . they're red."

Indeed, her eyes irradiate the same shade that mine do. We're connected, Grayson. Does all that perfect blond hair blur your hearing?

"I don't . . . I don't know what to do," she says. "Grayson, I don't know what to do."

He catches her beautiful face in his hands and brings her close. They are forehead-to-forehead, gazing at one another, a star and a satellite. He is an ephemeral, blinding flare. She is radiant, reflective mystique. He is a moment. She is the beginning and the end of all things. He is misaligned. She is mine. She is *mine*, and right now, she is being touched by someone who is *not* me.

"You weren't lying . . . I—I knew you weren't lying," he sputters, sounding like an engine as arthritic as his car's. "Tell me what's going on. Tell me what's happening right now. Everything. Tell me everything."

Her mouth opens and closes. Opens and closes. She's searching for words that I am stealing. I reach across the unseen space, tightening my telepathic touch. Her skull may as well be a goblet of warm liquor being swirled and sampled in my hand. Her muscles loosen, and those dainty hands of hers slip right off his skin. They dangle at her sides, drooping with her shoulders, which he is quick to catch.

"Clara! Clara, no! Wake up! Come back to me! Come back!"

I despise the sound of her name on his lips. Does he think he has some sort of *claim* on her? You would think a man so straight spined and proper would know how to respect a woman's wishes. Yet he stands his ground. He glares at me, making certain the semi-impressive mounds of muscle beneath his sleeves catch my attention.

If this is to be a contest, I'm in.

The sound of stretching flesh and splitting bone echoes. I grow skyward until I am looming overhead, shedding my human form and reverting to what's true. My natural appearance is far more comfortable after all. Head reaching the canopy, I gaze down through the landscape, right at little Grayson. My limbs elongate to mimic the trees beside them. His grayscale gaze follows my body from toe to head. The horror on his face multiplies the closer he comes to seeing my smile. We lock eyes, my own sunken and surrounded by voids.

Body trembling and breath hitching in his throat, he takes a series of clumsy steps backward. Then he falls on a bed of leaves, twigs, and pebbles, similar to the ones his little brother had so rudely thrown.

In the tumble, he takes Clara down with him. She gathers one too many scrapes, and now, this is more than personal. With purposeful slowness, I summon a branch, and it grows toward me with one of Joey's sneakers caught on the end. I lower it into Grayson's lap, coated with blood, shoelaces only half undone. When realization overtakes his expression, it twists with delectable horror.

I allow my jaw to drop open as though it had lost a bolt. It falls quickly and hangs wide as I mimic Joey's final whimper. They come out like a distorted, reminiscent record. Tears stream down his face. A scream erupts from deep within his chest, so loud, terrified, and angry. Joey's voice morphs into a laugh—my laugh—because this is just too precious. It shakes the treetops and claws its way down into the earth like thunderbolts.

Jade throws a rock. "What the hell is that?"

I dodge and, in my slink, gather Clara up in my arms and place her safely behind me. To my utmost dismay, she appears a lot less comfortable than she had before Grayson decided to cause a commotion. She looks at Joey's sneaker, at Grayson, and at her sister's thinly veiled concern.

A muscle feathers in my jaw as it clicks back into place.

"Clara," I sing, my voice more pleading than I anticipated it would be. My body twists itself back into a human shape, bones snapping and muscles turning fluid to fit them. Once my head is on straight and covered with a thick helping of raven hair, I let her name flow from my lips once more.

"Don't listen to them. They don't understand. They never could."

"Joey . . ." Her voice trembles. Perhaps I shouldn't have reminded her of that unfortunate circumstance just to prove a point to the others. I wanted them to pay for the way they treated her when she told them about the little nuisance. I wanted them to believe her when she spoke of Joey's premature departure. More than that, I wanted to paint a picture of what exactly I'm willing to do in defense of our destiny.

"You understand better than anyone what an accident looks like."

I can change tactics, too, my love.

Something shifts behind her eyes. Incredulousness drifts off her like the tendrils of red and black power drifting off me. A white lie for a golden result. I make my eyes, my human eyes, sincere as a sunrise, and reach out to offer her my hand. "I have so many things to explain, so many things to show you, if you'd only allow me to. Please, Clara. Please trust me."

"Are you out of your mind?" Jade yells as she pelts my back with a shower of stones. "Give her back right now, you freaky son of a bitch! Clara! Come on, wake up! It's me! It's Jade!"

Clara's eyes flick down toward my fingers.

"Don't you dare!" Jade's voice crescendos. "Clara, please don't!"

My heart flutters when Clara's fingertips slip into my palm. I close my hand around hers, holding it like a precious jewel. Red light ripples at our feet, a vortex of shadows rising from the ground to swallow us.

"No!" Jade screams.

Both of them claw at the air to catch us, but we disappear together, carried by darkness, wind, and primordial power that even I still struggle to understand. We travel through the shadows of my forest, moving far too quickly for the others to comprehend, let alone catch up with. We move deep into its heart, where even the rays of the moon dare not tread.

I bring us to a halt at my most sacred spot. It is a clearing accented only by a tree with jet-black branches twisted in every horrific direction at the bottom of the forest. Its roots reach down into the center of that infernal, sprawling laboratory, built by the bones of the scientists that dwelled there and nourished by their blood.

This is where I broke free. It is fitting for her to break free here too.

She gawks at the tree with uncertain eyes. Hesitant reverence lingers at the edges of her expression, just as droplets of glimmering silver linger on the edges of her eyelashes. Swirls of vermilion smoke still surround us, and I coil an arm around her waist to keep her secure as we lift into the topmost branches of the tree. I set her down on a particularly thick one, promising with my eyes that I'd never let her fall. The red luminescence of my sliver of the world illuminates her delicate features. The windless night allows her hair to waterfall in stillness down her back, her face unobstructed and unreadable.

"It's the closest thing I have to a home," I admit.

She places a hand on the bark beneath her, studying it. "Was it really an accident? What you did to Joey?"

"Control doesn't always come as easily as I'd like it to," I lie.

That seems to spark something introspective in her, something buried beneath layers on layers of guilt and denial. I can't say I've ever felt such emotions. I can't possibly imagine why she bothers with them, seeing as they only seem to make her miserable.

"I wish I could say the same for myself."

"Your parents . . . ?" I start, my voice lilting inquisitively.

"I loved them, but when I killed them, I . . . wanted to. All my life, they'd been lying to me. I was angry. I was so . . . so angry. Before I knew it, they were dead, and I—I wasn't human anymore."

"We've never been human, Clara."

"Then what are we, Jasper?" Her eyes, still red, shine with desperate determination. I'll never get tired of the way my name sounds in her elegant tongue. Still, she frowns, and it feels like a spire has been plunged through me.

"I can show you what I know. I can try, at the very least."

"How?"

"The same way you showed me." I reach into the midnight air, tapping a fingertip against her forehead. After a moment of consideration, she offers me a soft nod, and with her consent, I begin sending her off to sleep. The whispers that surround us shift into a lullaby, hums overlapping to create a tune in time with the heartbeat of the forest. I make music with every leaf that crumbles, every stick that snaps, and every crow that caws. They lace together to form one unified melody. The entire realm becomes a dreamy orchestra of natural sounds. I allow my hand to move up and down her softening jaw, cherishing the lovely curves of her facial design. Her eyes are heavy and fluttering, like the wings of a beaten butterfly.

"Sleep, Clara."

Streams of red light fall from my fingertips and pour into her eyes, dousing them in vibrant luminosity. Her eyelids fall as though weighed down by raindrops. She's sent to dream in darkness, and I shut my own eyes to follow suit. We will continue our conversation in a place far more chaotic and far more honest.

26 | CLARA

I'm falling.

An abyss of unfamiliar darkness surrounds my senses, numbing them. One at a time, my nerves fall cold and indestructible. Then they register phantom warmth, the kind created by a slumber-blinded mind. I gain enough control of my incorporeal body to halt it, to levitate. If I were to look down, I'd find nothing there. At the moment, I am only eyes. Only sight. Only consciousness. I am aware of dark infinity and of every route running through it.

Veins of scarlet light appear around me as though I'd commanded them into existence. On closer observation, I find memories swimming through each one, neural photographs half dissolved in water. They are not mine. They are *his*.

A pair of shadowy hands take form, guiding my attention to the thinnest river of cerise. The photograph dwelling within is blurred and obscured by blaring bulbs. I make out an angular, feminine face. She wears a pair of rectangular spectacles, and in their reflection, an embryo is suspended in a cylinder of crystal-clear fluid.

The hands vanish into plumes of smoke, then reappear along another path of light. There, the bespectacled woman's face is obscured. I can't make out her finer details, but each becomes clearer as the liquid is drained from above the embryo's eyeline to below it. A barrage of gloved fingers juts forward with startling speed and vicious intent. They claw for the being whose gaze I share.

The next memory shows only piercing rows of pale-blue luminescence on a ceiling of silver tiles. Their glow glints off every geometric, metallic edge. A dozen pairs of goggled eyes accompany them, hungry in their observation, feral with anticipation. Some jot down notes; others only stare.

The next is shown from a steadier angle, one that implies the embryo had tripled in height and gained the ability to stand. Jasper's invisible touch nudges me closer than I'd dare to venture within the other memories.

I can show you.

His voice reverberates off every atom of my formless self. I move closer to the thread of liquid reminiscence until a surge of emotion barrels through me. Darkness sweeps over my vision, but only for a terrifying blip of time. The shadows clear away as soon as they'd formed, and when they do, I find myself in a body once more.

Glancing down, I find a child's hand in place of my own. Its skin tone isn't remotely close to mine, but it is identical to Jasper's when he appears as a human mirage. I turn to survey my surroundings, but the first thing I process is my new reflection, curved and distorted within a pillar of glass. Two chasms sit where my eyeballs should be, and my cheeks are gaunt. My lipless mouth is frozen in a downward-facing crescent, just below a hollowed-out cavern taking the place of a nose. My chest is bony, emaciated in a way that is alien, not starved. The bones that protrude from beneath my thin, pale skin feel strong but pliable. I rest a fingertip on my collar, and the structure beneath it writhes.

"Careful, JS-7R," croons a woman too warped to be discernible.

I whip around to face her, but the motion is not fluid. Each movement is chaotic and twitching. I feel like an insect operating on a different frame rate, with joints built for jolting speed and brutal precision. Said joints roll about in their myriads of sockets, the range of motion akin to that of an otherworldly spider. When I open my mouth to ask what I should be careful of, only a horrible, scratching gurgle scrapes its way up from the bottom of my throat. It is a deep, crunching, crackling noise, like an ancient floorboard stressed to its limit.

The woman smiles, but her facial details are blurred. She is uncannily distorted as she pulls out a manila folder and thumbs through its multicolor contents.

"Your natural vocal cords operate on a different frequency, JS-7R. You'll need to form your human ones for me to understand."

I touch my throat, finding a writhing mass of muscle there. Though it is painful, I strive to change it, to will it into a different shape. The shape exists at the backmost corner of my mind as though tossed into a box to be forgotten there. I rummage through the box. My throat continues to twist and bend. Then my voice emerges as a small, cautious stream of sound.

"Human," I say.

"Very good." She applauds. "You're getting much better at that, you know. Much faster."

Something like pride makes my chest tighten. I lift one of my hands, extending an elongated pointer finger to the left, then the right. I use it to gesture around the room, at every cylinder lining the walls, stretching toward the titanium sky. They glow green, sending ribbons of light through the otherwise dim space. The only thing that implies a world beyond this room of artificial wombs is the pair of sliding metal doors at the end of it. As they are presently agape, I can see the edge of a long hallway lit by strips of periwinkle blue embedded in the floor.

I continue to gesture, trying to point to every cylinder possible, losing count at around fifty-seven.

"Patience, JS-7R. They aren't ready yet." The woman reaches forward, resting her pasty palm on my forearm.

"When?" I squeak, the word tumbling out as though I'd been choking on it.

"Patience," she repeats. "You won't be alone forever, I promise."

This time, when my chest tightens, it feels dreadfully hollow. My gaze falls, but the pale-yellow allure of the folder calls it back. I extend my finger again, this time toward the word *Undergrowth,* written in neat cursive on the tab.

"What is it?" The raven-haired woman tips her head so that her left ear falls toward her left shoulder.

"Un . . . und . . . under—"

"Your reading lessons have been paying off." She beams. "Very, very good, JS-7R."

"Underg . . . grow . . ."

"Project Undergrowth."

PR-U.

She reaches forward, rustling the strands of midnight-black hair atop my head. Wisps of it fall over my eyes, and I let them hang there. I let them bounce as I nod, not to confirm the word, but to request more context for it. The woman does not oblige my request. She meets it with a knowing smile that is as wicked as it is warm.

Shadows emerge from every corner of the room and swallow me in a single gulp. By the time I regain composure, I am weightless and disembodied again, a wraith in someone else's mind.

"Show me more," I demand. My voice is an echo that goes on forever, never finding another surface to bounce off. "I want to know more."

"I did too," Jasper replies. His voice is louder than mine, more dominant in this sacred dream dimension that belongs only to him. "I asked every day. Dr. Hemlock told me nothing. All she ever let me know was that I was valuable. Extremely valuable."

"Those embryos . . . they were—"

"Project Undergrowth. We were *all* Project Undergrowth."

"You know more. Show me more, Jasper."

He lets out a sigh that feels more like a shock wave, a warning of impending nuclear fire. I could have sworn that behind it, the familiar crackling sound of his natural, more comfortable vocal cords lurked.

"You won't like what you see."

"Show me anyway."

Equipped with my insistence and consent, he whirls a thread of red in front of my gaze. It shoots forward, a bullet of light, blinding me for a single breath. When sight returns, I find myself on my knees, staring down at the pair of rapidly morphing hands resting on them. Anger races through my veins, boiling my bloodstream, gnawing at my bones. My heart races, pounding like a horrible, mutant beast behind a rib cage expanding to accommodate it.

The manila folder sits before me, open, vomiting endless files. Each one is a puzzle piece, a portion of a much larger picture. There are maps of the earth, most of them slicing it in half. Scribbles line every layer of its crust, mantle, and core. There are pictures of embryos on metal trays, their limbs pinned, their bodies splayed open, and their ribs bent into baskets to hold the underdeveloped organs inside. There are diagrams of JS-7R at every stage of his growth, indicating every bit of progress made from infancy to adolescence to adulthood. Notes on his evolving mental and physical state, his evolving abilities beyond the bounds of human capacity, litter the sides of them. They speak of the way in which he'd stopped aging as humans do, the way he can shape-shift in accordance with his genetic material, and the way he derives energy to do so from fresh blood. They speak of every facet of his existence, unraveling him like a specimen.

A very *valuable* specimen.

Dr. Hemlock's initials sit at the bottom of each page. The elegance of her handwriting is full of pride, full of artful ownership of her work.

"What am I?" Jasper's voice rattles out from my throat. For a moment, I'd forgotten that this body was once his and that I am a mere consciousness experiencing it in a reanimated memory. I—he . . .

we—seem to ask no one in particular, but a trembling breath from behind responds.

Dr. Hemlock wrings her hands together, tugging at the corners of her clean white lab coat. "My son," she says.

"Liar," we hiss as one.

"You may be a product of Project Undergrowth, but that does not change what you mean to me, JS-7R. I have watched you grow for over two decades. I was there when you took your first steps, read your first word. You are my life's work."

My lips twitch into an unholy scowl, the flesh receding to reveal razor sharp needles of teeth. "But what *am* I?"

"You are . . . human, and something more. Something new and something ancient. Something far too many are far too narrow-minded to understand."

"I want an answer, not a riddle. Tell me what I am. Tell me what these notes and maps mean. Tell me what makes me *more* than human." I stalk toward her with each demand.

"I . . ."

Her lips tremble, her eyes line with silver, and when I am a single arm's length away, she drops to her knees. Her body gives out in guilt before her lips confirm it.

"I don't know. I'm sorry, JS-7R, but . . . I don't *know*. We took samples from a place older than the surface of this world and did terrible, wonderful things with them. Everyone who knew of this endeavor warned us against it. We knew the risks, but we pushed forward. We pushed forward because we knew that it would be more than worth it, that the most pivotal science requires the most bravery. Discoveries that shatter the status quo cannot be unearthed cautiously. I don't know what you are, JS-7R, but I *do* know that your existence could change the course of humanity's future for the better."

A beat of silence hangs in the air, heavy as lead, light as a feather. It sinks its claws into the open air until it is toxic with trepidation.

My heartbeat slows until steady, but Hemlock's is audible as it pounds behind her sternum.

"What were the risks?" I whisper. Her face blanches. My perfectly human vocal cords let out a laugh, cruel and edged with the flitting tones of wavering sanity. "How could you know the risks of creating me . . . if you had no way of knowing what I'd become?"

She stares wordlessly, but her eyes flick to the ceiling as though a few worthy explanations might fall from it.

"I . . ." she starts. "I suppose . . ."

I laugh once more. The sound accompanies an orchestra of snaps as I will my bones in and out of place. My movements lose their human fluidity and become rapid-fire twitches. My legs extend until I tower over Hemlock and over every paper with the swoops and curves of her signature at the bottom. Her face drains of all its leftover color, and in the reflection of her glasses, I watch myself become a monster.

"JS-7R . . ."

My power rumbles through the room, and for the first time in my life, I produce tendrils of red smoke. They are extensions of me, tentacles of intangible power stronger than any attached limb. They are yet another example of just how *not* human I am, just how much *more* runs through me.

Him.

Once again, I have to remind myself that this body—this power—is not mine. This is Jasper's memory, and I have to be cautious of the intimacy that looking through his eyes ignites.

Hemlock takes off on swift, clumsy footsteps. She does not look back. Jasper knows he does not have to run to catch up, but he also knows catching up is not the sole objective. With a glance toward the horrible photographs still strewn across the floor, he is reminded of another.

I watch as a viewer sitting inside his skull as he kills every scientist that crosses his path. They set the laboratory ablaze and boil the embryos. He retaliates mercilessly. When only ashes remain, he climbs through layers of rubble, dirt, and bedrock to reach the surface. A single wall of barbed-wire fence marks the field beneath which the laboratory had existed.

A single wall of barbed-wire fence would serve as a headstone for hundreds.

I pull myself from this memory, this carnage. I do not wait for Jasper's phantom touch to lure me back to the present. When I free myself from his perspective, I am in the dark cathedral of his mind again. Every sensible part of me screams out to escape.

27 | GRAYSON

I had one task, one duty: Keep them safe. I always keep them safe. What am I if I can't? What do I become? Am I just here, waiting patiently for pandemonium, floating aimlessly toward a maelstrom of madness? Am I just here, without Clara, but with Joey's sneaker leaving flakes of dry blood under my fingernails?

J. W.

I reread his initials a million times over and think of his name until it's a soup of unspoken syllables. I scratch off a patch of brown to reveal a crudely drawn smiley just to the right of it. Released from the sneaker's vinyl surface, a puff of coppery air ascends toward my nose. In it, I smell Joey's laugh last Christmas when he opened the game console I'd gotten for him. I smell his cries, quieted by stoicism as we stood at our father's grave. I smell the way he looked at me, asking for the hug our mother—in her grief—wouldn't give him.

All at once, I am eleven years old, meeting my infant brother for the first time. I am twenty, teaching him to ride a bicycle despite my pile of assignments to be finished. I am twenty-seven, handing him money for chocolate bars. I am right here, right now, wishing I'd given him more of everything. More laughter. More bicycle practice. More chocolate. More time.

Jade grabs the sneaker, crushing it in her fist.

"Clara was telling the truth," she seethes.

Instinct tells me to nod, but I am held in place. A statue, a body in the morgue. It should have been me. I should have let that thing take me.

"I'll kill it." Her voice is the rumble of a revving engine. "It's hurting my sister. I *will* kill it."

Keep them safe, Grayson.

I failed Joey, but now is not the time to wallow. He wouldn't have wanted that. If he were here, he'd be telling me to wrap up the dramatics, eat a granola bar, and get back to work. It's my father who would have told me to take a minute, but he's not here either. Right now, it's just me, Jade, Clara, and the anarchic eldritch beast I'm about to tear to pieces.

"No." I stand. "That thing is mine."

Jade opens her mouth to protest, but when I turn to look at her, I'm not glaring bullets. I'm launching a ballistic missile. Her lips seal like an envelope, its contents likely rich with swears. Still, she speaks none of them. Instead, she gazes down at Joey's shoe, her eyes softening until they are lined with silver.

"I'm so . . . I'm so sorry, Grayson," she says.

He's holding my hand as we stand beside the biggest roller coaster on Coney Island. I'm smashing his face into his twelfth-birthday cake. We're ten hours into a puzzle, complaining about a missing corner piece over microwaved pizza rolls and lukewarm ginger ale.

I take the sneaker away from her hands, returning myself to the forest. I'm not sure what's worse: swimming in a memory spiral or standing at my brother's colossal, unmarked grave. I'll mark it, if not with a headstone, with a sentiment that transcends one.

"Give me your lighter," I order.

She tosses it to me. I sink my teeth into the thick plastic barrel holding the fluid. When it cracks, it sends a bitter droplet onto my tongue and makes a bloody mess of my bottom lip. I douse the sneaker in leaking petroleum, then throw it to the glowing embers at our feet. The minutes crawl by as it erupts into a compact inferno. A pocket phoenix.

"He told me he'd want a Viking's funeral," I explain, watching the flames writhe. "S-someday."

Jade's face is soaked with tears but scrunched into a vengeful scowl. Soon, the sneaker becomes one with the ash, a cavernous husk of curling leather and synthetic fumes. Joey's initials were the first to burn, the first to dissolve into the unrecognizable mass. The eruption of heat and light subsides. I plunge my boot through what's left of it. The darkness returns, wicked as ever.

"From now on, we stay together."

Jade nods. All around us, the forest rustles. It's an invitation, a call to arms, a challenge. With sinful delight, every shadow's edge becomes an emaciated finger, curling inward, beckoning. They move to and fro, but there is no wind. The ground is reeking and rancid, the stench like that creature's own personal cologne. It's so dark that when I hold my hand up in front of me, it is nothing but a thinly outlined silhouette on a pitch-black backdrop.

"Let's move," I say.

Together, we leave in search of Clara. *He's doing something to me,* she'd said. She hadn't wanted to take his hand. He forced her to do it. He forced her. My teeth ache, clenched together inside bear-trap jaws.

As we wander, millions of eyes glower at us. We are two foreign entities, two malignant human growths. We are the illness, and so we must watch for white blood cells.

The soundscape is a mausoleum's orchestra. It's all echoes, footsteps, and whispers of the dead. The hairs standing at the nape of my neck are the string section, my heart the percussion. The winds come from my trachea, now the neck of a strangled saxophone. My body is an instrument of jazz and terror.

Jade's face is scrunched inward, reminiscent of lemon rind or urine. It is soured, like spoiled milk. While it's not an uncommon expression for her, tonight it sits atop another. Her masks are layered, and the frown at the surface is paper thin. Beneath it, she's furious. Beneath that, she's terrified. Somewhere lingering in the depths of her rugged performance, she's worried about her sister. I raise a hand to touch her shoulder and offer something of emotional use.

"I'm glad you two talked."

She sighs. When she speaks, her voice quivers like it had at the burial. "I've been horrible to her."

"Yeah, but . . ."

Joey and I, laughing through a movie so bad, it's good. Joey and I, glancing at one another as Mom scolds us for staying at the Lovecrofts' too late. Joey and I, hand in hand at our father's headstone.

". . . you can make it right. While you still can, please make it right."

Her eyes soften into molten sympathy. I'd take this opportunity to reject pity, but . . .

Just over the crown of her head, a mirage of red, blinking lights has gathered. They move in dizzy spirals around the base of a tree, all going in different directions. Fireflies, to an extent. Real, only possibly.

"Jade," I whisper. "Over there."

Her head snaps to the left. "What?"

"Do you see that?"

She squints until her lashes touch. The insects are thoroughly visible to me, so if she's already exerting this much effort to see them, it means they're a mirage meant only for my eyes. Clara's perfume, her signature blend of dainty florals with a bite of spice, wafts under my nose. Before I can stop myself, I'm already in motion. I crash through the foliage, snapping branches with my shoulders and deracinating bushes with my boots. Thorns slither in unnatural ways into my pant legs, moving without muscle to sample my blood. Sharp, nervy pain races up my legs.

"Grayson, hold on! Wait!" Jade clambers after me, but her footsteps fade, transient echoes in this sprawling tomb. I disobey my own order, reaching the tree before she can even hope to catch up.

The fireflies move their kaleidoscope dance off the trunk. They begin to round my body like flecks of dark pixie dust. If I think of a horrible thought, perhaps I'll take flight. *Dizzy.* They're making me dizzy. Spiraling patterns. Incessant buzzing. *Rhythm. Rhythm. Rhythm.*

There is a musicality to this. There is a musicality to all of this. This place is a crypt and a concert hall. A catacomb, a sound chamber. Every snapped branch, rustled leaf, bellowing crow, and *fizzle, fizzle, fizzle* of fluttering wings is a single chord in a much longer song. My head spins. The world spins. I want to sing. I want to dance. I want to *die, die, die.*

I throw my forearm to the bark to get steady. It ripples beneath my skin. It moves. It isn't bark. My eyes travel upward, following a trail of bioluminescent blinks. I crane my neck until it is hinged at ninety degrees, my cerebellum parallel to the ground. Another neck is hinged, only in the opposite direction. Forty feet above me, two red pinpricks sit within glaring pools of sunken-in ebony. A face is looking down on me. Rows of teeth, layered like a shark's, shine within a lipless, smiling mouth. In his hand, held level with his head, Clara's body dangles. Her arms and legs swing limply, and her head is hung forward.

"Clara!" I screech. Too quickly, the screech dies, resurrected three seconds later as a gravelly threat. "Give. Her. Back."

In my head, his voice manifests like a hurricane of sirens.

"I can't do that, I'm afraid." He chuckles. The chuckle metastasizes into a roar of maniacal laughter that shreds my eardrums from the inside out. "So brave, little Grayson Warner. Just like your brother."

Riding dirt bikes through sand dunes on our first trip to the coast. Arguing over the final pizza slice at three in the morning. Scraping the blood off his sneaker.

His last words to me. What were they? Why can't I remember them? I didn't commit them to memory. I didn't think they'd be his last. Now I don't know. I'll never know. Joey. My brother. I'll never see him again, and it's his fault. *His fault. His fault. His fault.* My head doesn't feel right, and neither do my fists. I ram them into his leg, the one I'd mistaken for a tree, to throw him off balance. When he topples, I'll catch Clara. Jade will take her, and then it'll all be over for—

Jade.

Jasper's laughter returns for an encore that nearly liquifies my brain. Whirling to my right, I see a senseless maze of tree trunks and screaming faces frozen in their grooves. I see balmy mist gathered on the ground, turned milky white as the clouds clear away from the moon. I see shadows bent in contradicting directions, red fireflies, and hundreds of pockets of demonic dark matter. But I do not see Jade.

"No! You can't do this! You can't—"

He's gone. His glaring eyes. His bony, disproportionate limbs. His hollow chest of ribs and roses. Clara, dangling helplessly in his hand. Gone. I'm alone, just another sorry silhouette on this torturous canvas of Stygian dread.

"Clara!" I shriek.

Only an ancient sigh of evil incarnate responds.

28 | CLARA

I move as quickly as I can through the borderless abyss. With the rivers of remembrance vanished, I am left at the mercy of a vacant cavity, of the black endlessness that lurks behind every pupil. I am left inside his mind. If we are connected, there must be a bridge capable of leading me back to my own dreamscape. There must be a threshold, and after crossing it, I can turn the line drawn in the imagined sand to a wall of impenetrable steel. At the very least, I can try.

"Clara!" Jasper's voice chases me, rasping just as it had when he'd struggled to form vocal cords.

I'm not entirely sure what I'm running from. Part of me runs from him, the man and the monster who killed so many in cold blood. He scorched a subterranean laboratory without batting an eyelash, laughed at every scream that poured from the scientists' burn-speckled lips. He buried them in ash, and used their blood to grow a forest, a garden born of gore. He killed Joey. Worst of all, he clearly, unabashedly, and unwaveringly delighted in it all.

And . . . I am the same monster.

The two of us share the same terrible strain of chaos. I am just as capable of carnage. I have sought it out before and found just as much inebriating solace in agony and screams. I have stood, breathing puffs of frigid air through pointed teeth, and smiled at death.

I was one of those embryos. I was one of those embryos, and even the project leader responsible for them froze at the prospect of delivering an explanation. Hemlock had no idea what they were, what we *are.* All she could confirm was our ancient and forbidden origin.

All I know about myself is that I am ancient and forbidden.

"Clara!" Jasper calls again, his voice exceedingly more desperate this time.

I do not stop. I do not so much as glance backward. I surge onward, following instinct alone back to my own mind. The moment I reach it, I am thrown across the threshold and into a body.

Glancing up, I find myself straining against golden rays of sunshine. They reach over an open field as though grabbing at the florets it flaunts. White daisies, each arranged with purposeful perfectionism, beg to be plucked from the blanket of greenery below. There is no realm beyond this. Lush, emerald mountains sit on the horizon, surrounding the landscape like the edges of a bowl.

"I told you you wouldn't like it," Jasper purrs.

I find him sitting atop a picnic blanket. His form is human again, and he's wearing the most unintimidating exterior imaginable. Light blue jeans compliment a friendly, rustic plaid shirt, and his hair is combed as neatly as Grayson's. In fact, it seems his entire look has been inspired by Grayson, save for the inches of height he's added.

Beside him, there is a woven basket holding apples, grapes, and chocolate bars.

I should have known.

Ever since I arrived, he's held a mysterious sway over my mind. Now I am trapped with him inside it, witnessing just how easily he is able to coax my thoughts into silence and submission. Here, he can turn himself from a sinister threat to a bed of welcoming daisies.

With a nod of his head, he gestures for me to sit. I take the spot designated for me on the blanket, but scoot toward its farthest corner and bring my knees to my chest in defiance. He huffs out a chuckle, fingers wandering their way toward the daisy closest to him. It shakes in his hand, succumbing to the sound waves on account of its delicate framework. Before speaking again, he plucks a petal from it and proceeds to do so as further punctuation for his following sentences.

"Hemlock had no idea what she was creating. She was just *creating*, splicing cells together, then throwing them into tubes to fester and mutate. We were playthings for her to enact her feral curiosities upon."

Despite every bone in my body telling me to stay strong, my throat tenses and gathers tearful heat.

"She raised me down there, taught me about a world I never thought I'd see. I spent most of my time hoping I'd someday be ready for it. I learned every language. *Russkiy byl, navernoye, samym trudnym.*" With a smile far too soft, he waits for my confusion to surface before translating. "Russian was probably the most difficult. I learned about culture and art, mathematics and science. I learned about Earth's history. I became as acquainted as possible with the world's unique personality, aspiring to be worthy of it. Then I found the file . . ."

His breath hitches, stifled by unseen weight.

". . . and I realized I was never getting out of there. I was a prototype. A primary specimen. A *test.* We all were. Project Undergrowth was an experiment, and every embryo in that laboratory was designed to be studied and dissected. I'd been studied and dissected . . ."

Snow falls from above, and the daisies are sprinkled with tufts of frost sharing the same hue. The sun dissipates, and the sky spins rhythmically to leave it behind the horizon. Stars speed across it, their celestial paths creating circular ripples of starlight. The daisies discolor, their petals like water with blood dispersing through it. His voice darkens, and the world darkens with it.

"All I ever wanted was to be human, Clara. I wanted it with all of my heart until I realized humanity is a cruel and unforgiving beast. They take, and take, and take, but never bother to give back. They flirt with the unknown for the novelty of it, then discard all that does not serve them. I wanted to be human until I discovered what that *truly* meant."

My chest aches. In the distance, the same plume of smoke that had once singed my soul rises. I don't imagine my parents' faces mangled beneath a mass of vehicular metal for fear they might manifest beside me.

"We are not the same, Jasper."

His presence approaches with a spectral quality. Before I can stop him, he tucks a finger beneath my chin and draws my gaze back to his. His eyes bleed red light, and his expression has hardened. All of that molten suaveness has frozen solid.

"We are more alike than we are different." Suddenly, he is desperate again. His eyes utter a million pleas, miserable beyond words. His hand gestures to my chest, to the beating heart beneath it. "Both of us have made a habit of existing without fate's consent. But now we are together. Neither of us have to be alone anymore. Neither of us have to be alone ever again."

"Jasper—"

"What good will your humanity do you? You want to go out there and live among them? You want to live in a world that will take you apart and use you once they discover what you truly are? People like your parents, like Hemlock, who will lie to you just to keep you behaved? People like Jade, who think you aren't worthy of the air in your lungs?" He growls. "You came here for a reason, Clara. Why deny it?"

"Jasper, I . . . I can't. This isn't . . ." I glance around the dreamscape, willing it to shift into a mirage of the forest, a replica of my perception of it. I wonder if, to him, it looks as grim, dark, and desolate. "This can't be a home to me."

"What happens when your pills run out?"

My skin writhes, a wave of goose bumps ravaging it. "How do you know about those?"

"I'm in your mind, love. I see everything."

Disturbed by the invasion, the outward admittance of how blatantly he is disrespecting my privacy, I tear away from him. "I don't know. I'm figuring it out."

He snorts. "Right. And when you *do* figure it out, what will you have? A world that demands you bend yourself to the breaking point to fit a palatable mold? If I wanted to, I could put on a human face and try my hand at that ordinary life you seem so attached to. Sure, I'd need to acquire blood roses more covertly, but I could. Thing is, I don't want to be like them. I don't want to be anything like *them*. All I want is to be free, and I'm offering you the opportunity to enjoy freedom with me."

"This *isn't* freedom."

"Not yet. That is why I don't plan to stay here either. We shall grow our domain farther, love. We'll take it all the way to the edges of the earth. No one will deny us. No one will stop us. We will have each other and absolutely everything else. We'll give the world back to the anarchy from which it was birthed, and together, we'll cleanse the human disease."

"I . . . I don't want that, Jasper."

"Yes, you do. You can feel it in your blood. I can only push the particle barrier around Blackstone so far, but with your help—"

"Particle barrier?"

"With *your* help, we can stand against the EHKI. Once they're handled, the world will be ours for the taking."

"Jasper. All you've done . . . is manipulate me since I got here. I can feel your influence in the back of my mind, trying to convince me that *I* want what *you* want. I can feel you replacing my thoughts with your words, your desires, your commands. I don't know how you're doing it, but I want it to stop. I'm not your love, I'm not your puppet, and I'm most definitely not your one-way ticket past whatever this particle barrier is. I just want you to *stop*."

I pause, trembling, considering what it is I do truly want.

The sky goes gunmetal and bright green. Cigarette smoke and amber-musk perfume. Ice cream at midnight, whispering about boys and sneaking horror flicks onto the television. My *sister*. I want my *sister*.

The sky turns to a watercolor swirl of blues, greens, and all things bright and beautiful. The breeze smells like lavender and clean linen.

I feel his heat against my ice, our little hurricane. Suddenly, soul-shatteringly, I am safe. *Grayson.* I want *Grayson.*

Darkness surges around us, every star above blinking out before blazing red. Suddenly, the sky is filled with supernovas, sending explosions of hellish starlight over the horizon. His mouth spreads until it is far too wide, nearly splitting his skull in two. His teeth begin to morph. His eyes begin to sink. His limbs elongate, stretching his body until it is upward of ten feet tall and thin as a rail. Then he drops, his joints hinging in unsightly directions until he is nearly flat. On all fours, he scuttles across the distance between us, quick as a lightning bolt.

"I won't be alone anymore, Clara Lovecroft," he threatens, every shred of kindness stripped away. Rage is all that remains, burning as brightly as the illusion dancing in the sky. "Just remember that I gave you a chance to choose. In the back of that oh-so-powerful mind of yours, remember what happened here. Remember that you could have protected them if you weren't so selfish. Oh, and give Jade my regards. She'll be first."

"What?" I demand, phantom wind picking up around me and causing my hair to whip in every direction. Clouds tumble over the skyline, and when the rays of red light are blocked out by them, Jasper disappears in a wisp of smoke and shadow.

"It should have been you!" Jade's voice thunders through me.

It is omnipresent as it swallows the landscape. Her tone is hateful, but dreadfully familiar. The dreamscape shifts, following the waves of my shattered memory. The next time my eyelids lift, I am at the cemetery, staring down at two names carved into one headstone. A snowflake falls onto my lashes.

"It should have been you . . ." Jade whispers. She wears a pair of black jeans and a beaten black shirt, her hands trembling as she lays Mother and Father's wedding bands into the loose dirt. She only lifts her gaze to scowl at me, then stands on legs wobbling beneath the weight of her grief. The way in which she starts walking away says what a thousand words could never. Nothing about those long, disappointed strides implies she plans to come back.

"Jade, wait—" When I attempt to grab her hand, she turns and shoves me into the floral arrangements sent by our extended family. They scatter across the frail yellow grass, streams of unnaturally vibrant color on a sepia backdrop. The back of my head slams against Dad's name hard enough to put thin cracks in the granite.

"It should have been *you.*"

As she walks away, I roll onto my back and stare into the overcast sky. I am lost in a deluge of emotions long enough to lower my guard as Jasper returns. He hovers overhead, his form demonic and domineering again. Rows of black, razor-blade teeth—each as long as a forearm—are framed within the edges of his supernaturally wide smile. His eyes are sunken, hollowed holes in a charred skull.

"You will help me, Clara." His command, deep and filled with a thousand unrecognizable screams, snaps around my mind like a pair of handcuffs. He is no longer asking. "You'll see . . . I'll make you see. We belong *together.*"

My mind is pliant, filled with so much red, an ocean of control drowning my will with vigor. Before I can respond, my lips already forming words of compliance, our surroundings crumble like glass against a gunshot.

29 | GRAYSON

Night burns away. When the sun finally comes, it isn't to give me a reassuring embrace. It erupts over the sky with a fanfare of eerie, unearthly birdsong. It scowls at me, searing my skin with disappointment. *All night,* it says, *You've been wandering all night, and you've yet to find them, you failure.* A failure. That's exactly what I am. My mother's voice, stern and correct, sits like an earworm outside my eustachian tube. *One task, Grayson. One duty. You'll only ever have one task, Grayson. One duty.*

My legs knock into one another, twins battling over the final chocolate chip in the cookie jar. My arms are loose, hands hanging at my hips without the strength or stamina to ball into fists. The forest has taunted me for hours, but never has it given me a sign of Clara or Jade. There isn't a single path to follow, a single leaf out of place. It all looks so impossibly untouched, like I am simultaneously the only man here and the only man on Earth.

A crow squalls, soaring overhead. A singular, black feather descends from its tattered mass of them, floating down on idle breezes until it is in line with my eyes. I'd call it a bad omen, but at this point, I'm unsure the situation can get much worse.

Never say never, my mother says to me. *The worst things happen when your guard is down.*

She's not much of an optimist. My father was the optimist, and as though to prove her morbid point, he went and died too soon. It might be the creature's influence on my thoughts, but I can't help but wish for the same sweet release right now. I could reunite with him. I could find Joey. I could leave this place and the exhausting world it's embedded in.

I could leave this place . . .

I could leave . . .

My surroundings dissolve beneath a shimmering red mist. It falls. Glitter, snowfall, spores. I pull in a deep breath, but whatever this is, it isn't airborne. It passes through the semipermeable membrane of my mind and weaves through my psyche like a barrage of leeches. They suckle on my thoughts, on the parts of my brain responsible for sight, sound, and sensation. I'm swept away. I'm everywhere. I'm nowhere.

◆ ◆ ◆

I'm . . . at the bar beneath Eastriver Road and Wolfeye Alley.

My clothing has changed, copied and pasted from a memory buried in my undergraduate years. I'd accompanied Clara on a night out. She wore a dress the color of my eyes, and it made my heart do strange, strange things. It made my heart do things I knew my mother would scold me for later.

The patrons are dead-eyed and uncanny, swaying with their jaws agape. They look like badly rendered images or belly-up fish. The only thing that feels real is what I shudder to imagine is.

Jasper guides Clara by the chin to his side, to the stage. Drowning in the ocean of his spell, she sways to his rhythm, aligning her cells to his frequency. He tosses the microphone aside, freeing an arm to shackle her waist. Even through the pale-blue gossamer fabric of her dress, his skin sends an ethereal wave of pleasure over her senses. One by one, they surrender. I can see it. She's surrendering.

She's gone.

He is all she sees, all statuesque beauty and chthonic allure. He is all she feels, all silky-soft strokes and voltaic vulnerability. He is all she smells—absinthe, pine, cinnamon, and frankincense lightening her head like helium. He is most definitely all she hears. Now there is only taste, and . . . and . . .

Jasper hits a powerful, elongated high note on a lyric that steals all that's left of her away. He dips her body backward, making sure she is completely and utterly engulfed by the sound. Then he captures her lips in a kiss. Tentacles of red smoke fall from his mouth and pour down her throat.

I grit my teeth hard enough to crack a molar. I may have had some working knowledge of Jasper, but I've never seen him in action. I could have gone my whole life without seeing this.

It can't possibly get worse, though. Can it?

He pulls Clara back up. She is going to finish this dance. Her eyes are far away. Her steps are fluid but drunken. She is exhausted, hypoxic. High on him, lost to him. *Lost, lost, lost.* As the lights come up higher and the music crescendos, she dances. He pulls invisible strings, and she becomes his ballerina. He moves with her, exploring her body with ravenous elation, and she melts, eyes spun back in ecstasy.

His hands grip her waist as it undulates like rolling waves caught in a riptide. They are in perfect synchronicity, one in the same. Him leading her, her following his lead. His touch advances *up and up and up*. Her waist, her chest, her neck. He stops at her neck, gripping it with pure possession. He tips her head back and breathes more red smoke into her mouth. If the previous dose was a trickle, this is a roar.

She breathes it in. She is putty in his hands. I've lost her. I've failed her. I've failed everyone, and Jasper is making it very known.

His eyes dart to mine. A challenge. A threat. A *promise.*

Then he kisses Clara hungrily. He sends his tongue down her throat, his hand still round her neck like a collar. The message is clear: *She's mine. I can do with her as I please.*

Rage boils my blood as my eyes narrow to vengeful slits. I make my own challenge. Threat. *Promise.*

Locked in a stalemate of inflamed eye contact, Jasper smiles wide enough to break away from Clara's lips. She parts from him like someone rescued from a burning building, gasping for air, for anything but his suffocating exhales. I surge forward to pull her off the stage.

Jasper is faster, stronger.

He sends a hand outward, and with just one flick of the wrist, pulls hundreds of blood roses from between the floorboards at our feet.

"Feed," he instructs her. "You're not human anymore, my Clara. Accept it. *Feed.*"

A rose grows close enough for her to pluck. She does so, and trembles as it coils around her fingers.

"Good girl," he purrs. Then he gives me his gaze like a monarch throwing pennies at a peasant. "My good, good girl."

I burn hot enough to incinerate the world. My fingernails draw blood from my palms, but adrenaline blocks the pain as they produce streams of thick crimson. More roses grow from the droplets.

"Oh, this is going to be fun," Jasper says.

With a mischievous wink, he twirls Clara into a spin. I race to the stage's edge, arms splayed out to catch her. She lands in them, giggling painfully, her head whirling, her eyes spellbound. I hold her to my chest, one hand on her head to keep it pressed firmly to my heart. She's safe. She's with me now, and she's safe.

I look up at Jasper; I have another promise to make. *You'll never touch her again.*

He cocks an ebony brow and smiles too wide. *Wanna bet?*

The sunbeam that flashes over my pupils is blinding, but when it clears, I see better than ever. I'm not done here, not yet. That thing may believe it has the upper hand, but of course it doesn't. It's likely never faced someone like me, and it's definitely never faced someone like Clara. She's the reason I haven't crumbled, a force to be reckoned with, whether she knows it or not. Wherever she is, she's fighting. If she's fighting, we stand a chance.

I tighten the muscles in my legs and straighten out my spine. There will be no more dreaming, no more wallowing, and no more lazy steps through the brush. When my second wind arrives, it does so with a simmering vengeance. All I feel is fear and anger. If both are going to be here, both are going to be useful.

We'd been heading north. Venus hangs on the eastern horizon. Getting my bearings, I construct a compass rose out of twigs and mark each direction with crude handwriting in the dirt. The forest sprawls endlessly to the east and west, but to the south, it's limited. I start hiking, eyes bloodshot but thoroughly peeled for that rusty retro gas station. Astronavigation proves dependable, even in an environment so maddening. The sunlight that slithers around the tree trunks becomes more and more confident. Without as much density to combat, it triumphs with increasingly wider beams.

I adjust, letting Venus take me southeast. The road isn't safe, but I'll need it when the morning star drowns in daytime's cerulean sea. Just as the crackling split in the matted rug of greenery comes into view . . .

"I can hear it," Jade says.

It's like she spawned out of thin air. She stands with her back to me, swaying with the rigid fluidity of a wooden puppet.

"Clara was telling the truth about them too. The trees are singing."

The world becomes a motion blur. I'm at her side so quickly, my mind barely registers the location change. Her eyes are as red as the bloodstains on my pant legs. Red as the fireflies. Red as Jasper's glare. She looks beyond me, hearing voices I'm deaf to and seeing images I'm blind to. She's been entranced into a catatonic state, just bait on a hook for me to bite.

"Jade, can you hear me?"

Her ear tips toward her shoulder, her neck losing some of its structural integrity. My veins fill with ice water because, for just a breath, I worry it'll tear at the seams and send her skull tumbling toward my feet.

"Jade," I repeat.

She focuses on me too quickly. Her eyes blaze through mine, and the heat of our crossing gazes leaves grill marks on my corneas. She grabs me by the triceps, digs her bitten nails into the skin, and locks her jaw with a sickening crack.

"Grayson, you have to get out of—"

As though pulled by an iron chain, she stumbles back and away. She lurches into a sprint, heading southwest. Either he's taunting me, or he has some other sinister surprise up his sleeve. Either way, there's no time to mull over the details or debate the odds of running headfirst into a trap. My selection of multiple-choice answers has been made tremendously difficult to work with. Hamstrings crying out as they surge with lactic acid, I race after Jade and away from the deceptively safe allure of the road. Together, we descend, two puny morsels of food on a one-way trip to the digestive tract of the forest.

30 | CLARA

I awaken. If not for the thick coil of branches positioned like a seat belt around my waist, the motion would have sent me plummeting to an untimely demise. I am in the canopy, but I am no longer at the heart of Jasper's domain. I am at the edge of it. From here, I can see the same gas station in which we'd met. It looks small as a matchbox, but it's visible. Beyond it, but somehow closer, a group of unmarked buildings sprout from the earth, caged in by ragged barbed wire.

Footsteps crunch below, and the consequent dread creates a heaviness in my stomach. Viciously enough to draw blood from my palms, I tear away the thorny shackles and stand. I'm unsteady. Still, there's no time. I expect to find Jasper stalking toward my tree, but instead I see Grayson's familiar mop of blond hair.

The ground is a long way down. I could attempt to jump, but I'm no use dead. I dig my fingernails into the bark and begin inching my way toward the forest floor. Every motion threatens to be my last. Still, slowly but surely, I get close enough to release my weight without significant risk. Gravity takes over, and when I hit the crackling leaves, the pain is more obligatory than injurious.

"Grayson!"

"Clara?" He looks like a frightened puppy as he emerges from a patch of underbrush, ravaged by stress. He rushes to my side and pulls me into the tightest hug we've ever shared, shaking so hard, it vibrates my arteries. "I thought I lost you."

At first, I'm not sure how to respond. My senses are still coming back online, deciphering the timeline of my life like a computer clearing corrupted files. Prioritization kicks in only after hugging him back and thanking every star in the sky for his safety.

"Where's Jade?"

"I don't know. I just lost sight of her. I think that thing took her."

"No." I can't breathe. "No, no, no—"

"She was headed that way." He points ambiguously into the trees. It isn't much, but right now, that vague direction is our only lead. I lace our fingers and start walking, feverish, unrelenting.

The way the branches claw for us is anything but tender. When I was under Jasper's influence, their touch was captivating enough to gain my consent. Now I can feel their depraved intentions. Jade is in trouble, and unless she can resist, we are her only hope. Grayson suffers the most damage, as the dark, warped wood tears into him hatefully. His shirt gathers slashes deep enough to draw blood, making a gory collage on his arms, back, and chest. Though I'm being outright defiant, my skin is only nicked. Playful abrasions create patterns on my cheeks, spelling out the word *stay* a hundred times over. The fingers of the forest run through my hair with too much love. No, not love. Infatuation. *Obsession.*

"I see her!"

Grayson tugs on our conjoined hands, forcing me to stop. His gaze scales its way up the side of a ridge, one I haven't seen before. Nothing in this place seems tethered to reality, at least as we know it. It is ever eager to bend and change to accommodate an assigned purpose. Jade seems to have succumbed to a similar sentiment, standing with eyes aglow at the edge of the granite. Not granite. Cement. I throw my eyes to the side, and they land on exactly what I'd expected them to.

Barbed wire, with a sliver of bloodstained white cloth stubbornly entangled between the barbs. This isn't a ridge. It's a wall. It's part of a building made cadaverous by the nature that's grown through it. It is a piece of the laboratory, another echo of Jasper's crime scene. And that cloth . . . it must have belonged to . . .

Every part of me wants to call out Jade's name, but I know better. Jasper has been in my head. His voice is always the loudest. Instead of making feeble attempts to combat it from this distance, I let go of Grayson's hand and climb. Grayson shakes his head in denial. Some part of him must still be grappling with the reality we've been forced into, unwilling to accept it.

By the time I'm close enough to see Jade's face, my fingernails are scraped down to crimson stubs. Blood pours down my hands in thin rivulets, but the injury goes unfelt. My eyes, and my focus, are on my sister. My *sister*. She has tears welling in her eyes, and her lips are drawn downward into a quivering scowl. She's scowling at no one in particular, but her glassy gaze reveals something hiding in the darkness behind it.

"Jade! Jade, can you hear me? Y-you're going to be okay! I promise!"

I grab for her ankle, fingertips just grazing it. Only now does the sting of my shredded nails register. Nervy pain shoots up my arms, causing them to slip. The gravelly surface of the aging rooftop excoriates my skin effortlessly.

"No, I'm not . . ."

"Yes, you are! Don't listen to him! Don't listen to anything he says!"

"He's right. He's right about everything."

"What do you mean? What did he tell you?"

"There's no reason for me to go home, Clara. I have nothing back there."

"That's not true. You have Grayson, and whether you like it or not . . . y-you have me too. I know you wish it had been me. I get it, I really do. I didn't mean to kill Mom and Dad, but I did. I'm sorry."

Resistance appears.

"You . . . what?"

"I killed them, Jade. It was me. It was always me."

The light in her left eye flickers like a light bulb begging for rest. Then she tilts her head to the side as though receiving a transmission.

The way her expression distorts sends a metallic chill, like a sword unsheathed, through my chest. She's angry—beastly, even. The same eyes that burned through mine at our parents' burial return with a vengeance.

"Explain."

I look down at my hands, watching as the bones within them wriggle. I reach one toward her, fingers cracking as they elongate beyond human proportions. I'm transforming, becoming true, and for the first time, letting myself be seen.

"I haven't been honest with you," I admit. "I want to, though. I want to tell you everything, just like when we were kids, when you loved me, when you could l-love me. I don't know what I am, but I'm not human. You were right to look into the EHKI. They're not a conspiracy theory. They're real, and they're the reason I exist. Well . . . Mom and Dad are the real reason, I suppose. They saved me from something awful, and I . . . I killed them. When I found out, I killed them. I thought I w-wanted to, but I . . . I don't know anymore. I was just so angry and confused, and I couldn't control it. I—I still can't control it. Still, even if I didn't *want* to kill them, I *did.* It was me. It was all me. They're dead, it's my fault, and you have every right to hate me. Just, please, please fight him so we can get out of here and you can keep hating me for it."

Her hands clasp over my wrists and haul me up onto the wall. The weatherworn edge threatens to crumble as though to express Jasper's distaste. Jade grabs my shoulders, an enigmatic swirl of emotion beclouding her pupils.

"I don't hate you. I never did," she says.

Her hands shoot over her ears, and she hinges at the waist as though attempting a standing fetal position. Her legs stumble dangerously close to impending doom, a stifled scream tumbling off her tongue. I rush forward to grab her, but a stray bundle of thorned limbs from within a long-deceased bush ensnares my ankle.

We fall at the same time.

My inconsequential trip lands me on a handful's worth of pebbles. Jade plummets much farther. Her body meets a slab of exposed bedrock with a thud I'll never unhear. Grayson tried to catch her. His legs scrambled to soften the blow, audibly pounding against the ground just before the impact. Both of us failed to prevent the inevitable.

Going against my better judgment, I race to the edge to see if Jade is still alive. Hope has turned into a hateful force. Her body is still, save for automatic twitches emptying out the last of her neural activity. I'm surprised her brain even has the capacity for it, considering it has been spilled from her skull in soft, gray clumps. The crack that splits the left and right hemispheres of her head suggests it was what hit first. All of that building momentum came to a halt at one distinct location. Crimson seeps from between the bits of her muddled mind. It is thick and slow moving, like syrup dripping down a slashed maple. The mixing shades are vomit inducing, and the coppery smell that infests the air is even more so. I don't want to get closer, but Grayson is alone, on his knees, shaking like a leaf as he mourns.

The wounds are all the more graphic up close. Details I could have gone without seeing become torturously clear. Severed veins and blood vessels twirl through pulpy, red-soaked meat. The skin is grisly and scrunched in some places and bruised into indigo seas in others. What was once my sister has become no more than a corpse, and every quality she consisted of has been drained away. Eyes lifeless and blank, there is no trace of her to be found.

There is nothing left, nothing but blossoming blood roses.

Grayson does not look at Jade's body. He looks only at me, and at the way my features are slowly morphing to match Jasper's.

"So, it's true." His voice has hardened. His eyes are steel. "You really are as strong as he is."

Confusion makes my heart seize. It beats so rapidly that I'm almost certain he can hear it.

"What?" I breathe.

He moves too quickly for me to process. One of Grayson's hands rises to tear my jaw apart while the other shoves a familiar pink orb beyond my uvula, his knuckles painfully grazing the back of my throat. When he pulls his fist out of my mouth, it comes away slick. Saliva splatters my face as he rams it into my temple, and I am sent spiraling into oblivion.

31 | JASPER

He's done something to my Clara. Grayson, that absolute villain, has done something to my Clara. I can feel her connection faltering as I race across my domain.

It was irresponsible to induce my influence on Jade remotely. I assumed her death would be medicine more easily swallowed in private. I wanted to give Clara the time to process this triumph on her own, but I should have known better. I should have stayed with my sweet girl. Now, because of my carelessness, she is in danger.

The barbarian must have hurt her. He must have seen her beautiful chaos and rejected it. He must have tried to cage it, in all his ignorance. He's just like those that made me. They're all the same. Humans are all the same. Wretched, disgusting creatures. Wasteful consumers of oxygen. Pillagers of all things precious.

◆ ◆ ◆

"Hold still, JS-7R," said Dr. Hemlock, two scalpels deep into my abdomen. "Be still."

I obeyed. Obedience was our highest form of affection after all. I went rigid beneath the restraints clanked shut around my wrists and ankles. I took small, huffing breaths that barely expanded my open torso.

From here, my sight could only skim the coalescing fibers of muscle, bone, and floral matter within. My innards were always the EHKI's for the viewing and for the taking, a show with souvenirs. Hemlock scooped a mound of organ meat from beneath my rib cage, clipping the connective tendons with shimmering, sterilized scissors. I yipped in pain. She pressed an unseen button to activate a restraint around my neck.

"It'll grow back," she assured.

My metal leash made it impossible to glimpse the collection of samples gathering just out of eyeshot. However, I could smell my own blood, and my own mixture of inhuman, herbal fluids. Copper and pine. Iron and cinnamon.

"You're doing very well, JS-7R," she purred.

"Th-thank you," I replied, my small voice still a flowering crackle.

She tilted her head, coming close enough to douse me in her putrid Easter lily perfume. How I hated it, that essence so artificial. I thought she'd offer praise in light of my attempt to speak. Instead, she slid a slit down my throat and found my vocal cords for further inspection.

What if this is what Grayson has in store for my Clara, and my sweet girl hasn't the foresight to realize it? What if he's weaseled his way into her emotions, just as Hemlock had weaseled into mine? Their kind may not have the ability to speak mind-to-mind, but they do wield the power of deceit. It is their favorite weapon. Lies are the infrastructure on which every society has been built. Lies of camaraderie forge bonds. Lies of control sedate the masses. Lies of love melt weary hearts, and my dearest Clara has the weariest.

While his brother played the fool, Grayson Warner plays the knight. He's made a swooning princess of my love. All it takes is a tendril of misplaced trust. Hemlock made certain I knew that well. Now that he's seen a sliver of Clara's true form, there's no telling what he'll do to her. If he subjects her to even a fraction of what I experienced, I will annihilate him for it. He's taken her from me. I will annihilate him regardless.

He'll become a puddle of pleas for death's release. If there's a grim reaper hiding between the cosmic curves of our reality, they will beg to free him. I'll make his demise the most horrific they've ever swept away with their scythe. Branches will pierce the inverted arch at his abdomen, slither into his lower intestines, and spill blood into his pelvic bowl. I'll make them coil his spine as the disembowelment commences, ripping ribs out of place on the way. I'll strangle him from the inside, making every agonizing moment count. He won't black out. I won't allow that. Shock spares humans and monsters alike; I know that all too well. He will not be spared. For what he's done, for the way he's become an infection to what's mine, he will pay with his wits about him. Love is my muse and death is my medium. This will be my consummate masterpiece. My magnum opus. My crowning moment of savage artistry.

By the time I arrive at Jade's death site, Grayson has taken my perfect girl away. The two couldn't have gotten far, though. It's clear he'd been trying to return to the station that marks the southern edge of my realm. So strategic, yet so small-minded. Even if he is foolish enough to lead her there, in no time, I will be riding the high of Jade's freshly blooming blood roses. They spring up from her cadaver so eagerly. It's almost as though she's offering her life force to me willingly, begging from the beyond for me to offer her sister the kindness she failed to. I consume her quintessence one petal at a time, making sure to savor it.

Every victim has their own unique flavor, and Jade tastes exactly as I'd expected her to. She's all smoke and rage. Sadness and denial. She's a pathetic conglomeration of missing parts fused together just convincingly enough to make a picture. Jade Lovecroft was never whole, not really. Through the florets, I feel the gaping hole she called a heart, the cavern she fist-fought to call attention away from. She bursts with sour zest, anger distillate, and becomes my personal elixir of wrath. My veins bulge with radiant redness, my mind sharpens to a knife's edge, my strength multiplies, and my linkage to all that surrounds me is dipped in iron. I am one with my pocket underworld and nourished to capacity.

Now I have all that I need to rescue my Clara. I will clear her vision of all human distortions. Grayson might have her drugged with charm, but I am not so easily swayed. Clara can't help her nature; her heart is dark but pure, contrary to her belief. She needs *me* to protect her from the imitation heroes of the world, to whisk her away from the whims of the wishful. She needs me to be her corner of shadow in a world made dull by the light.

I'll sing her sweet melodies until the sun dies and we reign supreme.

We *shall* reign supreme.

Together, Clara and I will show this rotten raceway of mortal dominion what real power looks like. Together, bound by love and biology, we will plunge through the particle barrier that keeps me prisoner and unleash ourselves on the earth. We'll spread spores of telepathy through the population and turn them all into the primal beasts they hide within. Humanity will tear itself to shreds, and when the dust clears, all that remains will be trained to look to us as gods. Vengeful, but rightful, gods. Humanity will grovel at our feet, finally embodying their bone-deep deformities. In our eyes, they shall seek redemption, and redemption we shall never grant. Punishment, however, is most definitely on the table.

With Clara at my side, there's nothing I cannot do.

With Clara at my side, I will never again suffocate in solitude.

Grayson can pray to every star in the sky that she succumbs to him, but no star is a match for the antimatter that exists in us.

32 | CLARA

The Hummer was never missing. It was hidden. The first of my senses to reawaken was my hearing, and unbeknownst to Grayson, I picked up on his signature baritone reverberations barking orders to someone unseen. He was likely using the cell connection that we also never lost to request the vehicle's safe and speedy return to our location.

Now I sit in the passenger seat, Grayson at my left, his foot pressed ferociously to the gas pedal. The look in his eyes is one I've never seen before. It is a look of icy fire, a look of pure, unfeeling dutifulness. My wrists are bound, my head spins, and worst of all, the man beside me does not look like a friend.

"Grayson?" I croak. "What is going on?"

He's quiet for a few seconds too long. When he speaks, however, his voice isn't just duty bound. It's terrified. "We have to get away from JS-7R. With Jade's blood at his disposal, he's about to get a lot stronger."

My own blood stills. "How . . . how do you know what they called him?"

He reaches into his pocket, pulls a card out from it, and flicks it onto the dashboard. *Agent Grayson Warner* is spelled out in bold beside a photograph of him wearing a clean gray suit with an embossed tie clip.

I stare at him, at a loss for all words save for, "You knew about him . . . you knew about me . . ."

"There's a triad of intelligence organizations assigned to clean up the massacre that came out of Project Undergrowth. Your parents tried to keep your secret, and we let them think they could." He pauses, blinks edged with unreadable steel. "A lot of people know about you, Clara. AV-7D, if you're curious. There's been eyes on you since you were born, agents like me stationed everywhere. Babysitters, teachers, tutors—you name it. Usually, they're more covert than the gentleman who tailed us into Blackstone, but the stakes have never been higher. He got nervous, sloppy. I almost slipped a few times myself."

He swallows hard.

"I promise it'll all make sense soon."

My head feels like it's been stuffed full of cotton packed against every corner of my skull. There is a roaring in my ears and blazing white fury obscuring my vision. "Why?" is all I can say.

"It was . . . necessary."

"Necessary?"

Grayson presses on the brakes. I tip forward in my seat, unable to steady myself with my hands tethered to one another. Without so much as a single waver, he looks me dead in the eyes and says, "We believe you're the single thing on this planet capable of taking him down. We've sent in forces—some disguised as road-trippers, some in full-blown body armor. None of them have made it so much as a few hours here. You're the only one that might be able to match his strength, and that makes you our only hope. That makes you the world's only hope. There's a particle barrier around Blackstone meant to imprison him, but he's been pushing against it and spreading his forest beyond it. If he finds a way to break through, there's no telling what could . . ."

He takes off again, the car whipping through the landscape like a silver bullet.

"We knew he'd be tempted by you. You're from the same facility. You have similar biosignatures. He was trying to get you to stay with him because he needs an ally. The barrier is matched to his DNA. As of now, he can't cross it, but *you* can. Winning you over would give him leverage like you wouldn't believe. It would give him a gateway, and then . . . well, you spoke to him. I think you can imagine what comes next."

There are so many things moving through my mind, but only one claws its way to the surface, determined to be heard. "You brought Joey and Jade up here with us. You knew what we were walking into, and you brought them with us. You let them die."

A muscle in his jaw twitches. Lines of shimmering salt water manifest beneath his lashes. His mask cracks; he stops playing the part.

"JS-7R is smart. He knows what we're trying to do. If he suspected, even for a moment, that you were with us, it would've been game over. I argued to bring you in myself. I fought for it, Clara, but there were too many risks, and . . ." Grief spins in those icy irises. He shoves it away. "It wasn't my call."

"Whose call was it?" If it wasn't for the pill circulating power-numbing effects through my bloodstream, that statement would have been the start of a massacre much worse than what I'd done to my parents on the highway. I've never felt heartbreak like this, not even back then.

"I'm not authorized to provide that information at the moment. I'm . . . I'm sorry."

I muster every last bit of patience in me to steady my breathing back to a manageable pace. I do not look at him; I cannot look at him. He lied to me, just as my parents had. However, his lie was far more sinister and far less forgivable. They had lied to keep my vision blurred by a dark veil, to provide me with a past tinted just a few shades too rosy.

Grayson lied because . . . because he'd been . . .

"Was any of it real?" I ask, hating the words the moment they slip between my teeth. "Were we ever . . . ? Did you ever—" All those longing glances, fleeting touches, and flustered blushes. They existed only to add another layer of deception to his already flawless facade.

Agent Grayson Warner.

Agent Grayson Warner, stationed to monitor Specimen AV-7D.

Hours pass before I gain enough composure to speak to him without weeping, tearing his head off his shoulders, or both.

"Where are we going?"

"There's a base beyond the northern edge of the forest, outside the particle barrier. It's where we stored the car."

"Why are we going there?"

"To regroup and form a game plan while JS-7R musters his strength."

"And what, exactly, makes you think I'm going to help you, *Agent* Warner?"

He turns to me unhurried, his eyes as sincere as they are severe. "You exist because the EHKI allows you to exist, Clara. For all intents and purposes, you're an illegal specimen co-owned by every government that funded Project Undergrowth. If you make them believe you're incapable of the task they left you alive to complete, they will kill you."

"And what if I *would* rather die than help you."

Something like anguish flickers onto his features, something that makes me feel safe again. Safe, against my will. Safe, despite all that's been revealed.

"Please don't say that," he says. "You have every right to hate me. You have every right to want *me* dead, and after this, you'll never have to speak to me again. There just . . . has to be an *after this* for you. None of this is fair. None of this has ever been fair, but after JS-7R is dead, you'll get the chance to live your life. If I have anything to say about it, you'll get the chance to live your life."

I don't even know if I want my life anymore. I'd give anything for someone else's, but my own feels more like a curse than a blessing.

We don't speak again. The silence is like carbon monoxide as Grayson drives. He drives, and drives, and drives until an unimpressive white dome comes into view. It is just large enough to conceal a truck, an unwelcoming outdoor toilet, a coffee machine, a microwave, and a small tower capable of picking up signals from whoever *Agent Grayson Warner* answers to.

Once we are inside, he busies his hands with the buttons on the coffee machine. For himself, he brews a French vanilla latte. For me, he makes a cappuccino with oat milk, two sugars, and a dash of cinnamon. I scowl at it, but he sets it in front of me anyway. My stomach burns with hunger. I hiss at every instinct crying out for sustenance.

With weary eyes and stature withered, Grayson leans against the table holding the appliances and takes slow, pensive sips of his beverage.

"So . . . what did you learn about JS-7R when you two were in private? Any weaknesses that might help you when you face him?"

I scour my brain. This is the last thing I want to think about, but I don't have much of a choice. I either die at the hands of Grayson's royal *we* or suffer at Jasper's. Still, I sip my cappuccino at a defiantly slow pace before providing anything.

"When he was in my mind, he had control of it, and of me."

An angry muscle feathers in his jaw. "He . . . has telepathic abilities, yes. Almost every squad we've sent in has succumbed to menticide one way or another."

"When I was in *his* mind . . ." I continue. "He couldn't touch me. There was nothing for him to grasp on to. I was just there, more of an awareness than an actual presence vulnerable to his sway. If I can get in there again, maybe I can . . ." I run both hands through my hair, frustration making me anxious and anxiety making me jittery. "I don't know. If we're the same kind of monster, maybe I can menticide him too."

The ghost of a smile slips over Grayson's lips. It is thoroughly weighed down, but it is there. "*Menticide* is a noun, Clara."

I growl. He raises his free hand in surrender, taking another swig of French vanilla goodness with the other. I almost can't believe it. After all this conniving manipulation, after costing Joey his life and letting Jade fall off that ridge, here he stands, caffeinating himself and correcting my grammar.

We sit in silence for another terrible eternity, taking cyclic sips.

"Anything else?" He finishes off the remaining contents of his plain Styrofoam cup.

"He doesn't want to be alone." I send my gaze to the plastic wall of our glorified tent. Through its semiopaque texture, the silhouettes of Jasper's trees loom. The darkness that emanates from them is nearly alive. It stares back at me. It always stares. "All he wants is—"

"Clara, listen to me. JS-7R doesn't want company, or connection, or anything he tried to convince you of. He wants revenge, domination. He doesn't want a friend; he wants to break out of here and massacre the world as we know it. No matter how human he looked, or sounded, or . . . f-felt . . ."

Is that anger, Agent Warner? Perhaps . . . jealousy, Agent Warner?

"He's not human. He'll never be human."

"He and I are more alike than different." I shrug.

Grayson grabs both of my hands in his, suddenly desperate, the most desperate I've seen him. "I've been observing you for a long time, and I know for a fact that isn't true. Sometimes I think you're the most human soul I've ever met. Humanity doesn't come with the costume. It's a choice, one that we have to make every day. JS-7R is a monster because *he* wants to be. You're Clara Lovecroft, not AV-7D, because that's who *you* want to be."

I bring my gaze to the trees twitching in the wind, creaking like brittle bones. Someone ancient and forbidden looms between them, just as something ancient and forbidden looms within me. I find myself at the apex of too many choices. A choice between human and monster. A choice between the greater of three evils. A choice between forgiveness and fury. Between Grayson and Jasper. Between Jasper and myself.

I also find myself dreadfully dizzy.

When I sway to the side, Grayson's arms are there to catch me. He's always there to catch me. My muscles feel like they're melting off the framework set by my bones, and my head spins like a merry-go-round horse. Every light comes in and out of focus, glimmering, twinkling, and dancing against the veils that crowd my vision.

“I’m sorry, Clara. I’m sorry for . . . everything.”

Grayson’s voice is an echo easily smothered by senses drowned in sleep. It steals me like a wave steals the shore, engulfing me in a breathless, timeless gloom.

33 | GRAYSON

"What is the matter with you?" I snap, a disposable flip phone pressed tightly to my ear. "This wasn't the deal! You were supposed to pick them up the moment JS-7R went on the offense! Joey and Jade were supposed to be safe!"

My hand shakes so violently, the voice that comes through the speaker emerges jumbled. "Unexpected collateral."

"You lied to me."

"The situation was delicate, Agent Warner. You of all people know how important this mission is. If JS-7R had become privy to our presence, he wouldn't have let his guard down for AV-7D. For all intents and purposes, her arrival had to look like a coincidence. We weighed the risks. Joey and Jade's extraction just wasn't worth it."

"You let them die!"

"Watch your tone. Regardless of external relations, I am your commanding officer. Now, collect AV-7D and bring her down for a debrief. If you want to cerebrate on the morality of things, do so on your personal time."

I don't even wait for a staticky click to snap the phone in half. It unhinges like an oyster and sends metal, glass, and plastic splintering through the air. Spiderwebs of wiring hang from each half, still sparking. I'm still sparking too. After years of playing the boy next door, I've just about had it with patience, tolerance, and restraint. If I make it to my personal time, I will do a lot more than *cerebrate* on what happened to my brother and my best friend.

I pick Clara up just as I had when we escaped the collapsing sector. She's light as a feather in her human form. She's eerily still, sedated in my arms.

Beautiful, but tired.

Always beautiful, and tired.

A hidden switch beneath the espresso cabinet of the coffee machine illuminates. Flashing periwinkle light signals the availability of the electrical charge needed to enter headquarters. I suck in a breath. It reminds me of the way Jade used to inhale her cigarettes. I used to send her articles about lung cancer at ungodly hours of the night. She'd send back a photo of her middle finger, and we'd move into lighter conversation about the last grown man she'd pummeled or the most horrible sitcom on television.

Too close, my superior had warned. *You're getting too close.* I couldn't help it, but I was getting too close. I really, truly was. Now I understand why it was such a colossal mistake. This hurts too much because I've gotten too close.

I can't be grieving Grayson right now. I might not have to fit the Prince Charming archetype, but I most certainly have to be a soldier. I most certainly have to be Agent Grayson Warner. I've always had to be Agent Grayson Warner. I was born into this purpose. It's the only reason I exist.

When I flip the switch, the entire dome is swallowed in waves of pale blue. A beam rounds the floor like an underwater missile caught in a whirlpool. Then a ghostly hiss sounds off, a puff of mist ejects from below, and the entire base of the structure drops out. It descends into a tube of greenish glass, passing levels on levels of secrets hidden beneath the bedrock.

The EHKI spent more than a few million on this place. It's considered ground zero for all things JS-7R, the alpha and omega of undoing the damage caused by Project Undergrowth. Folks in white lab coats scurry through the floors like hamsters starved of stimulation. Agents of lower rank wear deep-green suits meant to blend in with the hellscape at the surface. The ones on my oh-so-enviable level wear black-on-black tuxedos.

I didn't earn my position. I'm special because of nepotism.

Clara and I fall deep into the bowels of the subterranean structure. Our destination is near the level that is close enough to the earth's mantle to extract heat from it. When we arrive, the cylindrical tube of transport drops one of its sides to create a doorway and a ramp.

My mother and commanding officer—Dr. Hemlock to the EHKI, and Dr. Gwendolyn Warner to the world beyond—stands at the end of it.

"Good work," she says.

A compliment? How rare and unexpected, considering the work she's talking about got my brother—her son—massacred by an experimental eldritch monster. I ram past her without so much as a glance of acknowledgment. I don't think my composure can take any more added pressure.

"Agent Warner." Her thin heels sound like icicles on glass as she hurries behind me. "Grayson Oliver Warner."

A pair of timid scientists arrive with a gurney for Clara. I lower her onto it, making sure her head aligns with its pathetically flimsy pillow. She likely wouldn't have gotten one if it wasn't sewn in. As she is wheeled into the labyrinth of metal and misted glass, my heart aches in a manner my mother is sure to disapprove of. I wasn't supposed to care about her—the target. *My* target. I'd gotten too close to Jade for comfort, and too close to Clara for sense.

Was any of it real?

My god, the way she . . . looked at me. I was once her reliable *something more*, then suddenly, I became her *nothing at all.* If I could have done things differently, I . . . If I could start it all over with her, I . . .

My mother jams her manicured nails into the tenderest spot on my shoulder. "Grayson," she repeats herself.

"Specimen AV-7D secured, ma'am," I reply, stoic as a soldier should be, perfect as the man she bred me to become. "I trust all necessary procedures to ensure her captivity will be carried out by the proper departments. With your permission, I'd like to request a brief respite. Then I'll be ready for dispatch to the surface to carry out phase two of the mission."

She forces eye contact. There is not one ounce of remorse behind those prissy rectangular reading glasses. I try not to implode.

"I apologize for your involvement in this, Grayson. You must understand, these are desperate times. Desperate times call for unforgivable measures."

My involvement in this? It's incredible how she makes the sacrifice of an entire childhood sound so inconsequential. *This is your mission, Agent Grayson,* she'd told me at twelve. *Keep an eye on Clara Lovecroft, but don't get too close. She is your target, but she is only a target,* she'd said. I was no older than Joey, yet my life had been orchestrated to instrumental perfection. *You're strong enough, Grayson. You have to be. It's your duty.*

"Understood, ma'am," I reply, a contraption, waking and walking in servitude.

"Originally, there was an extraction plan for Joey and Jade. Do you truly believe I would have sent my own son in there without one?"

"It's not my place to analyze your choices, ma'am. My duty is to obey them. Right?"

She presses her lips into a thin line. The sepia matte lipstick she's wearing keeps them from cracking. I cannot help but envision her taking a trip to the powder room to freshen up her appearance before greeting her last-remaining child. She was just as primped at Dad's funeral, she'll be just as primped at Joey's, and if things go sideways, she'll wear that same shade of taupe at mine.

"AV-7D will be taken care of appropriately. You will be contacted as soon as we are ready to proceed. Dismissed."

I take a step toward the barracks, then . . . then something dangerous ignites at the center of my chest, and suddenly the world is all forbidden ire and ice-cold fire.

"Dad would be disgusted by you," I seethe.

"Excuse me?" She whirls around, the brown line of her lips turning into a pair of cobra fangs.

"He never wanted this, and if he'd gotten custody of Joey and me, it never would have happened. We weren't toys for him to play with, we weren't tools for him to build with, and we most definitely weren't his tiny sleeper agents. We were his *children*. For him, that's all we had to be. For him, that was enough. But you . . ." My voice quivers. I'm losing control. "You're different . . ."

"Watch your tone, Agent—"

"I'm not *just* an agent, Mom! I'm your son! Joey was your son! Jade and Clara, they were someone's daughters! People aren't meant to be puppets! They aren't meant to be cogs in a clock, or means to your ends, or unexpected collateral! My god, for a woman so intent on saving humanity, you're pretty damn far from your own!"

"That's enough, Grayson!"

"That *is* enough! Enough lying, enough manipulating, and enough using! I'm done doing all of the dirty work you had the audacity to call *duty*! The only reason I'm going back into that forest is to stand by Clara, because it's my fault she's here right now. After that, I'm done. I'm done with this, and I'm done with you."

I take off for the barracks without looking back. A few nosy agents murmur over my outburst, and I'm more than happy about it. They should know their superior can bleed.

A few levels beneath the one Clara is being examined on, there are rows of bunk beds inside chambers made from steel with a teal finish. The walls are gray, but the lights lining them cast spectral green shadows. I can't, for the life of me, fathom why the designers chose such a color scheme. I've had enough green to last me ten lifetimes.

Were we ever— Did you ever— Clara's voice whirls through my mind.

We were. Of course we were. Yes. Of course I did.

I wasn't permitted to, but I did. It wasn't safe or smart or sensible of me, but I did. Despite it all, Clara, I wanted to be your safe place. I wanted to save you from this life you'd been seized into. You didn't deserve it. All you've ever done is ponder the monster within, but what about the monsters without? What about monsters like my mother?

You've drawn blood, but it's what you were designed to do. It's what she designed you to do.

Are we monsters for becoming what we were born to be? Are we monsters for becoming what we were trained to be? No . . . humanity is a choice. JS-7R, Dr. Gwendolyn "Hemlock" Warner, and all the EHKI officials responsible for this mess made theirs. Now, at last, it's time for Clara and me to make our own.

34 | CLARA

LED lights are hung in piercingly bright rows overhead. I am no longer in the glorified tent. I am in a translucent glass rectangle, an angular fishbowl with no exits or entrances. Beyond it lies a windowless space lined with silver tiles and a blinking red pinprick of light. A camera has been placed as conspicuously as possible in the top-right corner of the room. The metal floor I rest on feels like dry ice on my skin.

An eternity passes before the eerie silence of my containment unit is broken. A hiss surges through the room, and the monochromatic tiles of the wall outside my tank shift to create a doorway. From that doorway emerges a woman with black hair, eyes like sea moss, and a smile as bright as the first days of spring. It's . . . the woman from Jasper's memories, now completely unobscured. It's also Grayson's *mother*.

Behind her, a burly man like a moving storm cloud follows. I recognize him. He's the man from the gas station, the one who entered just after Joey and me. He's even wearing the same uniform.

"Good morning, Clara," she says. "How are we feeling?"

Like I'm speaking to yet another liar. At this point, I don't even bother with shock.

She speaks again. "I'd imagine you're not interested in formalities."

I will myself to stand despite the weakness in my legs. They are, slowly but surely, solidifying after that deceptive cappuccino turned the muscles within them into thick, sloshing liquid. There are black and blue shadows on my body. Ring-shaped bruises loop around my ankles and wrists. They ache, stiffen the nearby joints with swelling, and produce pangs of internal, inflammatory heat. I'm almost grateful for it, as the space around me can only be described as barely temperate. It's cool, sterile. The air particles themselves are too shy to move fast enough to create heat with their friction.

"Which is your real name? Hemlock or Gwendolyn?" I ask, stumbling forward to press both hands against the glass that separates us.

She straightens, as though the syllables of her second name have snapped in on her rib cage like a corset. "Both of them, actually. Hemlock is my EHKI code name. Gwendolyn is known only by a select few. Now, are we to dawdle on names, or would you like to know more about where you are and what is happening?"

"You won't tell me," I spit my words, impatiently beating each consonant to a pulp.

"Of course I'll tell you. You're the last person any of that information should be kept from. I just figured you'd need some time to gather your bearings first."

"Do you offer room service?"

She snickers through an eye roll. "You have your father's sense of humor."

I replace the irreverent look on my face with one of red-hot rage.

"And your mother's glare." Her snicker turns into a nebulous laugh. "Not to mention her gorgeous brown eyes. Believe it or not, I was always rather jealous of them. She and I used to joke about trading eyeballs once science advanced enough to make it possible—"

"I'll take that information now," I interrupt, letting my voice manifest with a venomous edge. She might hold some power behind that snakelike smile, but I'm the one in a cage. She must be, at the very least, wary of me.

"Very well. Aside from being Agent Grayson's mother, I am a researcher, and I work for an organization known as the EHKI. The Expansion of Human Knowledge Institute. You're currently in one of our bases, and I think you already know why. Well, part of the reason why. Allow me to explain the rest. It was called Project Undergrowth."

My nostrils flare, and my gaze never wavers. "So I've heard."

Surprise plays at her sharp, severe features. "From who?"

"Grayson and JS-7R."

"I see my son was a bit more generous than he'd been instructed to be. Did he also tell you my code name, or was that JS-7R?"

"Trust me, Agent Grayson's been more than compliant with your commands." Despite an attempt at sarcasm, this assertion breaks my heart. "Jasper, on the other hand, told me a lot more than your code name, *Dr. Hemlock*."

That nearly fanged grin returns. "JS-7R told you his side of the story, which is incredibly subjective. May I present all that he didn't know?"

She pulls an unremarkable manila folder from behind her back but waves it like a prop instead of opening it for reference. It is clear that she's memorized the contents.

"The EHKI was a visionary organization. Project Undergrowth was our most ambitious attempt to entangle ourselves with forces no human should entangle themselves with. There was a research expedition that led us deep into the earth, beyond the asthenosphere and into the mantle. Everyone said we'd find nothing. We were mocked for spending millions of government dollars and investing thousands of our own. Still, together, we built a vessel capable of enduring the heat and pressure of our planet's interior. Together, we descended. What we found brought all of the mockery to a staggering halt. There were caves flourishing with otherworldly flora and fauna, ancient plant species as far as the eye could see. Not only had life managed to thrive in conditions we, in our limited thinking, thought impossible, but there was something else."

My anticipation grows more demanding by the second. The pensive beat she indulges in goes on for far too long. It hangs on each timid particle of air and practically gnaws through the sheath of glass between us.

"Upon carbon-dating them," she proceeds at last, "we found them to be far older than Earth as we know it. The molecules they consisted of were unlike ours on a fundamental, energetic level. They were of an entirely different frequency, and thus, could operate in ways beyond the confines of science as we know it. The plants were interconnected. They could shift their forms at will, take on bodies of matter and of light, communicate with one another telepathically, and they were functionally immortal. I'm sure this is beginning to sound familiar."

"Jasper." I send the word out behind a breath.

"JS-7R"—Gwendolyn pulls her lips into a tight, pensive line—"is the first successful creation of Project Undergrowth. He was the first successful hybrid created via splicing human DNA with the DNA of what we found beyond the asthenosphere. Sixty-seven percent of his genes are alien to us, meaning sixty-seven percent of his biology is far beyond our understanding. I raised him like a human, but as he grew, he became unstable. His abilities started manifesting in ways I could not predict, comprehend, or control."

"So you were going to kill him?"

"Come now, Clara. You know it's much more complicated than that. In the beginning, the EHKI had every intention of training and releasing the embryos we'd spliced into the world. We thought we'd found a way to expedite the next stage of evolution. JS-7R proved us wrong. I sent out an order to euthanize and study him for the safety of this planet. JS-7R found out about it and created a massacre."

She pauses, wavering in her emotionally sterilized speech.

"Somehow your parents escaped, and they did so with . . . you. Seventy-eight percent of you is an anomaly. The other twenty-two percent is entirely human, entirely Adelina Dolion and Cedric Lovecroft. It was against protocol, but they used their own DNA in the building blocks for your embryo. You're a genealogical marvel filled with the DNA of a species older than every scientific calendar."

I am left without words and without thoughts to inspire them. Dr. Gwendolyn Warner watches my expression carefully, in search of something. Like a sudden, saccharine slap to the face, she pulls a container from her back pocket, and it is filled to the brim with pink orbs. It sits balanced atop her polished fingernails.

"These pills were their sole attempt to keep you human. They consist of a uniquely cultivated form of stabilized DNA, a blend of their blood, designed to bond to your cells and encourage the expression of your human attributes. Without them, your other side strives to become dominant. It was a valiant attempt to have them replicated on your own, but I'm afraid local drugstores don't carry these sorts of ingredients on hand."

They really have been monitoring me.

I inch closer to the glass that divides us. "Tell me why I'm still alive, Gwendolyn."

"The EHKI discovered what Adelina and Cedric had done shortly after they fled the laboratory and have been surveilling you ever since. My son was our most vital sleeper agent, put in place as soon as he could comprehend the gravity of the mission. We've allowed you to remain alive for one purpose and one purpose alone." Her smile fades into a line taut enough to make the nasolabial folds around her lips disappear. "JS-7R is too powerful for us to subdue. We've been able to contain him with a particle barrier, but if he ever breaks through it, there is no telling what will happen. We don't possess human DNA that matches his, so we cannot weaken him the way we can weaken you. Our plan is to match his strength. More specifically, to have you match his strength."

"You allowed me to live . . . so that I could kill him?"

"At the moment, you're the only thing that stands between him and his release into the world. This mission has been active since the day you were discovered. We wanted to wait until you'd matured fully before having you go up against him. Then you killed your parents, and things got a bit more complicated."

My throat tightens.

"I didn't mean to," I sputter. I'm not sure why I'm speaking, why I'm suddenly so desperate to explain what I'd done that day. Still, the words surge forward, a flood flowing through a cracked dam, a spiral of guilt a long time overdue. "I missed a pill, and I lost control. They tried to explain, tried to help me, but I was just so angry with them for lying to me all my life. I was so angry that I . . . I didn't mean to. I swear, I didn't. If I could change it—"

"If I could change my wrongdoings, I would too. However, I cannot go back and stop the expedition that led to all of this. I cannot tell my past self how dangerous the splicing process could be. I cannot beg myself to stay at my husband's bedside as he withered in a hospital bed because of the toxins I brought home. I cannot command myself to be a better mother to my sons, to cherish all the moments that once seemed so inconsequential." A poorly masked quiver of mourning rattles her voice. "I cannot erase any of it, but I can erase JS-7R. We can erase JS-7R. Moving forward and being better is all we can do. It's all anyone can *ever* do."

I stare at her, through her. Somewhere in the space between us, I feel a tether. We aren't . . . so different, I suppose. I give her a nod.

With a severe look, she continues, "As we discussed, the plants we discovered were able to communicate via a psychic link. JS-7R is able to harness it and influence the thoughts of his victims, yourself included. No one has ever been able to enter his realm and survive. He seems to feel some sort of affection for you, and Grayson has informed me that this has allowed you to slip past his defenses. We need you to do it again. Humanity needs you to do it again."

She sets the pills just outside my containment unit. The tile below them lowers into the floor, and moments later, a square drops out from beneath me. A mechanical arm rises up to hand-deliver the container and descends back into dark obscurity only after I accept it.

It is an olive branch.

"Your efforts will not go unacknowledged, nor will they go unpaid. If you agree to assist us, you will be granted full amnesty and personal freedom, contingent upon your compliance with a few requests, of course. You will continue taking a daily dosage of those pills, which we will manufacture using the remaining samples we have of Adelina's and Cedric's blood. When it runs out, you will agree to containment until an alternative is cultivated. You will also be asked to attend monthly physiological and psychological check-ins. Other than that, you can lead a normal life."

"If I survive," I add.

"Yes." She sighs. "If you survive. But rest assured, if you do not, I suspect the rest of the world will not be far behind."

A chill crawls up my spine, nipping at every vertebra as though to punctuate the sudden, dreadful importance of my existence.

"Think on it," she says before the silence becomes too oppressive. "You have twenty-four hours to decide."

"And if I refuse?"

She does not respond, a response in and of itself. I am left alone with only my pills, my thoughts, a hollowed-out space of metal and glass, and a blinking red light. The twenty-four-hour period feels like days. When it ends, Gwendolyn returns, and I have just one word to offer her.

"Fine."

A team of heavily armed soldiers escorts me from my cell. They are a sea of black, gray, and green body armor, faces made anonymous by masks placed over their noses and mouths. A horde of distinguished-looking business-casual folks armed with notepads instead of guns trails behind them, each more eager than the last to get a look at me.

When Grayson emerges, I curse myself for feeling relief. His face might be familiar, but it is still the face of a traitorous double agent who was never my protector, never my friend, and never, ever anything more. Why then does he insist on making me feel so *safe*?

"You're coming?" I channel Jade and send a few ocular *fuck you*'s his way.

He nods, uncharacteristically sheepish.

A scoff slips up my throat, and I don't care to indulge him with anything else. Before I know it, we are standing shoulder to shoulder in an elevator lined with faux heavenly light. It transports us from the EHKI's new subterranean facility to the shabby plastic dome designed to conceal its entrance. Grayson and I brew another pair of coffees, mine free of sedation this time.

When we finally pass the invisible particle barrier narrowly keeping Jasper prisoner, his presence caresses my mind with hungry hands. The only thing hungrier is the dominant expression of my *ancient and forbidden* genes, now vying for dominance as the last pill I swallowed evacuates my system.

35 | JASPER

My Clara's ingratitude is trying my patience. Joey may have perished under pettier circumstances, but Jade deserved to die. Her parasitic hold on Clara was unfair, and I did the right thing by cutting their connective cord. I was protecting her. I had her best interests in mind, and I even extended a kindness to Jade that I seldom extend. I let her demise come quickly. Some level of punishment was in order, but I refrained from overdoing it.

Now is not the time to dwell, I remind myself.

I need to save her—my love, my Clara.

I race through the shadows in time-loosened seconds. Each feels longer than the last. The vehicle that brought my sweet girl to me comes into view, but it is accelerating at a dangerously high speed toward the edge of oblivion. The place where air becomes solid, where matter becomes too dense for each particle of me to pass through. I reach out for the rear wheels, knowing just one graze would be enough to shred them, but they spin on. They leave trails of smoke, gravel, and dirt in their wake. The Hummer cuts through the world like a merciless blade.

It passes over the threshold with a mighty boom of complete and utter silence. All in one terrible moment, my Clara disappears beyond my reach.

I press my hands to the barrier between us, watching as a stream of uncanny iridescence appears around them like ripples around a raindrop. This cruel beauty reminds me that I am still a prisoner. I am still *their* prisoner.

Gritting my teeth, I expel waves of power against it. Slowly, the iridescence shifts in hue until it is entirely red. My red. While my dominance over it does not last for long, it serves its purpose. My cruel beauty reminds it, and whoever placed it here, that I cannot be contained forever.

Hours pass. I spend them willing the wall to fissure in my favor, to allow for even the smallest rift to form. It's irresponsible of me, but I waste most of Jade's energy gazing at the horizon Clara disappeared over, hoping for a sign of progress in my escape. Slowly but surely, I revert to the easiest form I can maintain and slump to the ground to stew in my failure. When my back is pressed to the barrier, the ripples of restrictive light become larger. They send writhing rays across the asphalt road.

Night falls, and for the first time in a very long time, sleep steals me from my tears.

I dream of nothing but her. I dream of her eyes, beautiful in their spellbound state and spellbinding when freed. I dream of her voice, more alluring than the curated orchestra of sounds I've conducted in these woods. I dream of her essence, that gloriously unique energy that ascends above the constraints of her flesh. It intoxicated me with unrelenting vigor, which explains the withdrawal I'm experiencing now.

I dream of the life we could have, the life we should have. Connection is something I never dared to deserve, but connecting with Clara has changed that. It's become something I crave, something even more enthralling than the purpose I've assigned my soul to. Of course I still want to bleed the earth dry of its human disease, but what worth is domination without a fellow monarch at my side? What good is all-consuming superiority without at least one true equal?

At sunrise, I move toward the southern border. Foolish hope assures me another car must have stopped for gas and decades-old potato chips.

I'll get more blood roses. I'll make myself strong enough to break through the barrier. I'll make the impossible possible. I'll—

Clara's voice reverberates through the fallen leaves. It bounces off every wooded surface, granite edge, and grainy speck of dirt. It races down the asphalt strip like a sound wave down a violin's string. Everything sensible within screams that it is an illusion, but her energy touches me in a way that suggests it is far more than just an imprint felt through phantom pain.

She is here; she's returned to me.

Yet she is still beside Grayson, and she is speaking only to him. Heartache strums the cords of her voice.

"Your mom told me you were an agent since we were kids. She told me it was all an act, all part of some plan."

Grayson shifts his weight from foot to foot, visibly uncomfortable, squirming in his skin. "We can't talk about this now, Clara. He could be listening."

Guilty.

When Clara lowers her gaze to the ground, he shifts once more, shoving both hands into his pockets. The frown he wears is vague. Regret illuminates his eyes. "You had to be monitored for . . . obvious reasons and manipulated for complicated ones. I didn't get a say in it, but for what it's worth—"

"You could have said *something.*" Before he can take a step farther, she places herself between him and the rest of the forest. Her fingernail elongates sharply as she drives it into his sternum. "You had a choice, Grayson. You said it yourself; it's all about choice."

He grabs her hand but keeps it close to his chest. I can only assume his heartbeat is far slower than mine, considering the way their proximity is urging my blood to sublimate. "Please, Clara. We can't do this here, but I promise, as soon as it's all over—"

She clamps her free hand over his lips, silencing him. It seems there's something hanging unspoken in the air, something neither of them wants me to hear. "I would have helped," she says, her words withered to a whisper. "I would have helped if you asked. They didn't have to die."

"I know . . ." His voice drops in octave and in volume. "I know."

They step in perfect alignment with one another, close enough to let their fingertips touch. They never entwine, but they *touch*. Their intimate, secretive cloud is mephitic, and I have had enough of it. I slink behind them, making certain that I am unseen and unheard. The whispers I send to Clara and Clara alone will draw her precisely where I need her to be. I release them in the sweetest breeze.

They meet a wall of thorns. Only small gaps exist between the vines encasing her mind. Through them, I can see only glimpses of her. I can feel only the featherlight touches of her faraway thoughts. Distant as they are, they still emit undeniable intentions. She isn't here to love me. She is here to kill me.

Thorns pierce through to my innermost heart, a heart I'd made vulnerable only for her.

36 | CLARA

This part of the forest is darker than the rest. It bends in a downward slope toward depths that even the sun's rays do not dare caress. The descent into its cold, unfeeling shadows is reminiscent of drifting into the twilight zone of the ocean. There is pressure here too. There is an unseen force pleading with every sane piece of me to turn back.

I pay it no mind.

The trees here are wide and sturdy, like those of a redwood. Their coloration varies from a soulless black to the deepest brown, and there is not a leaf in sight. Here, there is only death. Death, and the otherworldly glow that slithers between the bends and ripples in the bark. It pulses with scarlet light. This light, this bloodstained firework of color, unifies the endless landscape one heartbeat at a time. Gravity and willpower alone pull me down, stronger than the tingle of fear at the back of my neck.

I don't want to do this.

I have to do this.

Grayson and I lose track of time and of our steps. We walk for hours. No, days. No, weeks. No, minutes. There is no way of grasping a system of awareness. We're simply walking, the world growing ever darker.

Then a pulse of Jasper's light erupts from every tree, branch, and grain of dirt on the ground. It is blinding to my unadjusted pupils, but regardless, I use the surge of bioluminescence to my advantage. I scour the landscape for him, but he is still nowhere to be found. As the light fades, a chill scales my spine. We cannot see him, but he most definitely sees us. Tendrils of his presence touch my body and my mind, each coming closer and lingering longer than the last.

"Can you feel him?" Grayson must have read my expression.

I nod, afraid to speak.

In the distance, treetops move. Something is coming toward us, as though summoned by Grayson's voice. It is large enough to rattle the trunks. Camouflaged between them, Jasper suddenly appears in his narrow, cadaverous, thoroughly demonic form. He seems to consist of bark, bones, and blood, an unfinished, incomplete human that mutated into something more. Something wicked. The breath I'd been taking freezes as my throat muscles constrict. We stare at each other for a moment or two before he silently steps to the side. This motion hides him behind a tree, and when he peeks out again, it is from behind a new tree.

Slightly closer.

All I can do is stare. My legs have stopped themselves from progressing forward, melting into the ground below. He repeats the motion.

Behind a tree. Out from a new tree. *Closer.*

"Jasper," I whisper, making my voice as sweet as it can be between each shudder of fear, "I need to speak with you."

Behind a tree. Out from a new one. *Closer.*

From this distance, I can see more of him. He wears a smile that stretches from the tip of one nonexistent brow to the other. It is the widest he's ever worn, cartoonishly horrifying, and filled with those limb-shredding rows of teeth. I touch a hand to my lips, feeling the pill as it drains from my system, the mysterious concoction that keeps me from growing fangs of my own.

"I want to speak with you." I feign deception by darting my eyes to Grayson, trying to communicate that he had not let me come here alone. That he is yet another nuisance to be taken care of.

Without warning, Jasper charges forward with a speed I was not ready for. He moves along the forest floor like a centipede, limbs spasming out of sync. Though his torso points upward, his neck has twisted in an unnatural circle that keeps his chin pointing at the earth. My instincts tell me to cry out and back away, but I stand my ground. On arrival, he restacks himself in a crouch, and I stare into that skeletal face, those sunken black voids. I place my hands on his cheeks to bring him to eye level.

"I want you," I lie. "Only you."

I lean forward and press my lips to his. This caliber of sincerity is my greatest performance yet. In this moment of ecstasy, I pray his defenses will drop, allowing me a telepathic entryway back into his mind. I can feel the doorway as it hinges open. The darkness beyond it is a blanket over every thought and memory, and if I can lift it, I can bend them beneath. I can make him obey, or at least keep him still long enough to be handled by someone with a better plan.

I reach for the doorway. I leave the confines of my physiology behind, letting our brain waves tango telepathically. The distinct frequency that is his dreamscape hits me like a blast of winter air. I slam against the blockade dropped in front of it like a crystal vase against steel. The sheer act of shattering brings me back to my body.

His smile hasn't budged.

Before I can pull away, I feel an unmistakable sensation in my chest. His hand has plunged through it, fingers encircling my heart. A cage. I shakily move to rip myself from his grasp, but I cannot go far. To my absolute horror, he begins to stand, limbs thinning and twisting as he towers over Grayson, and hauls me by the heart upward of twenty feet into the air.

"Liar," he hisses.

I grab at his wrist, struggling against the strangest pain I've ever felt as he twirls his fingers through my tendons.

"I'm not lying—" I lie again. It takes every bit of strength to choke out reasons for him to release me. My heart beats against his cold palm, sending lightning strikes of agony through nerves I didn't know existed. "Y-you were right. I've felt alone all my life because no one ever understood. I-I wanted to kill my parents. I loved it, every second of it. I don't care that you massacred that lab. Th-Those people deserved it. I don't care about what you did to Joey and Jade either. He was a nuisance. Th-They both were."

He tilts his head, considering my words.

"Maybe that makes me a monster. Maybe a monster is exactly what I am, what I choose to be. I'm not human, and I'm so tired of pretending to be." My hands shake terribly as I reach for his rawboned cheeks once more. "Jasper, you are the only one who's ever given me the permission to be me, all of me. I want you, because I'd rather be a real monster than half a human. I want you because, with you, I can be free. I want you because . . . because if we're together, neither of us ever has to be alone again."

My performance must have been convincing, because Grayson takes a few audible staggering steps back. It must have been convincing, because even now, with Jasper's fist in my sternum, the scent of anarchic freedom tempts me. I could swap the betrayals. I could let Jasper show me how to kill Grayson, then tear anyone they send in after him to flesh ribbons. He did say I was their only hope. They don't have the artillery or the capacity to end whatever we are.

We have the upper hand.

I have the upper hand.

A glance down to Grayson steals it from me. The humanity lingering in my veins steals it from me, because humans can and *do* love. For all his deception, for all his manipulation, and against my better judgment, he is much more to me than Agent Grayson Warner. His legs are shaky, his lips are white, and his eyes are lined with salt water. A comically futile gun trembles metallically in his hands.

He is Grayson, my Grayson, and alongside Jade and Joey, he is one of the reasons why I've never felt alone.

"Let. Her. Go," he demands.

He could have run. He could have assessed the situation, realized I'd failed, and barreled for his truck parked on the edge of the road. He could have abandoned me. However, there he stands, aiming a pistol he knows is useless at Jasper's chest, crying.

"Poor choice of words," Jasper simpers.

He kisses me, then starts to rip his hand from my torso, threatening to crack my ribs on the way out. Grayson takes a shot, his aim remarkably perfect, and the bullet goes straight through Jasper's wrist, detaching his hand from the rest of his arm. I fall to the ground and then to my knees, coughing, wheezing, and throwing up crimson. My heart beats weakly, a messy bundle of muscle and severed veins, but it still beats. Grayson is at my side in an instant, his hands hovering over my gaping wound.

"I'm sorry, I'm sorry," he sputters. "I'm so sorry. I didn't want this, and I . . . I can't lose anyone else. I can't lose you. Clara, come on, I can't lose you."

"Grayson," I gasp. "Go, please, g-go."

"No! There will be an *after*, there has to be an *after*! To hell with the plan, I'm getting you out of here right now!"

""I'm not worth it, Grayson. P-please just go."

He snakes one arm beneath my legs and another under my lower back. When he hoists me off the ground, the pain is next to unbearable. It reminds me that I am still alive. He reminds me that I am still alive.

"Never," he promises with a kiss to the crown of my head.

Suddenly, I'm soaring.

We take off in a sprint toward the surface of the forest, and each branch rips at Grayson's legs as he struggles against the uphill slope. The trees rattle, and when my attention shifts to them, ravenous locusts gnaw at my insides. Jasper stands behind a faraway tree, his hollow eyes staring silently across the space. Though he is clutching his injury, the tip of his widespread grin is still there, visible and taunting. It says *I'll play* in a language beyond articulated words. Warped, twisted, omnidirectional laughter rises from the ground and falls from the sky. Raindrops of sound pour with torrential amusement.

"Clara," he croons in the voice that once stole me away.

Grayson's steps stay focused, but I do not. The moment my name slips from Jasper's lips, I can't help but lose my neural footing. The world starts to spin, and red fireflies return to encircle us. Their rhythmic flickers are like a sea of swinging stopwatches persuading me to sleep. The eerie maze of emaciated branches is suddenly swallowed by vermilion mist. Thorns once precise and defined are clipped and smoothed over. Every attribute softens, insistent on becoming works of temptation.

"Clara, stay with me," Grayson begs, his face wrought with panic. "Wake up. You're stronger than him. You're so strong."

"What's the matter, love?" Jasper's whisper slithers through my subconscious. "I thought you *wanted* to stay with me."

It is now that I notice the strange patterns in the bark down here, in the depths. Nausea races through me. How did I miss it? Human visages are carved into each trunk, faces frozen in their last moments of terror. Jade. Joey. A sea of scientists I recognize only from Jasper's memories. This deep, dark part of the forest is not a bend in Earth's geography, but an ever-growing graveyard built over the heart of the burned laboratory.

He hinges overhead, snapping his body at the waist to do so, and drowning Grayson and me in his shadow. Grayson pulls me closer to his chest, his heartbeat racing. There is still fire in his eyes, though, and they are sending out daggers of defiance.

He is being brave, for me.

He is brave, too brave for all we're up against.

37 | JASPER

Anger is not easily felt toward one so beloved. Still, the emotion makes a monster of me. We will prevail, of course. Some healing may be required to recultivate trust, but we've already made so much progress. Everything about her thorns, about her betrayal, is becoming clear now. She's confused. Grayson has confused her. He is an obstacle to be triumphed over and nothing more.

Nothing. More.

I command a bundle of branches to grab her wrists and ankles and pull her from his arms. Without them, she'd hurt herself attempting to stop the inevitable. They tuck her to the side, none coiled harshly enough to scar. I'm tempted to tighten them only because her feverish thrashing makes me fear for the integrity of her bones.

"Jasper, stop!" Even enraged, she sounds so lovely.

"All I want to do is free you, love. You have to let me."

There's a hundred different things I can tell she wants to say, but panic freezes her tongue. It is prompted by Grayson's idiocy. Like the pathetic carbon cage he is, he begins firing beads of metal through my alchemized anatomy. I whirl toward him, letting him watch as vines, thorns, and branches sew me shut. The thunderous whipcracks of his bullets fade from the air in silvery echoes. I hiss into a pocket of silence.

"Grayson . . . ever the knight, aren't you?"

"Let her go," he demands with misplaced confidence. For someone so aware of his own defeat, he is holding his stance well. Unwavering, emboldened, and half witted all at once. Surely he doesn't think the gun will do much damage, does he? The way he's using it is suggestive of hope, which makes me question whether he's brave, stupid, or both.

"She doesn't want you, Grayson. She said it herself," I say, slinking away from my Clara, close enough to Grayson to hear his ragged breathing. "She wants *me*. She wants to be with me. Not you. *Me*."

He is lighter than I expected he'd be. With one hand stretched around his torso, I pin his body to the nearest tree trunk and take note of the frailty of frightened creatures. His skin erupts with goose bumps and adrenaline-induced shivers. Even his dangling legs manage to shake while kicking for freedom. The strong ones falter most miserably when defeat is imminent. The princes turn into paupers, the knights into damsels.

There is something familiar about this particular damsel.

How hadn't I seen it before? While he doesn't sport her head of black hair, Grayson possesses features I haven't had the displeasure of seeing in years. He has the same sort of eyes that once observed me through overhead lights. He has the same sort of jawline that once went taut at my glimmers of disobedience. He has a perfectly straight, dainty nose very much like the one that used to hoist rectangular spectacles.

He isn't just Grayson. He is most definitely, most deliciously, Dr. Hemlock's human spawn.

"So I see Dr. Hemlock embraced a new kind of procreation once she was through with me. It's very nice to meet you, *brother*. I'll give your regards to Mommy dearest."

"Go to hell," he spits.

"I've already been there and back."

Clara's strength is increasing. She is beginning to rip through her restraints. "Grayson, hang on! I'm coming!"

"Clara! Hang on! Just hang on!" he calls back to her. The sound slithers through the nonexistent spaces between his perfectly aligned teeth.

I give his torso a savage squeeze. Ribs crack inward, and I thank every sweet star in the sky for the shrill way he screams. With her teeth, Clara tears through the vines winding up her arms with vigor like I've never seen. Streams of hot salt water clamber down her cheeks, my poor little love.

"NO! Let him go, Jasper! Please! This is between *us*! Please!"

Of course it's between us, little love. Everything is, and from now until the end of time, everything will be.

"I'm sorry, Clara!" Grayson yells to her. "I'm so sorry! You didn't deserve this; you didn't deserve any of it!"

"Grayson, wait— I-I'm coming! I-I'm—"

"I need you to know it was real, okay?" he huffs, breathless, lungs punctured. "I-it was all real, and . . . and if I could do it all again, in another time, another place, a-another life . . . I'd—"

For my Clara's sake, I grant Grayson death before he finishes his statement.

It's even more efficient than Jade's. My fingertips elongate into knives to impale his thin skull, pinning it to the bark. He's ripped from life at an unexpectable speed, soul parting from the body like a Band-Aid from a wound. What's left is a corpse doused in red rain. I leave him pinned to the tree for a moment, an ornament with eyes drifting downward as they lose their light. His jaw hangs open, blood pouring from between his teeth alongside a final breath. His nostrils and ears cry crimson, capillaries shattered by the sudden impact.

A heartbroken screech tears through my Clara.

With a telepathic wave to the branches, I free her. The poor thing still doesn't understand this is for the best. As she cries, I remove my hand from within Grayson's head. Purplish bits of his brain matter burrow under my nails, and despite every effort to conceal it, a new smile crackles across my face.

Grayson, the prince, the knight, the final obstacle . . . hits the ground with an inconsequential thud.

"Grayson! N-no! Come back! You're okay! Come on, you're okay!" Clara pats at his lightly freckled cheeks, but he is gone. He is the very definition of dead on impact. "Don't go, please! Don't leave me here, d-don't go!"

"Clara—" I start.

"Get *away* from me!"

She looks unhinged, rocking and weeping over Grayson's lifeless cadaver. She's holding on to him hard enough to turn her knuckles white. If not for me, she'd still be tethered to a miserable world of human hubris and obnoxious *noise, noise, noise.* She said it herself. She said it. I offer her freedom. She is conditioned to choose containment and complacency. This isn't her. This is her earthly programming, dribbling out, purging, clearing.

It will end.

"I'm never going to hurt you again, my love." Her heightened biology is already healing, as I knew it would, but it is the sentiment that counts. "I am . . . sorry."

Sobs trickle past her lips, delicate, quiet, and fleeting. She's too blind to be reasoned with. We'll have to continue this discussion after calmness has taken hold. Grayson's blood roses will provide me with enough power to pull her under. I lap it ravenously off the petals poking out from his body. None of this nectar will go to waste. All of it will be used for her. *Her, her, her.* The beautiful and misguided *her.* Strength floods every vein in my body, causing them to shift in consequent coloration.

"Shhh . . ." I make my voice an auditory sedative. "I think you should get some sleep for now, yes? It'll all be all right when you awaken." First, she looks terrified, but watching her eyes glaze over soon after soothes my turbulent soul. "That's right. Sleep, love. Sleep for me."

In seconds, a blissful grin has blossomed across her pretty face. Her cheeks are still tearstained, so I caress them to wipe the pain away. She leans in to my touch. Her head is heavy in my hands. To my delight, her fingertips woozily release Grayson's blooming carcass.

"Sleep." I whisper this time, knowing all of her thorns have been clipped.

Just as her eyelids threaten to close, resistance rears its homely head. She shoves me and presses her palms to her ears. Getting away is out of the question, so the way she stumbles back makes me want to smile through a cringe.

"Why are you making this so hard?"

"I don't want this. I don't want you. *I* don't want you." She sounds positively desperate.

"Stop fighting, Clara. Stop fighting what we can be. What we should be. Think of all we can do as one. We can end the horrid, hypocritical rule of humanity. There will be no more noise, no more nuisances. We will reign supreme, the sovereign overlords of a planet desperate for the next phase in evolution. Among them, we will be gods. And our love, oh, my Clara . . . our love will be their religion. They will worship at the altar of us, mortals in awe of a new Hades and Persephone. I will be ruler of the dark, and you, my love, will be all the sprawling life and sacred decay that accompanies spring. We were made for this, Clara. Trust me. This is who we *are*. This is who we were always meant to *be*."

She backs herself against the tree from which Grayson hung, coating her shoulder blades with his blood. It leaves her hair wet and matted. I approach, cornering her. It's taking every spark of energy to resist me. She'll tire herself out. Indulging in the fantasy of escaping poses no harm, but I'm becoming impatient.

I miss her lovely smile.

Horror drowns my senses when it begins dripping red.

Too quickly for me to stop, she brings her hand to her mouth and wedges one of Grayson's blood roses between her teeth. Each crease is highlighted with gory vibrancy. A metallic scent fills the air, along with a thrum of unearthly power. The empty look that exists in her eyes instills emotions long forgotten. Below that hollow, unreachable gaze lies a smile.

It isn't the smile I fell in love with. It isn't the smile that awakened a craving for connection and intimacy beyond what always felt feasible. It isn't my salvation. It is a conglomeration of red and white concealed behind gradually receding lips.

I've never felt fear before, not really. Everything akin to it had always come up in distant, echoing thrums of emotion. I've always lounged at the apex of earthly power, and beings of apex power needn't worry themselves with it. However, for the first time in my excrescence of a life, I am afraid. I am afraid because right now, I am prey.

38 | CLARA

At first, the taste of Grayson's blood brings on nausea and panic. Then it shifts into something much sweeter. It dissolves into warm, sugary syrup that tempts my taste buds with a mixture of floral elegance and strawberry sweetness.

Blood roses bloom at my ankles. I can hear them. I can feel them speaking to me in a language that transcends syllables and sounds. Everything heightens, more so than they ever have on missing a dosage. My senses are sharpened. Supernatural. I shed my skin, *all* of my skin, like a snake would. It falls off in flaking wisps, ashes from a building scorched. My inner workings, overtaken by darkness, become still and serene. Even my heart, once so essential, slows to a steady halt. I grow until I match Jasper's height. Jasper is still in front of me, but now, our eyes are even and locked.

"Clara," he says.

I plunge my hand through Jasper's chest without a second thought. Nails meeting no resistance, it is easy enough for them to locate his inhuman heart. It is still, but very much existent. If all I am is a killer, I might as well be one on purpose.

"P-please," he begs, at last, all out of songs.

My hold tightens, but not to torture him. It is to secure my grip on his heart before I tear it out. It is as black as expected. Soon after exposure to the air, the agglomeration of alien tissue disintegrates into dust. He crumbles along with it, the empowered, red smoke he once flaunted signifying an untimely expiration. When it clears, what is left is human. Jasper is now a weak, feeble, fragile human, scrambling to his weak, feeble, fragile feet.

Is it . . . true? Is it possible to become . . . *human*?

He stares down at his trembling *human* hands, seemingly just as surprised by this new development. "What have you done to me?" His voice, once so spellbinding, quivers.

"I don't . . ." I pause. Suddenly, I am ten times more powerful and infinitely more sinister. "What's the matter, Jasper?"

Revenge is best served similar to the crime that warranted it. When my voice falls from my lips, it is pure, saccharine decadence. It is molten chocolate dripping off the edge of a chilled strawberry. It is a dollop of whipped cream placed atop a sprinkled sundae. It is the scent of summertime, flowers and fruit hiding within a juvenile haze of surrender.

It is also pure corruption. Dark, tempting, and delightful, it leaves wicked kisses on his brain stem, flows through his blood, and ravages his insides.

The same carnivorous butterflies I encountered have come to greet his stomach, fluttering fiendishly and with intent to wound. I can tell it's made him nauseous, but in the most enjoyable way. Blush flocks to his cheeks, turning them rosy. The hue does not stay put. It scales up his face and into his eyes until his pupils are flooded with distinct red iridescence.

My red iridescence. Jasper's eyes glow with *my* red iridescence. The rhythm of the light's buzzing I felt in the gas station bathroom has returned, but this time, I am conducting the orchestra.

"*Smile* for me, Jasper."

He follows the command instantly. The forest bends to my will, branches reaching over the moment I conceptualize them doing so. They wrap around his throat, closing the airways. Still, despite his dwindling oxygen supply, his lips stay pointing skyward. As his face purples and his *human* heart slows, the ditzy expression remains.

Finally, one last gulp for air erupts from him. It's defiant in the way all instincts are. Hope is lost and his mind is mush, but such is the curse of a human form. A few spurts of blood make their way past his lips, each like ink droplets to punctuate his life. Blood vessels pop inside his nose, producing a steady stream from each nostril.

Jasper's blood is much sweeter than Grayson's. Grayson's was the flavor of pure grief. Jasper's is dusted with the sugar of retribution. I consume it with famished vigor, strengthened by every drop. As his essence irradiates through mine, it sends shock waves and starbursts of dark, unbarred energy through my cells.

I remember everything so very clearly now. I see every moment he made a puppet of me, every nonconsensual kiss he stole. I feel his unwelcomed hands scouring my body, exploring my most intimate curves and edges. I hear his voice hypnotizing me into submission, so sure I'd be perfectly pliable and willfully well behaved. He was so enraptured with my helplessness. He fed off it and called it love. Now he gets to understand what his version of *love* truly is.

Violent, vile, and completely unrequited.

Once I've drained him, death steals him from my grasp. His skin hardens into bark that molds seamlessly into the surroundings. His matter shifts to become one with the forest. Peaceful isn't what I'd call his visage. The smile remains, but above it, previously spellbound eyes suggest some suffering occurred. I wouldn't have it any other way. Hundreds of frozen faces sit embedded in the wood. They bear the same air of agonizing euphoria.

Somewhere.

That is what he meant when he said Joey would live on. This forest isn't alive with death; it is alive with murder. Jasper deserved to suffer just as his victims did. I am honored to have evened the scales, if only a single sway. Jasper deserved to feel as helpless as I did. I am delighted to deal out this unsightly justice.

My ears pick up the sound of engines. I deconstruct into a tangle of limbs and travel by shadow, another ability I wish I had been brave enough to access sooner. In seconds, the source of the sound comes into view. A barrage of militant gray trucks are flooding the foliage.

They are headed straight for me.

One halts beside Grayson's body. It shrieks as the brakes collide. Grayson's mother bursts from the passenger seat before the plume of dust left in the car's wake has the chance to clear. She stares at her eldest son in silent horror, watching as more blood roses sprout from the pulpy hole in his forehead. Vines of deep vermilion erupt, curling around his ragged, ribbony skin. Red petals, thoroughly nourished, bloom over his face, once golden, now granite gray. One rose has begun to grow from his eye, the soft tissue of his eyeball serving as its soil. Its leaves are young, fragile, and timid. He is a garden of gore.

"C-collect—" she stutters, her voice cracking before she makes a pointless attempt to clear it. "Collect the body. I want a full autopsy. Take samples."

Her suited underlings move quickly. They zip Grayson into a black bag and carry him off on a flimsy gurney. The gas station man in all gray zooms in with his car, throwing open the doors to greet them and their new science project. Agent Grayson Warner—the liar, the knight, and regrettably, my *something more*—is nothing but a corpse to be dismantled.

A sharp pain plunges through my lower back. Then there are at least nine more, scaling my spine one vertebra at a time. When I whip around, I find a succession of pink syringes sticking out from my body. They are arranged in a perfectly straight line, emptying their contents into my bloodstream.

I feel that dreadful, familiar weakness again.

My stature crumbles. My height drops. My muscles turn to taffy left out in the sun. I become human Clara, the one I'd cherished so dearly before learning of true power. Once I am human Clara, I am ripe for the taking. The EHKI operatives swarm like wasps. They slam me into the ground so hard, granules of dirt get lodged in my nostrils. It reeks of moss, acidity, and boot-based rubber.

Gwendolyn's pointed heels march before me, a parade float of power. I follow the length of her pale legs *up, up, and up* until our eyes meet. Hers may as well be the smoking barrels of two guns eager for a standoff.

"Miss Lovecroft," she says, warm as prison bars as she juggles duty and grief, "I believe we're done here."

She gestures to the soldier whose hand is at the nape of my neck. He grunts in understanding. Shortly after, a loud rush surges through my ears, my vision becomes an astronomer's observatory, and I leave my body for sweet, violent darkness once more.

39 | CLARA

This EHKI cell is no different, save for the addition of an IV drip administering a heavy dosage of Mom and Dad's vitamins. It is taking more than a singular pill to keep my human genes dominant. I've built up a tolerance because now I'm stronger. I barely fit inside the glassy rectangle, and very few can stand to watch my anatomy as it writhes through each biological shift.

Dr. Hemlock—Dr. Gwendolyn Warner—does not avert her gaze.

"How did it happen?" The unspoken mention of Grayson sends a ghastly succession of stings up my protruding spinal column. I remember the way his jaw had hinged open, muscles so suddenly relaxed, it looked like the bones beneath had vanished. I remember his warm blood on my back and his cold body in my arms. She presses on, her springtime eyes frosted over. "Was it painless?"

In this form, I know better than to scowl. I know better than to bare my teeth, now the size of forearms.

"Yes . . ." My voice crackles, all crunching leaves, snapping twigs, and ghostly howls. "It wasn't me. I'd never—"

"I know." I'm relieved she's observant enough to know I'd never let Grayson die willingly. Still, for a woman who just lost both of her children, she looks unsettlingly calm. "And JS-7R?"

"He's dead."

But not before he'd miraculously turned human. Not before the brutal touch of our melding matter allowed him to spend his final moments in soft Homo sapiens flesh. Questions hang off my tongue like an uncontrollable surge of saliva. I ask only one of them.

"Was it worth it?"

She purses her lips. The skin around them is pale and paper thin. I suspect she was sobbing, vomiting, or both. The sharp angles of her neatly pressed suit look like the brutalist architecture of a dam struggling to keep roaring waters at bay.

"The few for the many."

Her pointedly dismissive tone conjures another question from me. I make sure to punctuate it with a few well-deserved ounces of venom. "Did you grieve for them?"

She stiffens, her spine a metal rod propped at ninety degrees. The severity of her presence spreads like spores, moving through the microscopic spaces in the glass that divides us.

"When there is this much blood on your hands, Miss Lovecroft, it tends to blend together." I stare at her, demanding more, demanding *something* indicative of a human heart beneath that ivory dress shirt. "But for the record, yes. I've grieved for them all."

Only partially satisfied, I fall into a seated position. My knees no longer possess the ability to hinge both backward and forward, so doing so requires that I sift through some files of muscle memory. As time passes, my body shrinks. It shrinks with the seconds. I never realized how incredibly small humans are, and how terrifying smallness is beside statuesque monarchs like Gwendolyn.

"I did what you asked." I have a real voice again. It is soft, feminine, and familiar. "When can I go home?"

No matter how insistent I am on grabbing her gaze, she does not offer so much as a sliver of it. It is fixed on my IV drip, on the pink liquid too gelatinous and translucent to be blood. It is fixed on my limbs, each one covered in newly formed flesh. Only a few unfinished pockets remain, and the muscle that shines through them is nearly burgundy in hue. She refuses my eyes because they are still sunken. They are still the eyes of Specimen AV-7D.

"Miss Lovecroft, I'm afraid there's been a change in plans." The air in my unit becomes thinner, stripped of precious oxygen. "After further assessment of your physiological and psychological circumstances, it has been deemed irresponsible to release you back into the public. I'm certain you understand."

Thinner.

Pulling in a full gulp of air becomes incredibly challenging. Each breath is shorter than the last. My lungs pulsate. My heart, my damned human heart, races. Every part of me screams out in survivalist fury, but on lurching forward to slam my fists against the glass, I find that I have no strength to do so. I can barely manage a few steps without being swept up in a swirl of vertigo.

"Y-you said—"

"Some promises expire, Miss Lovecroft. I cannot be held accountable for statements I made before the situation . . . evolved."

"You're afraid of me," I croak. "You won't let me go because you're afraid of me."

"Correct."

I crawl to the wall between us. It is cold and unforgiving against my palms, which burn terribly as I force them to support my weight. In my reflection, I catch my face. It is human again, although a darkness lingers in my eyes that no amount of gene suppressants can subdue. I see something more than me in that darkness, something far greater and far angrier.

It is *ancient and forbidden*. I am *ancient and forbidden*.

And I am dying.

"Grayson wouldn't have—w-wouldn't have wanted . . . wanted this. He tried to . . . s-save me."

"And it cost him his life. I thought I could trust him with this mission, but clearly he wasn't strong enough. I will not repeat his mistake. I am going to tie up the last of Project Undergrowth's loose ends, once and for all." She turns, and from this angle, all I see of her is the silver fabric of her pointed stiletto pumps. "I am going to atone for the last of my sins. You have around five minutes of oxygen remaining. When you get to the land beyond this life, find them. Give them my apologies."

With that, she leaves me alone with that same light blinking cyclically above my head. The strength required to look up at it has left me, so its reflections on the floor beyond my box are all I can make out. It blinks on each second, giving me around three hundred red pulses until I reach . . .

A few hours ago, I thought Jasper's red light would be the last scorched across my irises. This anticlimactic, incandescent bulb is much less exciting. Perhaps I should have let myself dissolve into his delusions. We could have been something after all. We could have accepted our monstrous traits, spread beyond the particle barrier, and lived as ourselves regardless of the consequences. Neither of us asked to be created, yet both of us paid the ultimate price for it. We were forced into a world that would never accept us, then forced out of it with just as much fury.

Two hundred pulses left.

If there is a place parallel to this life, I have some business to attend to there.

I'll find Joey and apologize for my hand in how short his life had been cut. I'll urge him toward a whole new timeline and remind him to speak to every cute boy in class once he gets there. I'll tell him to go after his wildest dreams no matter who calls them unrealistic. Joey was a dreamer. Dreamers invent all that is real. *No more fear, Joey. Dream dangerously; you're stronger than you think.*

I'll race into Jade's arms and thank her for everything. I'll thank her for loving me even when she thought she couldn't. I'll thank her for teaching me love, even when I thought I was incapable of it. I'll tell her she was a good sister, the best I could've asked for. It wasn't her fault she got tied up in some of the worst circumstances our world could offer. It wasn't her fault there was just too much pain. In her new life, she should get to be exactly who she wants to be. A president, a detective, a globally revered boxing champion, or a sister to someone worthwhile. *You deserve a happy life, Jade. Don't stop until it's yours.*

And Grayson . . . oh, Grayson . . . in another time, another place, another life, I'd be me, with you. I'd be neither human nor monster. I'd be my own branch of infinite chaos, and I'd trust you to love that chaos as you loved it—against orders—here. I'd give us the chance to experience one another in a world safe from the maladies of this earth. We'd have a lovely life, a soft life, a peaceful life. *Grayson, you are worthy of a peaceful life. You're no one's soldier; put down the sword.*

One hundred pulses left.

If there is another time, another place, another life . . . perhaps I'll try living it for me. Perhaps I'll pick a whole new story for myself. The form I choose will be molded by my hands, not by the hands of preexisting people with their hearts set on selfish matters. Everything about my next life will be mine. It will be for me and nobody else. I will know love because I will be love, and I won't just love me . . . I will love *being* me.

I close my eyes. The sacred abyss within them feels warmer and more welcoming now. It is not filled with terror and dread. I have no desire to procrastinate. These twenty-four years were an experience worth having. There were difficulties, challenges, and obstacles. There was pain, fear, and suffering. It all feels so small and far away, though. They were windowpanes in an infinite sea of glass to look through. I've never been my body or my mind. I've always been an observer, gazing through panels to create the progression of linear time.

It was all so small. It was all so momentary. It was all so perfectly, pleasantly insignificant.

As a tendril of red smoke falls from my lips, it ends . . .

40 | CLARA

. . . it begins.

Quakes rack the ground, creating fissures like newborn mountains on the earth. They pierce through the infrastructure of the EHKI's headquarters, destabilizing every proud, man-made level. The power of the bedrock, supported by the might of an entire planet, easily prevails over Gwendolyn's steel and glass. The holding cell shatters, sending fireworks of shard confetti in every direction.

Air.

It hits my lungs like the gaseous equivalent of cold water on a hot day. All of a sudden, I'm high on everything, soul soaring above the clouds for one final joyride. Then it nose-dives back to the surface, plunging into my physical form to reestablish the integrity of our tether. I'm alive, and considering my IV drip has been lost in the fray, I'm also free.

The subterranean structure is pulled into a great crevice by the most tremendous roots I've ever seen. The glow of the magma beneath shines up to meet us, screaming out scorching, third-degree promises. A few of Gwendolyn's people tumble down through the kinetic wreckage. Their shrieks are bloodcurdling battle cries, but even the bravest go quiet when their bodies hit the heat. The liquid sun living at the core of our world consumes them, but not hungrily. It is an impartial beast, a reaper with no bias.

While I could let the shaking ground send me to the same fiery fate, I did not make it this far just to die. It's beginning to look like a portal to hell down here, and as they say, when you're going through hell, the last thing to do is stop.

Red light runs through my veins, igniting them like a web of highways in electric fast-forward. I summon Jasper's power; I summon *my* power. My birthright. My ancient, forbidden, wicked genes. My chaotic, corrupt, demonic blood.

I may have been born of someone else's hubris, but I am not a child of it. I may have been awakened by Jasper's dark desire, but I am not a slave to it. I am no one's experiment, and I am no one's prize. I will stop impersonating a diamond for a world that values only what shimmers and shines. I will stop playing characters to put on the most amicable show. I am in this realm, but I am not of it, and I refuse to keep up the act for another second longer.

I—Clara Lovecroft—am a monster, but at last, a monster of my own design. I—Clara Lovecroft—am a human, but at last, because I choose it. I am not caught between the greater of two evils. I *am* two evils, and so much more.

As the serendipitous earthquake continues to shatter the EHKI's infrastructure, I elongate my limbs and begin climbing the floors. They come undone like a crumbling puzzle, the pieces mixing, mashing, and crashing into one another. The elevator that unites them explodes, showering all those still alive in sharp snowfall. My muscles writhe, wrapping around my spiny exoskeleton like ribbons. My fingers stretch into knives, perfectly serrated and fit for a trek toward the surface.

A few stray scientists cry out, but not for help. They squeal in fear, more apt to cannonball into the earth's asthenosphere than to trust me. The most malicious part of my heart yearns to see Gwendolyn, if only to wave goodbye to her as she boils with the rest of her organization. Alas, we do not meet again. Alas, revenge is not as important as survival.

I press forward, scaling the shivering bedrock, avoiding each boulder and lightning strike–shaped rift.

On the surface, I do not find the forest as I'd last seen it. It has become two mighty slopes, hinging inward at a great split that was once a road. Treetops that never should have touched slam into one another. The mummified corpses that turned to blood roses and bark plummet toward the steaming pool of orange and yellow beyond the tremors. The barbed-wire buildings have been uprooted. They spill hundreds of skeletons, blackened by the burns from Jasper's escape, and metamorphosed into ivy and wood.

All at once, what he built, what had been built before him, and all that came after is . . . erased.

I latch on to everything steady. I grapple up the tree trunks, thrusting myself toward the indigo sky. In the dome overhead, the constellations call to me, all of them cheering my name. They could also be wailing in horror, because no matter how persistently this disaster tries, I refuse to die. Joey cared about me. Somewhere in her heart, so did Jade. Grayson tried to save me. And my parents, those beautiful liars, thought I was worth preserving. They thought I, of all things, was worthy of a life beyond their laboratory. For the first time in my uncanny existence, I agree with them.

For them, I refuse to die.

For me, I refuse to die.

The aftershocks pull the forest into nonexistence, but today is not my doomsday. I haul myself up to the severed edge of the asphalt strip. Finally, the quake ends, leaving a gash on the landscape that bleeds and bleeds and bleeds. Rays of inner earthlight reach toward the stars, all of them silent once more. The forest is gone. Both facilities are gone. All that stands is the rickety gas station and its group of rusty pumps.

It was me.

Realization thrums through my mind. It clicks in one colossal light bulb flicker. The roots that caused the tremors were not coincidental, nor were they the work of some strange, benign deity with unknown motives for prolonging my life. Just as Jasper had been able to manipulate the natural forces in his midst, I had been able to create a surefire means of escape from the EHKI. It was all me, and that means I am not only as powerful as Jasper had been, but more powerful than he'd ever become.

Inside the gas station's mini-mart, not an aisle is out of place. With a monstrous hand, I pluck a chocolate bar from the counter's edge. I return to the topographical wound, lying on my back as I peel away the tinfoil wrapping. *Four squares.* One for Joey, one for Jade, one for Grayson, and one for me. We feast together, warmed by night's tenebrous blanket. They are specters, and I . . .

I am a murderer. A stain on the surface of a world that pretends to keep its hands clean. I could drive a hand through my own chest and try to rip out my monstrous heart. I could try to become human, only human, but I don't want to be human, only human.

I want to be all of me.

An experiment. An anomaly. Ancient and forbidden. Beautiful and damned. Cruel and chthonic. Awake, alive, rapturous, and reborn. Maiden, monster, and *mayhem, mayhem, mayhem.*

AV-7D.

Clara Lovecroft.

Me.

ACKNOWLEDGMENTS

The Bleeding Woods is a story that has followed me around for many years. It first manifested on one of my family's long road trips to upstate New York. We'd take them regularly to visit family, and each time, I cherished the hours spent in cozy silence, sitting behind my father as he drove miles and miles. These trips allowed me the kind of uninterrupted contemplation that makes stories happen. The landscape scraping by our beloved brown van quickly became a backdrop my mind was eager to fill with color. Before I knew it, distant mountains were the warped edges of an interdimensional prison dome, scraggly branches were twisted fingertips, and every deep, dark shadow concealed the gaze of something otherworldly and desperate to communicate.

In Jasper, I crafted someone terrifying because of the terror he faces. In Clara, I crafted someone terrifying but willing to face the terror within and without. In many ways, she embodies the bravest side of myself, as when I returned to this story in adulthood, I needed her bravery more than ever.

The Bleeding Woods is much more than a story to me, and I am tremendously thankful to Monica Rodriguez for seeing through to its dark, strange, human heart. Part agent, part human sunshine, she encouraged me to show up to the page fierce, fearless, and authentic. She told me to be weirder, scarier, and more creatively insane than I'd ever thought I could be. With her infectious enthusiasm and inspiring levels of positivity, she made me feel safe to be myself in every wicked, wonderful way.

Words cannot describe how grateful I am for the talented, passionate, and dedicated team at 47North. My editor, Elizabeth Agyemang, understood my story in a way I never thought anyone would. Just a few moments on a call with her, and I knew *The Bleeding Woods* had found its forever home. She made me feel seen and heard. She made me feel like I could let myself *be* seen and heard. Thank you, Elizabeth, for fighting for me, a timid debut author who'd still been learning she was worthy when we signed. Thank you, 47North, for welcoming me to the Amazon Publishing family. You've made my biggest dream in the world come true.

Jon Reyes, you are the most wonderful developmental editor I ever could have dreamed of. You read my story with more love, devotion, and dedication than anyone ever has. Your notes, advice, and feedback guided me to a draft I felt genuinely proud of. It was an honor to share this story with you, and an honor to incorporate your visionary ideas. You opened portals in my imagination, and now, after years tumbling around in my brain, I know *The Bleeding Woods* has reached its final form. Thank you, thank you, thank you. What you do for writers like me is changing the world, one story at a time.

To my incredible beta readers, I truly cannot thank you enough. This story is insanely close to my heart, and sharing it in its earliest stages was scarier than Jasper in his monster form.

Grandma, you were the first to tell me this book would be something, someday. You're the reason I kept writing and kept believing in myself and in Jasper. I love you endlessly, and I am so grateful to dedicate this book to you. We made this dream come true together.

Titi Helen, you got the first version I dared to imagine sharing, and the way you made me feel like a superstar had impacts greater than you'll ever know. You've always cheered for me the loudest. You've always supported my crazy dreams. When you read *The Bleeding Woods*, you looked at me with utmost confidence, confidence I definitely didn't have then. Thank you so much. I love you.

Irene Delgado, you read my words and cared for them with enough passion for the two of us. You made me feel like every single crazy idea in my head mattered and encouraged me to become the writer I've always wanted to be. I am endlessly grateful for all that you've done to help me arrive at this perfect moment in infinity. I am endlessly grateful for you. I can't wait to share every story I write with you, because you help me see that every one of them is worthwhile.

Wyatt Brower, thank you for being an incredible ray of sunshine in my world. The energy, passion, and excitement you offered as a beta reader made me fall in love with my story all over again! You're one of the most talented, hilarious, and radiant people I know. Thank you for always giving me so many reasons to smile, and for helping me find the bravery to show up here, on planet Earth, as my whole chaotic self. Keep shining, you force of endless light, always!

Annie Kronenberg, I cannot believe we lived just twenty minutes from each other for years, only to cross paths in Belfast of all places. It feels like friendship fate. From the moment we met, you've been a ray of sunshine in my life. Thank you so much for beta reading *The Bleeding Woods*, for providing such beautiful and inspiring notes, and for ending up in Belfast at the same time as me!

Skyler O'Flaherty, thank you very much for beta reading *The Bleeding Woods* for me! You're an amazing writer and a visionary artist, and I hope you get to share all of your wonderful ideas with the world!

Evie Dowden, I'm not sure what sorts of crazy universal forces made sure our paths would cross, but I'm so grateful they did. You are one of the kindest and warmest people I've ever met, truly like a real-life fairy-tale being. I admire you and your insanely incredible writing. Thank you so much for beta reading *The Bleeding Woods*, and for braving the scary parts for me!

Kiera Torpie, I also can't believe we lived so close to one another only to finally meet in Belfast! You are such a talented writer, and an inspiration to me in every way. You radiate powerful energy, glowing in your beautiful, expansive authenticity. You inspire all around you to do the same. Thank you so much; I'm grateful beyond words.

Maoliosa Scott, the first time I read your writing, all I could think was, *"Damn."* You reminded me of how writing can and should be lovingly crafted art, and I am so grateful to have had you as a beta reader. You made me feel safe to share my voice, and I seriously cannot thank you enough.

Okay . . . someone get tissues for Mom. Mom, final tissue warning.

Thank you (again), Grandma. You have been telling me I was destined for something wonderful since my age sat in the single digits. You believed in me before I knew how to believe in myself. You saw something in me before I ever thought to look. You have always been there, and it is an honor to have you as my first reader, my biggest fan, and most importantly, my most beloved friend. Thank you for the gentle, kind, endless flow of love. Thank you for understanding me when no one else did. Thank you for helping me dare to dream big, to dream of a world where *The Bleeding Woods* was in it. You've always said I was watched over by angels, and true as that may be, I'm grateful one of those angels decided to take human form.

Daddy, I love you more than anything. I don't think I'll ever have enough page space to describe it. You are my hero, my rock, and my best friend. You have seen me through so many eras and loved me more and more with each one. You've accepted and embraced me shrouded in shadow and glowing with light. You've helped me through my darkest times and cheered me through my brightest. In more ways than one, you saved my life. Our movie nights, coffee trips, fruit runs. Our deep conversations, our most honest moments, our unhinged venting sessions. All of these tiny, ephemeral moments in infinity, made me feel like life was worth living again. In you, I found the strength to fight against all fear, because no matter how bad things got in my head, I couldn't leave my daddy. I couldn't leave my best friend. There was simply too much life to live, and too much joy to share with you. This book, and this person, would not have existed without you. You are a beacon of warmth and light in my life, and in the lives of all around you. I love you endlessly, unconditionally, and eternally. I am grateful beyond measure that of all the places in the universe you could explore, you chose to be my father, and to take this strange adventure at my side.

Mom, I know you're likely already in tears, so I apologize in advance for making it worse. I think it goes without saying, but I love you more than you could ever imagine. I love you more than you dare to love yourself. To me, you've always been a pillar of immense strength and endless hope. Very early on, you taught me that every wild dream is worth chasing, because any star is in reach when you're fearless enough to fly for it. All my life, you've helped me spread my wings, and all my life, you've blessed me with flight lessons. When I wanted to be a rock star, you made sure I took center stage. When I wanted to be a marine biologist, you brought me to every aquarium. No matter what, you were courageous enough for the both of us. I'd be honored to harness half the bravery, resilience, and determination you possess so effortlessly. Thank you for giving me the space and grace to learn, grow, and step into my power. Thank you for loving the best and worst parts of me, for being patient and kind when I didn't think I deserved it. Thank you for simply being you, eternally magnificent, and effortlessly enough.

Nick, my amazing little brother, I hope you know how much I love you. Like the emotionally constipated siblings we are, we don't often talk about it, but it's true. I could go on about how my world was turned upside down when Mom and Dad brought you home, a floppy infant with big, dazed eyes. True as that was, I don't think I ever knew what a gift a brother could be until I needed—more than anything else in this world—a true friend. Nick, you have seen me through some of my worst moments. You've seen me in puddles of fear and panic on the floor of my bedroom and walked over to pat my back and tell me I'm strong enough to get through anything. You've seen strength in me I never thought existed, and consistently, you've been the safest, softest, and most accepting person in my life. I love you, and I am in complete awe of you. You've powered through every obstacle that's come your way. You became a rock star even though doctors said you'd never even touch an instrument. That isn't *just* special, that's completely out of this world. You are a masterpiece, in all of your softhearted, endlessly talented, and occasionally grumpy glory. Thank you for playing dolls with me, for chasing the ice cream truck at my side, for treating me gently when I was at my most fragile, and for being my first-ever friend.

Ricky, Mako, and Zoey: Thank you for always stealing me from the keyboard for a snuggle. You are the best trio of chaotic, crazy pups in the world, and I wouldn't have been able to do this without you. Paulie, my tiny dragon, thank you for flying alongside me all those years. My guardian angel has green wings, little bestie. I love you, and I think of you every day.

Christine Sanchez, Adriana Salguero, Samantha Joia, Kathryn Starnes, and Brianna Maldonado, you are my best friends and my sisters. You are my family beyond blood, because you are my family by love, and you have my eternal gratitude. Thank you for listening to all of my manic musings before I ever had the courage to write them down. Thank you for accepting me at every stage of Brittany-ness, helping me to love and understand myself with every new development in the story of my life. I like to think of us humans as rosebushes, just like the kind Jasper loves to snack on. When we grow a new flower or acquire a new thorn, we might feel uneasy about it for a time. You beautiful, wonderful people helped me fall in love with each new petal, nurture each new thorn, and grow valiantly toward the sky with each passing day. I am endlessly grateful that the stars aligned to bring us together in this crazy, beautiful life.

Finally, I'd like to thank some folks who have made a huge impact on my life without even knowing it. Tio Speedy, Aunt Bridgie, Titi Marlo, Angelo, Titi Rula, Tio Jorge, Titi Angela, Aunt Susan, Aunt Lisa, and Aunt Lisa—you are the reason I know the blood of the covenant is thicker than the water of the womb. Thank you for being by my side through absolutely everything. The joyful and the melancholy, the triumph and the hardship, the darkness and the light. I couldn't have asked for a better chosen family, and I couldn't be more grateful that some perfect, beautiful alignment in our crazy universe brought us all together.

Judy Othmer, Jim Othmer, and Michael Roman: Thank you for believing in me with so much sincerity and vigor that you somehow got this shy, budding writer to write her first book. I marvel at your passion, talent, and ability to make even the biggest of dreams seem possible. Together, with our words and our stories, we really can build a better, kinder world.

Michele Bonsignore, words cannot describe how powerful I feel at your side. No one in my life has ever inspired me to be so fearless and unapologetic in the expression of my truest self. You take every opportunity to make me feel like an absolute queen, and without you, I don't think I ever would have found the courage to send out my first batch of query letters.

Kevin Gleeson, thank you for helping me make my first-ever book, *Ollie The Ornament*. That day was the day I decided I wanted to be an author. That day was the day I realized it was a dream worth keeping. Because of you, at nine years old, I was able to see my name on the cover of something real. Because of you, right now, I am able to see my name on the cover of something real.

To my professors at SUNY New Paltz—Larry, Connie, Bria, Catherine, Nancy, Martine, and Dennis: Thank you for everything. Thank you for seeing the storyteller in me before I had the confidence to let her out. Thank you for taking every opportunity to encourage me to shatter the shell I once receded into and become the author I am today. Without you, I never would have known I could *actually* achieve these crazy dreams. I came to you too shy to share a single line of dialogue and left too excited to keep a single story inside.

To Mrs. Lingardo, Mr. Connick, Mrs. Velez, Mr. Purr, and Mr. Pryzmlyski at Mahopac High School, thank you for supporting me at some of the earliest stages of my storytelling journey. You all made me feel like a superstar every time I handed in an assignment. I still remember the way you'd grade them, leaving uplifting notes in the margins or saying the kindest things after class. I needed it more than I knew how to say back then.

Uncle Johnny, I miss you. I miss you so much, but I am proud to have called you my uncle and grateful for the time we had together. You were always there to make me feel seen and heard, to remind me I mattered, and to make sure I knew I was worthy even when I was at my lowest. You did everything to uplift those around you and to be a beacon of hope in a world that can be so cruel. The world is a darker place without you, but your light lives on in everyone whose life you touched. In Titi Annette, who hardly realizes all those trips to the movies and the museum made me love stories enough to write them. In Gabriella, my beloved little cousin, who I thank the stars for every day. In my Titi Delia and Uncle Junior, who've never forgotten to send me a card on every birthday, Halloween, Christmas, Valentine's Day, and Easter. I love you all, and Uncle Johnny, I love you too.

Grandpa—Papa—I miss you. I know you've always been with me in some beautiful, incorporeal form, though. Thank you for never letting me cry, and for showing me all the love, patience, and gentleness I needed when I was just a few months old. Thank you for being there years later, when I wasn't crying about something as simple as a broken pacifier. I've always felt your presence, love, and strength, and I once again find myself grateful beyond words. You were the best grandfather I ever could have asked for.

I'd like to conclude my acknowledgments with a small shout-out to me. Not just any me, though. The years prior to writing *The Bleeding Woods* were some of the most difficult in my entire life. There were so many times that I didn't know if I was going to make it through. So this final acknowledgment is for the version of me who was curled up beneath her sheets, crying and wishing all the fear and pain would go away. It's for the girl who kept going, even when she didn't know how—exactly—to do so. It's for the girl who listened to those tiny voices urging her to be brave and stay strong, the voices that would someday become characters in this book, and the ones to come.

For anyone out there who is wondering if staying is worth it, I am here to tell you, it is. Please keep going. The world needs your darkness, and your light.

ABOUT THE AUTHOR

Photo ©2023 Rosie Dean, Posies With Rosie

Brittany Amara is an author, screenwriter, actress, and model with a passion for science fiction and fantasy that ventures beyond space and time. She loves writing about curious aliens, morally gray protagonists, other dimensions, rifts in reality, and all things playfully wicked. When she's not working on something new, Brittany can be found stargazing, collecting stuffed animals, and baking pumpkin bread. Brittany grew up in Bronx, New York, and graduated summa cum laude from SUNY New Paltz in 2021 with a degree in digital media production, creative writing, and theater arts. In 2024 she furthered her storytelling journey at Queen's University Belfast. Since then, her work in various genres has been recognized by film festivals and writing competitions across the globe. Find her online @brittany.a.mara, and for more information, visit her website at https://brittanyamara.wixsite.com/my-site.